Collected Christmas Horror Shorts

Tales for a Terrifying Christmas

Collected by Kevin J. Kennedy

Collected by Kevin J. Kennedy

Edited by Brandy Yassa

Cover design by Lisa Vasquez

First Printing, 2016

Table of Contents

Foreword

By

Nev Murray

"It's the most wonderful time, of the year." – Andy Williams

"I've got all the company I need, right here!" – The Grinch

Christmas eh? In my experience, people fall into one of the two categories above. Oh, you didn't realise they were categories? Well let's face it, you either love it or hate it. I don't think there is any in between.

There are people who start planning for Christmas from last year's Christmas. They love everything about it. Absolutely everything. These people fall under the Andy Williams category.

Then you have the people who hate it. They hate everything it stands for and would like nothing better than to poke the Andy Williams people with a big shitty stick. These people fall under the Grinch category.

Which do you come under? I know where my loyalties lie.

I used to love Christmas. Well, one part of it in particular. It involved presents. Now, before you think I am materialistic in nature, I'm not. There was always one present I looked forward to every year. I would say it came from my parents but my Dad had nothing to do with it. It was all down to my Mum. I know this because of what it was. I always got my main presents but as well as being delighted with whatever the main present was, I was always secretly looking for one of the smaller ones.

It was a very modest thing. Not the latest craze and nothing overly expensive. It was quite simply, a book.

Every year my Mum would buy me a nice big hard back book. I never knew what it would be, only that it would be something that was just out, so I had to be careful with what I bought in the run up to December. She knew I was a horror freak so it was always something scary. I honestly don't know how she knew which one to get because she was a *Mills and Boon* woman and knew nothing of horror. She always managed to pull it off, though. I knew it was her alone that picked it because my Dad would have nothing to do with those evil horror books. That's a story for another day, however.

So, Christmas used to be wonderful. Every year I would get excited about opening that book to see what I got. Then, one year, all my Christmases came crashing down around me, in one rip of that tacky wrapping paper. It was the first year I had ever cried upon opening a present. It wasn't a flood of tears of joy, oh no, it was a rampaging torrent of tears of absolute terror and sheer hell.

It was still a book, but, I can hardly bring myself to tell you, it wasn't the latest James Herbert or Shaun Hutson or Graham Masterton. It wasn't even horror. My mother, had bought me, deep breath, *The Da Vinci Code* by Dan Brown!

What the actual f……. I looked up at my Mum and she saw my tears. She started crying. She thought I was so ecstatic. I didn't have the heart to tell her that she may as well have went out into the street and picked up the nearest lump of dog mess and wrapped it for me instead. The fact that I didn't get my yearly horror book was horrific in itself.

From that day forward I threw off my Andy Williams jumper and painted myself Grinch Green!

But what has that got to do with the book you now hold in your hands I imagine you are asking? If you're not, I will tell you anyway.

I have never been able to get into the Christmas spirit since that experience. You see Christmas is about being nice, and friendly and singing and pulling crackers and garish jumpers. I hate all that. I just want to sit in the corner and read a book, so I always see Christmas as boring.

I love reading a good anthology at Halloween because that's when you get the best collections of horror stories. It's the time of year that weirdos like me actually fit in. Not Christmas. I mean how can you make an anthology of Christmas horror stories that will be genuine horror? Seriously? It doesn't fit, does it? Christmas is jolly and nice, not evil and nasty.

Or is it?

Enter Mr. Kevin J. Kennedy. He mentioned to me a while ago that he was planning on putting together a Christmas horror collection. My initial reaction to that was *good luck mate*, although I didn't tell him that, of course. To me, it just doesn't scream '*scary theme'* for a horror book. He persevered though, and the result of his labours is now in your hands. I'm just sorry you have to read my ramblings before you get to the stories.

There is one simple reason for this: Mr. Kennedy has pulled together a collection of stories that has given me my scary Christmas back. I feel that, for the first time in about thirty years, I can smile again at Christmas.

The stories you are about to read are a mixture of tales that will make the 'Andy Williams' ones amongst you poop your pants and make you rethink everything you thought about Christmas. A cheery time of year for all to enjoy? Think again. Everything you ever believed about Christmas is going to be turned on its head and left there to think about what it's done, like the stereotypical naughty child.

For those of you in the Grinch camp, you will just want to lock yourself away in your own little world with your own little thoughts because they will not be as scary as reading some of the stories within these covers.

The big friendly fat guy with the beard? Turns out he may not be so friendly. Turns out he may not be anything like you would have wished. The term polar opposites springs to mind.

The wonderful sights and sounds of the Christmas Market you go to every year? Forget it. Once you read this book you will do all of your shopping on line. Sod the egg nog and sod the wonderful winter smells you get when you venture out in December. Stay indoors or the only thing you may be smelling is the coppery tang of blood. Masses of blood.

Those beautiful Christmas songs that you hear every year? With a subtle twist and a little change of the lyrics, their possible true meaning comes out and they will never sound the same again.

You know the extra roll of bin bags (trash bags for you American types) that you buy every year to cope with the enormous amounts of rubbish you accumulate? Switch them for body bags.

Christmas being the time of year to spread happiness and joy? Forget it. For some people Christmas brings so much pain and misery that they feel they must share it with others. For revenge.

Have you got the picture?

What you hold in your hands is, indeed, a celebration of Christmas. The alternative Christmas. The Christmas that all us horror freaks dream of. We can be happy people, but we are at our happiest when we read about all the nasty, gory, sadistic, horrifying scary stuff.

Kevin Kennedy and the host of authors who have contributed to this collection have made sure that for those of us who have darker tendencies, we can learn to love Christmas again.

I finally forgive you, Mum. Thanks to Kev.

Nev Murray.
November 2016
Confessions of a Reviewer
Scream Magazine

Better Watch Out

By

Willow Rose

1.

"I guess I have always been afraid of Santa."

The man in the chair in front of Sara is sitting up almost too straight. It looks awkward. Unpleasant. She's guessing he's as uncomfortable with this situation as she is. Doctor Hahn doesn't look up from his notepad, which is leaning on his knee as he talks to her.

"Really?"

"Yeah. It was sort of my thing growing up. Other kids were scared of the dark, or monsters, or clowns. For me, it was always Santa."

"Really," he repeats, this time more as a statement than a question.

"Yes. Really. I mean, what's not to be afraid of? He's creepy. He sees you when you're sleeping. He knows when you're awake. That's really scary. Don't you think?"

She knows it will be an uphill battle with this guy, but she needs him to understand where she is coming from. She doesn't need him to judge her or even look at her the way he is right at this moment.

"And why do you think you feel that way?" he asks with a deep sigh, as his eyes return to the notepad.

"I guess it started when I was eight. The first memory I have of Santa is from when my mom took me to the mall; you know Merritt Square Mall on Merritt Island…?"

"I know that mall, yes."

"Well then you probably know that every year, they—like most malls—have a Christmas exhibit where you can meet Santa. And that year my mom decided to take me. Well, that's not exactly true. She decided we should go Christmas shopping, and then I saw the exhibit with Santa and his elves up on the big stage and started to beg her to let me go sit on his lap and tell him what I wanted for Christmas."

"Like most kids do."

"Yes. Exactly."

"So you weren't afraid up until then?"

"No. But I have no memories of any Santa in my life earlier than that."

"You never saw him at your house? You never accidentally snuck out and saw him eat the cookies and drink the milk?"

"No. I was always sleeping, I guess."

"Okay. Let's get back on track. So, you got in line, and then what happened?"

Sara sighs. She really doesn't feel like telling this story, but she has to. She *needs* to.

"I got in line and waited for a very long time till it was my turn. It took maybe half an hour and I was dying of excitement. I wanted to tell Santa how much I wanted a Gameboy. My brother got one the year before and I wanted one so badly. It was like the biggest thing back then…"

Dr. Hahn clears his throat.

"I'm sorry; I'm rambling," Sara says. "I do that sometimes. I'll get to the point."

"Please do."

"When it was finally my turn, I walked to the man in the big red suit, my stomach exploding in butterflies, and sat in his lap."

Sara pauses. She sucks in air between her teeth and prepares herself to go back to that day, even though she doesn't want to...even though it scares the crap out of her.

2.

Ho. Ho. Ho. So, what do you want for Christmas, little girl?

"The words and the laugh were both perfectly normal for a Santa, and everything about the situation was familiar and seemingly very innocent. I started to talk, to tell him about my brother and how he has a Gameboy, and how my parents say they can't afford one this year and I am really upset about that, and that's when I see it."

"See what?"

"His fingers."

"What's wrong with his fingers?"

Sara wrinkles her nose in disgust. "He had these…these long nails. I noticed them when his fingers were drumming on his thigh. They were crooked and pointy and brown and so…so long."

Dr. Hahn shrugs. "What's wrong with that? Isn't he allowed to have long nails?"

"Yes, of course, but there were other things as well and, curious as I was, I asked him about them. I asked, 'But, Santa, what long nails you have?'

"And then he replied, 'That's to better be able to scratch myself on the back when it itches.'

"Then I said, 'But, Santa, what red eyes you have!'

"And he answered, 'That's because I work so hard around Christmas and don't get enough sleep.'

"So then I said, 'But, Santa, what long teeth you have and pointy as well and…and…and what is that in your white beard? It looks like blood!'"

"Blood?" Dr. Hahn asks and looks up from his pad.

"Yes, blood. There was blood in his beard."

Dr. Hahn shrugs again. "So maybe he bit himself or something. What happened next?"

"He told me to go back to my parents. My mom said I was shaking when I got back to her. She didn't believe me, of course, and told me I was being silly."

"It does sound like you exaggerated a little or let your imagination get the better of you," Dr. Hahn said dismissively. "As children tend to do."

"That's what my mom said, but it gets worse. A lot worse. I'm not done with my story."

"How so?"

"That Christmas night, I snuck downstairs when I heard a noise, and I saw him. In my living room."

"Was he kissing your mom?" Dr. Hahn asks with a chuckle.

Sara ignores his remark.

"I saw those…those long dirty nails sticking out from his sleeves. I was terrified of him and ran back to my room and shut the door. Panting, I leaned my ear against the door and listened. My parents slept in their room downstairs, so I couldn't get to them. I heard steps on the stairs and, at one point, I think he was right outside my door, because I could hear his heavy breathing behind it. It was almost like a wheezing."

"Maybe he was out of breath from the stairs," Dr. Hahn says, still sounding amused. "He is quite heavy."

"Later, the breathing disappeared and it all went quiet. When I thought it was safe, I opened the door and snuck into the hallway, my feet quiet across the thick carpet. I walked to my brother's room, where the door was left ajar. I pushed it open and looked inside; that's when I saw it: there he was… Santa bent over my brother's bed.

"*'Santa?'* I exclaimed.

"And that's when he turned his head and looked straight at me, smiling from ear to ear, showing me his pointy teeth. They were covered in blood. My brother's blood."

3.

"It says here in your file that your brother was found dead in his bed on Christmas morning, 1992. It says nothing here about blood. There was no obvious cause. They concluded it had to be Sudden Infant Death Syndrome."

"But he was five, doctor. He was no infant. Santa killed him," Sara says and lifts her head up from the couch.

"So you claimed, even back then when you were questioned about it by the police."

"Here we go again," she says and rolls her eyes. "All of my life I have had to live with this. Everyone believed I had done it. The kids and teachers at school, the doctors, the police. Even my parents believed I had somehow killed my brother. Just because I was in the room. Just because my parents found me there, bent over his dead body."

"Well, you were awfully jealous of him, weren't you?" Dr. Hahn asks. "You said so just before when you mentioned he had gotten a Gameboy and you didn't."

"Who wouldn't be jealous? He was always their favorite. Three years younger than me and he gets a Gameboy when it was my biggest wish. Of course I was jealous!"

"So it is safe to say you resented him for being favored?" Dr. Hahn concludes, taking off his glasses.

"I know what you're getting at," Sara says. "Not falling for it. Santa killed my brother. End of story."

"Except it's not, is it? The end of the story?"

Sara sighs and leans her head back on the couch. "No, it's not."

"Tell me the rest."

"Okay. Well, after the death of my brother, I developed a fear of Santa and dreaded every year when Christmas came around and he was everywhere. When I was sixteen, I met a boy I soon started to date. Rob was his name, and he was gorgeous: captain of the lacrosse team and tall and handsome. He was perfect; even had good grades. And he loved hanging out with me. It wasn't easy getting the boys to like me when my nickname was *Sara the Slaughterer,* and when everyone thinks I killed my own baby brother. But with Rob it was different. I met him at my high school, Merritt Island High. He was new in town and he didn't know those old stories; luckily for me. Then that year, when December came along, we were out for a walk in the park with my dog, Scotty. It was almost sunset and it was getting darker as we walked and talked about our future and how it would be awesome to live closer to the beach, maybe in Cocoa Beach on the canal one day; you know, buy one of those houses that are so close to the beach that you can ride your bike there or walk. Anyway, there we were, walking, chatting, and laughing when suddenly I spotted something between the trees-something red. I stopped and pointed, my hand trembling.

"'What is it?' Rob asked.

"'It's…it's…'

"'It looks like Santa,' he said and waved. 'Hi there, Santa!'

"Santa waved back and pulled up his big stomach while exclaiming, 'Ho. Ho. Ho!'

"I grabbed Rob's shoulder.

"'Don't go there. Don't go to him.'

"'Why not? It's Santa. He's the merriest guy on earth. You know…reindeer, the North Pole, and presents and stuff.'

"My heart was pounding in my chest. I couldn't believe Rob didn't find it odd to meet Santa out there in the park late in the evening. There were no kids there at that time. The playground was empty. Why would he be there?

"'Maybe he has a present for us,' Rob said, smiling and pulling my arm. 'Come on.'

"'No! Don't!'

"'What's wrong with you? Santa's the best. Don't you know that? Here, let me show you.'

"Before I knew it, Rob ran towards Santa. I yelled at him to come back, then whimpered when I realized he was not going to listen.

"He turned around to look at me again, to make sure I knew it was going to be all right. He gave me a thumbs-up and winked. And that's when it happened. Before Rob realized what was going on, Santa stuck three of his long nails into Rob's throat, pierced them through his skin, and poked a hole in an artery. Blood started spurting out, like a sprinkler sprinkling water."

4.

"It says here Rob Wilson disappeared on a walk with you in Osteen Park on December fifteen, the year two thousand. According to the police file, you reported him missing at five minutes past six in the evening and you stated, 'He was taken by Santa Claus.'"

Dr. Hahn looks at Sara above his glasses.

"I know. I know what you're thinking. No one believed me that time, either. No one else had seen Santa between the trees; no one had seen him attack Rob."

"There wasn't even a body," Dr. Hahn remarks.

"No. They searched everywhere, but never found him."

"And why is that?"

"I watched Santa drag him in between the trees and never saw him again. I screamed, but no one heard me. When Santa had taken him away, I was all alone with Scotty. I called my parents and they came to get me."

"But since there was no body, you weren't convicted of anything. You did spend time in a mental institution, though?"

"My parents told me they couldn't have me at the house anymore. They were scared of me, of what I might have done, so they sent me there, yes. I spent two years in there, telling the same story over and over again, but still no one believed me. I eventually gave up on convincing people that Santa was dangerous and started telling them what they wanted to hear. That I had imagined the whole thing. That there had been no Santa. They let me go, stating I was cured of hallucinations and paranoia. I moved away, to Cocoa Beach, and started working as a waitress, then moved on to become a secretary at a newly-started company that shaped surfboards. I stayed under the radar and tried to forget everything about my past. I kept in scarce contact with my parents, since they were terrified of me. Little by little, I put it behind me and convinced myself that I had just imagined things; that none of it had ever happened.

"Some years later, I met a nice guy, John, and we moved in together, then later married. He had been a professional surfer, but had to stop because of a back injury. He was running a surf school. I became part of his business and we worked together with the kids. It was awesome. I never spoke to him about my past. Luckily for me, he wasn't too fond of Christmas either, so we didn't really celebrate it and would often travel to places like Costa Rica, where he could surf instead. For a long time, it was all good and I didn't have to worry.

"But then Molly came along."

"Your daughter, right?" asks the doctor.

"Yes. Our precious baby girl. Never had I been happier. It was like everything bad went away and life was good again, like it had been when I was a child. The world was a good place. Having a child even improved my relationship with my parents, since they wanted to be closer to their only grandchild.

"When Molly was an infant, it wasn't really a problem, but soon she started to ask questions. It's hard to ignore Christmas when you have a four-year-old who sees the decorations and hears the carols on the radio. Even the TV is filled with cartoons about elves and, of course, about Santa. Not to mention all the stuff they fill them with at preschool. Soon she was asking about him, wondering if he would come to her house this Christmas. What was I supposed to tell her? She quickly learned he only gave the good kids presents, and one night when I tucked her in, she grabbed my arm and asked me if she had been naughty all of her life. She asked if she was a naughty kid. What was I supposed to say? I told her she was a very good kid, but she didn't believe me.

"'Why doesn't Santa come to my house, then? Doesn't he like me?'

"So I told her Santa wasn't real. I told her we didn't believe in Santa. Just to make it easier. To avoid the questions, I lied."

5.

Sara covers her face with her hands and tries to not let herself get too emotional. Telling this story is tough, a lot tougher than she thought it would be. She can tell by the look on Dr. Hahn's face that he doesn't buy into it, but she is used to that. She learned that at a very young age. Under different circumstances she would just lie to him, but she can't this time. She needs to tell him the truth. People need to know what really happened; they need to know what they're dealing with, what kind of evil they're letting into their homes at night while they're sleeping.

Finally, she lowers her hands. "Can I get some water?" she asks. "All this talking makes me thirsty."

"Of course," Dr. Hahn says, gets up and walks to a small table with bottles of water.

He hands her one and she sits up. She drinks greedily with her eyes closed. Her hands are shaking. Some of the water spills on her chest.

"So, you told your daughter Santa wasn't real?" Dr. Hahn says when she puts the bottle down.

Sara swallows the water and lies down again on the couch. She closes her eyes and tries to go back.

"At the time, it seemed like a good idea. John didn't agree with it, though. He didn't like lying to her. He didn't understand how anyone could dislike Santa. But I had to lie to her. To protect her. I told her the man at the mall was nothing but a man in a suit, dressing up as Santa…that Santa didn't exist. Of course, Molly went and told everyone in her preschool and I was called to a conference, and later had to tell her to not tell anyone, since she made all the children cry. But other than that, it didn't pose any significant problems."

"I have a feeling that it didn't remain that way."

"No," Sara says. "For about two years, she let it go. But as she grew older, she started to talk about him again, stating that everyone else believed in Santa, why didn't we? Telling us that if we only believed in him, he would come. He would bring her presents too. She begged us to take her to the mall to sit on Santa's lap. I forbade it, but when she turned seven years old, John couldn't stand the pressure anymore. Without my knowledge, he took her to the mall and told her not to tell Mommy, because Mommy didn't like Santa."

"So how did you find out?"

"I saw them. I drove past the mall on my way home from yoga class and saw John's car in the parking lot. I don't know why I stopped. I mean, they could have just been shopping. But something told me I had to stop. Maybe it was the fact that they hadn't told me they were going to the mall; maybe it was intuition. All I know is, a small voice inside of me told me something was up. And I was right.

“I parked the car close to theirs and rushed inside the mall. I didn't have to look for long before I spotted them. I will never forget the shock I got. Can you imagine? They were in the line to see Santa."

"How did that make you feel?" Dr. Hahn asks.

Sara sits up. "How do you think that made me feel? I was angry. And scared, of course. Terrified."

"You didn't think you were overreacting slightly?"

"No. Not after what I’ve been through. Haven't you been listening to my story?"

"I have, yes, but...didn't you think about the hundreds of kids that sit on Santa's lap every year that nothing happens to? Couldn't you let it go? For Molly's sake?"

Sara leans over towards Dr. Hahn and points a finger at him. "Listen to me, doctor. I know what you think of me. I know you think I am a cuckoo, and I’m fine with that. But don't for one minute think I am letting any of this go. I am not letting him get away with this. Never. I will tell my story till I can't speak anymore."

6.

"So what did you do?"

"I ran to them. It was Molly's turn and the elf had grabbed her hand and told her to follow her. I watched as she approached Santa and he smiled at her. With terror rushing through me, I stormed towards her, yelling for her to stop. The crowd heard me and several heads turned. A mom pulled her son away from me. I knew I sounded like a crazy person. I knew I risked that everyone in my neighborhood would see me, but I didn't care. I simply couldn't let her go to him."

"Why not?" Dr. Hahn says. "It was out in public. What did you fear would happen?"

"Would you let your child sit on the lap of a vicious killer?" Sara asks. "If Ted Bundy lured your child with promises of candy and presents? I don't think so. I know how this all sounds to you, doctor; believe me. I know. But you asked me to tell the story, so if you'd just let me tell it…"

Dr. Hahn nods. "Go ahead."

Sara exhales. "Okay. Well, I ran towards the stage where Santa was sitting in his chair, his hands with his long nails already reaching out for my daughter as she approached him. I didn't make it to her before she turned and sat in his lap, his red eyes lingering on her throat.

"'*Ho. Ho. Ho*,' I heard him say, as she leaned back into his beard. '*Have you been good this year?*'

"Molly leaned over and whispered in his ear. I couldn't hear what she was saying, but I could tell Santa nodded and smiled, showing off his pointy corner teeth as she spoke.

"Then he laughed. That deep rolling laughter and said something back to her, whispered something in her ear, his long claws grabbing her hair and pulling it aside so she could better hear.

"I screamed and clawed my way through the crowd, pushing moms and dads and even children aside. For a second my eyes locked with my husband's and I could see the terror in them.

"'NO! Sara. Stop!' he yelled.

"I didn't listen. I ran past him. He tried to grab me and stop me, but I managed to get past him, then I stormed onto the stage. I was panting and out of breath, but still managed to yell at Santa sitting there in his red suit, black shiny boots, and white beard. I grabbed my daughter's arm and pulled her away from him.

"'You get your dirty claws off of her, you bastard!' I yelled.

“Molly ended up on the floor. She was crying and my husband sprang to get her. Meanwhile, I clenched my fist and slammed it into Santa's cherry red nose, knocking him backwards so hard the chair tipped, causing him to fall into the curtain behind him, and down from the stage.

“A loud gasp went through the crowd, someone screamed, children cried and yelled at me, and soon two or three of the mall's security guards were on top of me, pinning me down. The police came and everything. They kept me for hours, asking me questions. It was even in the newspaper that a crazy mother had attacked Santa at the mall. They had pictures of the poor chubby Santa with his bloody nose. I never spoke to them. Luckily, no one pressed charges against me. I was told to never come back to the mall and to stay away from Santa; that was all."

"But that is not where the story ends, is it?" Dr. Hahn says with a tired sigh.

"Not at all, Doctor. Not at all."

7.

"John never forgave me for what happened at the mall. For two weeks, I was the talk of the neighborhood, and at school the other moms told their kids to not play with Molly. They took away my status as volunteer because I had been arrested, and none of the other moms wanted to power-walk with me on the beach or meet up for coffee like we used to.

"I had one neighbor who came to my door and asked me if I had time to talk out on the porch. We sat in the swing.

"'You do realize everyone around here is talking about you, right?' she said. 'They're even planning on not letting you go to the Christmas parade, you know, since Santa rides the fire truck. You have them all scared. Why? Why would you attack Santa at the mall?'

"I stared at her for a long time, not knowing what to tell her. I appreciated that she was the only one who dared to confront me about it, instead of just talking about me behind my back like everyone else, but I had no answer at hand, not one she would accept. My silence made her draw her own conclusion. She leaned forward smugly and whispered, 'So, it is true, then? John really is gay?'

"'What?'

"'It's really none of my business anyway. But just a piece of advice. If John sleeps around, then you should punch *him* instead. That's what I did to Steve when I found out he had that affair with our cleaning lady. Never slept with anyone else again.'

"And then she left me. I was sitting on the swing staring at her as she left, realizing I had no idea what just happened. I knew then that no one would ever believe me, no matter how loud I yelled, that all I could do now was to protect my own family.

"But not even my loved ones believed me. After the incident at the mall, I told John everything. I told him about what happened to my brother and about Rob and that I believed Santa had killed them both. I thought he would believe me. I really did. I thought he would understand, but I was alone in this. And he made me promise to never tell Molly any of these crazy stories. He never looked at me the same way again. To him, I was simply a lunatic. And so it happened that three weeks after the incident at the mall, three days before Christmas, he left me. I came home from work that Thursday, carrying presents I had bought for him and Molly, and found the house empty. It was the scariest thing in the world. To open the front door and yell, '*I'm home!*' and then have no one answer. At first, I thought they were just out--of course I did-- but then I found the note. He had left it on the kitchen counter, next to the sink. He simply wrote that he had left and taken Molly and that they wanted to have a real Christmas this year, that Molly had written Santa a letter to excuse my behavior and invited him to come. He also wrote that I shouldn't try and find them and that with the record I had, there wasn't a snowball's chance in hell that I would ever get custody of our daughter. So, if I wanted to see her again, I had to prove I wasn't crazy. That was basically what the note said. Oh, and it ended with a *Merry Christmas.*"

8.

"Of course I didn't stay away. Are you kidding me? How could I?

"The first two days, I stayed at my house, wondering what to do, but by Christmas Eve, I knew I couldn't leave it alone. John had written in the letter that they would stay with his mother till they found a new place, and so I went there--to protect my daughter. It was, after all, Christmas Eve.

"I drove to John's mother's house at nightfall and parked the car outside on the street, hoping they wouldn't see me. Through the windows, I could see them eating dinner and see how Molly was having a great time. She enjoyed being away from me; it hurt like crazy to watch. Part of me wanted to leave them, to go drive into the river, because I missed her so much and couldn't bear having to live without her, but I knew I had to stay and protect her. I knew I was the only one who could.

"I had bought a sandwich that I ate and washed down with a Coke, then I watched as they played charades. I enjoyed seeing my little daughter and the man I loved, but it also crushed my heart that I couldn't be with them.

"At some point, I must have dozed off because I woke up to a dark house, the lights completely turned off. That was when I exited the car. I walked to the house and found the back door that I know John's mother never locks; don't ask me why she doesn't, but it worked out well for me. I used it to get inside. I walked to the living room, where the decorated Christmas tree was standing next to the fireplace. I walked to the cabinet where I knew John's mother had her shotgun ready in case someone tried to intrude maybe that's why she never locks the door. I grabbed the gun and sat in the recliner, ready for him. I was prepared to stay up all night to make sure he didn't get to my daughter. I knew it would cost me the rights to her if John found me there, but I didn't care. Her life was worth it.

"I almost dozed off again a few times, but I was brought fully awake by the sound of a loud thump on the roof of the house. My eyes grew wide and I sat up in the chair facing the fireplace, cocked the gun, and pointed it at the fireplace.

"'Come on, dear Santa,' I whispered in the darkness. 'Come to me. Guess now you're the one who *better watch out*.'

"Ash fell from the nooks and crannies of the chimney. It landed in the bottom of the fireplace and sent out charcoal smoke, filling the room with a strange burnt smell. For a few seconds, I wondered if I should light a fire, but then realized I wanted to face him. I wanted him to see me. I wanted to look into his bloodshot eyes.

“An explosion of grey smoke followed. Big lumps of ash fell to the bottom of the fireplace. It was followed by something big, a loud thud, and someone groaning.

“I thought, *Is that how he makes his entrance? Not very elegant for someone who has done this for centuries.*

“As the smoke and ash cleared and I spotted his red suit amidst it, I lifted the shotgun to my shoulder and sighted him.

“Santa grunted again, got back on his feet, brushed off his suit, then coughed. I realized there was blood. It was coming from Santa's head. He had hurt himself in the fall.

“He wiped it away with another grunt, then grabbed his bag, turned, and looked directly at me.

“And that was when I pulled the trigger.”

9.

“I swear I didn't know. I swear. It wasn't until Santa fell backwards into the fireplace, a hand to his chest, blood gushing from the wound I had made, that I realized his beard had slid to the side.

“That's when I knew I had done something awful.

“I ran to his body, grabbed John's head, and put it in my lap. He was barely able to speak.

“‘…she was terrified of Santa. After…the incident…you scared her…I…I wanted her to know…to show her…there was nothing to be…afraid of.’

“To make matters worse, Molly had heard the commotion and, thinking it was Santa, which it sort of was, she had run down the stairs and was now standing behind me, screaming her lungs out.

“‘DAAAAD!!!’

“What have I done? I thought to myself, completely devastated.

“‘Please don't die, John,’ I whispered, while I stroked his hair. ‘Please don't die on us. We need you.’

“John opened his eyes once again and looked at me with a sly smile.

“‘I knew you'd be my death one day, Sara. I just…knew it.’

“Then his eyes rolled back in his head and his head fell to the side.

“‘NOOOOO! DAAAAAAD!’ Molly screamed.

“Seconds later, John's mother came out as well. Her screams were terrifying and pierced through my bones.

“‘John! Oh, my God. What did that awful woman do to you, John?’

“She pulled me away from him and took him in her arms, sitting on the floor, getting blood on her hands, crying, my daughter at her side, crying her heart out as well. I had no idea what to do, how to react. I was devastated. Completely broken. I couldn't stay in that house anymore, so I ran outside, threw up on the lawn, and went for my car."

"But you didn't make it very far," Dr. Hahn says.

"No. One of the neighbors had heard the shot and called the cops and, seconds later, they had surrounded my car and I got out."

"From another perspective, one might think you were trying to escape," he says. "To run from your actions."

"I wasn't. I just had to get out of the house, to get away."

Dr. Hahn clears his throat. "One might argue that it’s the same thing."

"I wasn't trying to run from what I had done," Sara says. "I really wasn't. I knew I had done something horrible, but it was an accident. I promise you it was. You have to believe me."

"And just why do I have to believe you?" Dr. Hahn asks. "Why is that?"

"Because you're the last one I'll ever get to tell about all this."

Dr. Hahn clears his throat then leans forwards. Sara doesn't like the look in his eyes.

"Okay. Here's the deal. I was asked by the court to make an evaluation of you. To see if you were even fit for a trial, mentally that is. Or if they should simply lock you away in a mental institution for the rest of your life. You're being charged with first degree murder of your husband. You've told me your version of the story. Here's what the rest of the world believes: They believe you killed your baby brother because you were jealous of him, then came up with the story of Santa killing him afterwards. When it comes to your boyfriend, Rob Wilson, you conveniently left out an important part of the story, didn't you? In your file, it says you had recently learned that he had cheated on you and slept with a cheerleader after a game, so that provides a very good motive for you to get rid of him as well. You learned at an early age how to get away with murder, so you thought you could do it again. Blame it on everyone's favorite person: Santa. The good and jolly Santa Claus. Finally, it is obvious you were angry with your husband for leaving you and taking your daughter away, so you went to his mother's house and killed him. What do you say to that?"

Sara sits up straight, folding her shackled hands, and placing them in the lap of her orange jumpsuit that is two sizes too big.

"I know exactly how the world sees me, what they think about my story, but what I need to know is that *you* have listened, that *you* have understood it."

"Why me?"

"Like I said. You're going to be the last one I can tell. I know what the world thinks of me. I know they'll condemn me. I know I am heading for the needle. But what's important to me is for you to know the story and tell it. I need you to keep warning people about this monster. We let him into our homes! Every year, people welcome him like he is the cuddly teddy bear we are all taught to believe he is. But he's not. He's a vicious monster. I need to know that you'll tell people, that you'll warn them."

Dr. Hahn looks at Sara like he doesn't really know what to think, then he points at her.

"Oh, you're good. You almost had me convinced there that you were, in fact, crazy, but you're not. You're just really clever. I'm not falling for it. You're perfectly fit for the trial. There you have it. That's my verdict."

Dr. Hahn presses a buzzer and in come the two guards who have been watching them through the one-way window. They grab Sara by the arms.

"Please, Dr. Hahn," she screams desperately. "Don't let him get away with this. He's a vicious killer and people should know!"

"Take her away."

"NO! Dr. Hahn, please listen to my story. See the facts! Don't let your kids sit in his lap! Don't let them trust him!"

Her arms are hurting as they drag her out of the room. Just before the door closes she yells, “Can't you see it? He's got us all FOOLED! Santa is just an anagram for Satan!"

10.

Dr. Hahn is still shaking is head as he crosses the parking lot. His Toyota is the only one left outside the prison. It is getting late. He can't wait to get away from here. The woman's story still gives him the chills. To think that anyone could be so cold as to blame Santa. To make up that kind of story about everyone's round and joyful childhood hero?

Tsk. A bloodthirsty Santa. What has the world come to?

Dr. Hahn has met many killers in his life, many of them coldblooded, but this lady tops them all.

He finds his keys in his pocket and unlocks the car. He gets in and puts his briefcase on the passenger seat. He thinks about his daughter, Trisha. He has promised to take her to see Santa at the mall this coming weekend and can't wait to see her precious face when she sits on Santa's lap.

Dr. Hahn shakes his head again. What a day. He doesn't like to have to send people to Death Row, but that is where she'll be going. He had really hoped this woman would turn out to be insane. But she was way too collected to be crazy. He didn't see the traits of someone hallucinating or any paranoia in her. Nope, none whatsoever. She had just made up this story to make sure she wouldn't have to go to trial. But she hadn't counted on meeting him. He's the expert when it comes to evaluating people like her. He has so many clients at the prison he has his own office there.

Dr. Hahn sighs and is about to put the key in the ignition, when he spots something on the dashboard.

What is that? A note? I don't remember leaving a note there.

He picks it up and reads it. It simply says:

BETTER WATCH OUT

Dr. Hahn wrinkles his nose and reads it over and over again, but still can't make any sense of it. Is it some cruel joke?

That's when he hears it. It's creeping up behind him, slowly sneaking closer. The sound of someone laughing. But not like normal people laugh. The way only one person in this entire world laughs.

He looks into the rearview mirror and sees him. There he is, wearing his red hat and with his cherry red nose, bloodshot eyes, and pointy teeth, grinning from ear to ear, his chubby hands lifted, the long claw-like nails ready to rip into his throat.

"S-S-Santa?"

The End

Tommy's Christmas

By

John R. Little

I was being noisier than I should have been. Goddam kid. I never even heard the little bastard come into the room until he cried, “Santa!” Then, he ran over and hugged my leg.

“Hi there, kid.”

He rubbed his eyes and yawned. He was maybe three years old -- four at the most. His hair was brown like a sparrow and stuck out at odd angles.

I swallowed and slowly put the silver candlesticks back on the mantel over the stone fireplace beside me. The burlap sack was almost full anyway. If I could just get rid of the damned kid, I would leave the rest of the loot and just split.

“Did you bring me toys, Santa?” He was wide awake now and staring up at me in awe with big blue eyes.

Christmas Eve is usually my busiest night of the year. The parents are all too drunk to wake up, and the kids are normally too worried about scaring off Santa Claus to get out of their beds if they hear me.

“What’s your name, little boy?”

“Tommy.”

“Well, Tommy, has Santa ever disappointed you?”

He shook his head yes. “Well you di’nt bring me a Hot Wheels Road Race set last year like you promised.”

The place had seemed like a perfect setup. I had cased the joint pretty good -- the parents were sleeping in a small bedroom in the basement, and only the two kids slept on the main floor. Maybe I hadn’t been careful enough because it had seemed so easy.

The house was all decorated for Christmas inside, and the family had gone to bed with all of the lights still burning on the tree. There was a set of Royal Doulton figurines in a china cabinet in the dining room. I had been careful to wrap them up so’s they wouldn’t chip.

There was also a good heavy crystal set and a couple of hundred bucks stashed away in an oak bureau drawer.

A grey and white cat was meowing loudly around me when I first got in. That’s probably what woke the kid up. I picked the cat up by its neck and tossed it out the back door onto the porch overlooking the yard. It looked at me and hopped down the steps.

I had drunk the glass of milk and ate the oatmeal cookies that the kids had left out for Santa Claus. A can of Green Giant niblets corn was sitting on the coffee table beside them; I guess it was a snack for the reindeer. The milk was warm.

“How come you got Danny next door a Hot Wheels set and not me?”

“Can’t have everything you want, Tommy. You’d be spoiled.”

"That's what my mommy says."

I bit my lip. Never did like to deal with little kids. "You'd better get to bed, you know. You ain't supposed to be up when Santa comes."

"You really Santa Claus?"

"Sure I am, kid. Why?"

He twisted his head and scratched his ear. "I dunno. How come you din't know my name?"

"I always get you mixed up with your brother, kid."

He thought this over and said, "You don't look like you did in Sears. Maybe I better get my mommy."

I grabbed his shoulder. "Hell, no, kid. Don't do that." He looked scared. "Big people don't believe in Santa. You know that, don't you?"

He nodded slowly. "Aunt Betty does."

"If you wake up your mommy, I'd have to leave and take all of your presents with me."

He eyes brightened and grew wide again. "Presents! What did you bring me?"

"Why, I brought you a Hot -- "

I looked behind Tommy and saw an older boy walking down the hall toward us. "Oh, damn."

"Tommy?" he said. Then he saw me. "Hey, what's going on?" He looked to the staircase leading down to the basement.

I grabbed Tommy and covered his mouth with one hand. "One word and I'll break his neck." Tommy squirmed and tried to get loose, but I kept a tight hold on him.

The older boy was about ten, tall and skinny for his age with short blond hair. He wore a light green robe over brown flannel pyjamas.

"Put those candlesticks in the sack for me. Fast."

He walked over and did as I asked, frowning with dismay as he saw the rest of the silver and china I had lifted.

"What are you going to do with Tommy?"

"I'm getting a bit old for this business," I said. "Need an apprentice. He'll be okay if'n you don't try anything stupid."

The idea hadn't occurred to me until I said it, but maybe it was time. Whoever heard of a fat old man like me breaking into houses?

"You just stay put, kid. One move and your brother's dead."

I grabbed Tommy, picked up the sack, and quickly climbed up the chimney. Prancer and Vixen didn't like him at first, but they'll just have to get used to him.

The End

Naughty or Nice

By

Veronica Smith

As Thanksgiving approached, all the impending signs of Christmas were apparent. Even before Halloween had arrived, the Christmas decorations had taken over the seasonal area and shelves. The leftover bags of Sponge Bob & Bratz Halloween candy now sat next to all the new flavors of candy canes and marshmallow Santas.

Working in the local Kmart was a crappy job but it still was a job. It paid the rent and girls really went for guys that actually had a job. Robert was thinking about girls again as he adjusted the white and green artificial Christmas trees in the display. They had them packed in so tightly you couldn't get a postage stamp between them. It was thirty minutes after closing so he could loosen his smock and relax a bit. He took pride in his department and wanted it to look the best. He decided to put some of the trees back in storage; it would make the rest look more appealing. As he mulled it over, deciding which ones to put away, he heard odd clopping noises; like horses walking down the center aisle.

He looked around for the prankster; Lou was way over in Housewares, straightening up the Tupperware and small appliances. Susan had the worst department – Toys! After a day of all those brats going through there, it looked as though a tornado had hit. He didn't envy her one bit. Usually his department, Seasonal, truly only got bad when they had a huge sale on ornaments or cards, as it did today. After straightening up those shelves, he wandered over to the yard displays and came to a sudden halt.

The inflatable Santa and reindeer were gone! No nylon puddles sat on the floor; they were just missing. Someone had turned off the air pumps and unplugged them from the figures, then toted them off.

"Have you been naughty or nice?" boomed a loud voice.

Robert turned to see Santa in all his blown-up glory, without the aid of any air pump!

How was this possible?

"Well?" Santa asked again, "Have you been naughty or nice?"

His round air-filled belly shook like a bowl full of jelly, bigger actually – like a huge manhole-cover of jelly. Santa had one arm behind his back and brought it around front now. In his huge gloved hand he held an axe. It still had the $10.88 sale tag on it. His jolly mouth was turned down in a frown of malice. He smacked the axe flat-wise in the palm of his other hand.

"You haven't answered me!" he bellowed at Robert.

Robert opened his mouth but couldn't speak – couldn't do anything except stare at the axe bobbing up and down. He turned and fled down the aisle that let towards Linens.

Clop. Clop. Clop. He froze when he saw three inflated reindeer walk out from other aisles to meet in the aisle in front of him. He let out a scream of terror!

"What's wrong?" he could hear Lou call from a distant part of the store. Without stopping to answer he turned down the next aisle and headed in Lou's direction. He almost stumbled upon another two reindeer. They had knocked down several shelves worth of towels and were locked together on top of them like two dogs, mating. In shock, he tripped and picked himself up.

He managed to get to Housewares and ran right past Lou, who was covertly picking his nose and wiping the boogers on the spatulas hanging next to him.

"What's the matter with you?" he asked Robert.

"Santa!" Robert panted, "He's got an axe!"

Lou looked at Robert and smiled. "Oh, you've been nipping at that spiked eggnog, haven't you?"

"No really!" Robert yelled, "He's coming!"

"Sure," Lou sang, "Santa Claus is coming to town! Ha ha!"

"Have you been naughty or nice?" boomed Santa, who had caught up with Robert now.

"Holy shit!" Lou shouted, "What the hell is going on?"

Santa didn't answer him; only swung the axe up and back down through the top of Lou's skull. It split in half and he dropped to the floor like a stone. He chopped at him for a while, momentarily forgetting about Robert. Robert's mouth gaped in horror. He had to get out of here! But he had to get Susan out before this homicidal Santa found her. He ran to Toys, careful not to make noise this time. He literally ran into her near the Barbie dolls. Any other time that much pink would make him puke. This time, however, he didn't even notice.

Rather than try to explain about psycho Santa, he whispered to Susan, "We have to get out of here. There's been a break-in and they have guns."

He knew that would get her going. She nodded and put down the toys she was arranging. As they were sneaking through Hardware, three more reindeer stopped them short. Amazingly, they snorted smoke from their nostrils and bellowed like bulls. Suddenly they charged like bulls! Robert dropped and rolled away, smacking into a hanging rack, and suddenly rained on by small tools.

Susan only screamed once, was knocked down, and all three reindeer stomped on her viciously. Robert suddenly noticed the air valve on the back hindquarters of each reindeer. He grabbed a pair of pliers and ripped them out of the package. He used them to grab the valve and rip the entire thing off. Immediately that reindeer deflated before his eyes. He couldn't believe that it worked! He grabbed a screwdriver and jabbed it into another one; it burst with an audible pop! The third one ran off, trailing Susan's blood and gore down the aisle.

He sobbed silently as he quietly made his way to the front. Passing the rack of posters, he stopped when he heard a noise. Out stepped Santa, bigger and badder than ever!

"Have you been naughty or nice?" he bellowed at Robert.

`"I've been nice!" Robert screamed hysterically, "I'm always nice! I'm a good guy!"

The axe flew past his head and buried its head into a poster of Johnny Depp as Captain Jack Sparrow, splitting Jack's head in two. Robert almost pissed himself.

Smiling, Santa pulled out a notepad from his pocket and cheerfully said, "Nice! Good, got you down now on the 'Nice List'. No lump of coal for you. Ho Ho Ho!"

Santa put the notepad back, stood still, and promptly deflated.

The End

All Naughty, No Nice

By

Michael A. Arnzen

The letters had stopped coming long ago.

But he still had his magic list. He still checked it twice. He hoped for a change, but still it proclaimed: the kids were all naughty, no nice.

Yet it is still Christmas. And Santa is still Santa. He rides, his sleigh loaded up with gifts for those who no longer deserve them. The big bulky bag behind his seat remains full and this weight slows down his flight. But still he must make his journey. Still he must deliver joy.

If he can find it.

He travels above rooftops, searching for someone, anyone, deserving of his finely wrapped packages. The air is always choppy and cold. It's a different kind of winter now -- one that never ends. It's always Christmas for Santa. His work never ceases. It can't.

The reindeer snarl and snap at each other while their bone-grey legs angrily churn in the snow-laden air. His heavy red sleigh courses through dirty orange clouds, moonlit and musty.

Rudolph's nose no longer glows. It fell off weeks ago. Blitzen, three rows back, is dead in the air, a corpse hanging loosely in its harness across the sky. The others have chewed his dangling legs to the bone. All of their eyes are dead and grey, but they remain fuelled by his magic -- and a growing resentment he tries hard to ignore.

Santa Claus cracks his whip on backs of the reindeer as he crosses the Canadian border. He scans the houses below, seeking any telltale signs of Christmas joy. But there are none. No fireplaces crackling smoke up to the sky. No decorated trees in city streets or fancy light displays. Just rundown factories and empty houses. Shattered glass and crashed cars. Empty shopping malls and city halls. Fallen flagpoles and overgrown hedges.

Everywhere, always, desolation.

But the people -- if they even are people anymore -- are still down there. Harried and gaunt, they rove in bands of ugly starvation. Sometimes he spots children, loping among the hungry hoards of the undead. Sometimes he imagines they look up at him above, smiling in the Christmas starlight. But he knows those sparkling teeth are just open-mouthed cries for food.

For flesh.

For him.

Sometimes, out of pity -- and other times, out of boredom -- he'll toss a colourful box down into the throng of creatures. They never pay attention to it, and keep ambling en masse, kicking through its ribbons and wrapping paper. Instead of playing with their toys, they just raise their hands up toward the heavens, crying out at him for the one gift he refuses to give them. Himself. His body.

The sole survivor's flesh and blood.

Sometimes he considers teasing them, leading them all up to the North Pole, like some insane Pied Piper of the Damned. He knows he could shepherd them all -- the whole world of these hungry monsters -- into one giant crowd of chewing mouths, a pile of creatures he could leap into. He would deliver to mankind a final gift of his fatty flesh and it would make for a fine Christmas meal, yes it would.

But he refuses to believe he is really so abandoned. So alone. He keeps hoping he'll find someone. Anyone with a soul left to serve.

His magic does not help him understand what has happened.

It just keeps him alive, in flight, sailing in the sky with his hideously transformed reindeer, and all those wasted gifts.

He keeps searching for survivors.

And checking his list.

Checking it twice.

He hopes for a change, but it always proclaims:

The kids are all naughty.

No nice.

The End

Slay Bells

By

Weston Kincade

Mr. Chokoteh reaches into the large, hand-sewn leather bowl, his hand shuffling around inside. He is a jolly man with a rotund belly the size of old Saint Nick's and a beardless grin almost as wide. The only real difference between him and the merry holiday depiction is Mr. Chokoteh's darker complexion, a common enough trait for the Aleut, Haida, and other Inuit tribes that reside here in rural Alaska. Otherwise, he is the greatest reflection of human duplicity our northern brethren could create, a man after the heart of any flamboyant circus ringmaster.

"Get ready!" Mr. Chokoteh says happily, his hand still swirling.

The inhabitants of our small town all stand in front of the raised platform, backs straight, eyes drilling into the mayor as they anxiously await the verdict. It is this way every year, to decide who will be given to the Saumen Kars, the offering that has kept our little fishing village intact since the earliest stories of legend told by our elders.

Lifting one solitary strip of faded paper from the bowl, the mayor stares for an extended moment. Each person in the village has a slip. It's the first thing filled out by medical staff after the birth certificate.

Come on, come on, I plead silently, staring up as he stands before us, two feet above the ground.

Fists clenched, I'm not sure why every orifice is threatening to let loose at the same time. For fourteen years, as far as I can remember back, it's always felt this way, on this day--this very day--a day that stands in memoriam: Ma's first and last Christmas Eve that I can recall. Every day since has been like this. Her name didn't come up, nor did mine or Pa's, but she died nonetheless. Now every Christmas Eve the feeling returns.

"Well…," Mr. Chokoteh says, clearing his throat, "I did not expect this."

A uniform gasp grips the crowd of nearly two hundred people, filling the crisp night air with orgasmic anticipation. Who will live? Who will be this year's "volunteer"? The one donation every resident makes each lifetime. "Some just have longer to grieve," or so say the old-timers at the local trade store when I stop in.

My voice fills my skull. *Get on with it!* There are murmurs in the crowd, questions and even a few spat words.

"It is always with grief and pity that I look upon our token, the gift for our Saumen Kar protector on Quviasukvik, our winter feast and celebration. But all must eat." Mr. Chokoteh's eyes search the crowd, coal-black but glistening with flecks of deep brown. They find me, and stop.

Really? No… this is not happening! My knees tremble under his stare.

The mayor frowns and nods, his gaze never leaving mine. "Do not fear, child," he says, coming down the steps. "I am here for you." He lifts his hands, gold chains and a pocket watch dangling from his red vest as both arms rise, outstretched. "We are all here for you. You are our savior in our time of need," he recites, the words stretching back before anyone can remember. Only legends remain to explain our archaic predicament. "We thank you for your gift on this hallowed Quviasukvik." His words continue in the traditional right given every Christmas Eve.

His words echo in my mind, then dissipate into a burbling murmur behind my thoughts. My hands clench. Eyes dart left, then right.

Mr. Chokoteh's plastic smile holds no emotion, no pity, no understanding. It is one of acceptance of his place in the world as he descends the few steps from the platform and anchors himself a foot ahead of me, where the crowd has opened up.

Run! Run! Run… run… run… The words meld into my mind forming a mantra, but instead of moving, I stand, my back erect, hands tightening then loosening. *Move, dammit!* I tell myself.

The mayor stares down at my simple body; no more than five feet tall, my feminine curves are more akin to a youthful adolescent boy's. Other children in the village call me *Tilagisich*, or broom. "Slender and petite," my father calls it. "Just give it a few years, little nivi." It's always been his nickname for me. Under Mr. Chokoteh's bushy gaze, the chill in my gut spreads like a plague of icy butterflies.

Fingers flex and flutter. And I'm off, dashing to my left, between family friends and acquaintances who watched me grow up. Men and women tower over me.

Mr. Chokoteh clucks disapprovingly, taking slow steps to follow. "Miss Yazzie, what do you think you are doing?"

In my panic, I can't even acknowledge him--I don't dare. Concentrating on forcing myself through the slim gaps between people, my focus is on the edge of the clearing. The town's many compact buildings line the center of our small village, beckoning with places to hide like an oversized granny ushering children beneath her ample skirts.

As the villagers realize what I've done, arms reach out, fingers pluck at my deer skins and wrap around my thin arms. My progress slows with the drag and I glance around, assessing their looks. Dark, matching Inuit eyes stare down from a myriad of faces, pity held within their depths, but also determination. If I don't make the sacrifice, it will have to be one of them. I chew my lower lip as dozens of gazes stare into mine, slowing my progress further, condemning my fear and selfishness. Glancing around, I find Pa. His honey eyes meet mine, a few mere feet away. Unshed tears glisten and his face is slack, but his lips mouth "I'm sorry."

"Miss Yazzie, we thank you for your gift. No need to run. We are here for you." The mayor stops and turns back toward the platform.

No, no, no! This is wrong, I tell myself. *Run, Inuk.* I push forward through the throng of people closing in around me until one firm hand grips my shoulder, unwavering. My gaze follows it from wrist, over my shoulder, to its owner. The hand belongs to Pa. He shakes his head sadly and my eyes widen. Pushing forward, I try to pull away but other hands take hold of my arms, elbows, and both shoulders. Forward momentum stops altogether and I'm jerked backward, toward the mayor and his Cheshire cat grin.

The words finally find their way out as I scream, "No, no, no! Stop! You can't do this." But the words die on my lips as I'm pulled past Pa, his own hands betraying me as I drift backwards. "Pa…! Pa…!"

My pa's gaze wavers on mine momentarily, then drops to the trampled grass, dirt, and snow below.

"Pa," I mumble, exhaling as he drifts from sight, his fur-covered form mixing with the mass of people.

Before I know it, my perspective changes. The ground falls away from my feet and I'm staring out above the heads of my people, those I've grown up with all my life, lived with, cared for, and been scolded by when my little brother Miki and I ventured into town for a sweet pie with nothing to pay for it. Miki is nowhere to be found in this scrum of people, but at barely eleven years old, he is still shorter than me. He would be nearly impossible to find amidst so many adults. The common snow covering is clearly visible now, coating houses, stores, porches, and the makeshift street and town center. For a pregnant moment, swirling air from the mass of people drifts up and over the crowd in an entrancing dance, mixing with the clouds above and the darkening sky beyond. Night is coming, and with it Christmas Eve, or Quviasukvik as the tribal elders call our winter feast. I have enjoyed that feast every year for as long as I can remember, at least the food. Otherwise, the holiday is a constant reminder of our family's loss--the first of a series if today is any indication.

"Miss Yazzie, it is good to see you've changed your mind," Mr. Chokoteh intones once my feet settle onto the platform and he turns me around. As though oblivious to my plight, his plastic smile greets me once again like the worst frenemy one could have.

"I... c-can't..."

"You can," he assures me, his grin never wavering. "It is time."

A second later, footsteps echo behind me and something pierces my neck. Darkness quickly follows.

Cold wind courses over my exposed skin, chilling my already numb nose, cheeks, arms and legs. The feel of tiny hairs battling the wind wakes me from my anesthetized slumber. Then the cold seeps into my consciousness. Opening my eyes in a stupor, pine tree limbs hang overhead, northern lights playing in the background like LSD-infused fairies in tie-dyed tutus. Sitting up, every joint screams with the movement, shooting pain up and down my legs and torso. Something jingles too, but the sound is muted in my current condition. I barely hear it, but the pain of everything colliding in my mind at once overwhelms me.

What happened? Where am I?

Fluffy, wet flakes continue to drift down. Shaking off God's dandruff, I force my limbs to work and stand. A shiver sweeps through me as wind buffets my scantily clad form. My furs are gone, leaving only a thin shift that barely covers my thighs. It clings to my body, frigid and soaked through.

"What the hell?" I can't help but ask the shadows. My voice cracks like an iceberg leaving port and I grimace.

Beneath the dark canopy of trees, an enormous downed pine catches my attention. Under its exposed limbs, the black depths of shelter catch my eye. I tread closer in bare feet, stumbling forward only to fall to my knees and shuffle inside, unsure if I'm intruding on something's lair. However, the question doesn't even come to mind till after I'm curled beneath the great tree, huddled within its arms and fallen snow.

The makeshift cave is only a few feet deep, but it blocks out the biting wind. For the first time since waking up, I can hear my own uneven breathing. The temporary housing is a blessing though. Closing my eyes, I focus on balanced breathing, something Ikiaq taught me while out hunting. Ikiaq is only a few years older than me, but he is like an older brother, stepping in when Pa couldn't… or wouldn't. "When in danger," he had said, "keep control. Control your breathing and you will control the situation." I do as he said, thanking him silently for the training he'd provided over the years. It was what had allowed me to hunt for the family, to provide when times were tight. *Pa was never good at that--still isn't,* I correct myself. *Although he delivered me to Mr. Chokoteh, he is still alive. I can't just dismiss him. He's my pa.* The thought threatens to break something deep within my soul, something that hasn't revealed itself since it was first cracked open the night of Ma's death. Since then, Pa never ventured too far from home, especially at night. He works for Mr. Chokoteh at the trade store, pulling in just enough to survive but nothing more.

Breathe in, breathe out.

My teeth chatter. I can't stop them. With it comes the familiar sound I heard before, the jingling of small Christmas bells like Saint Nicholas is near. With the eerie silence of night filling me, the curious sound piques my interest.

Where is it coming from?

A shiver courses through me once more, and with it a chorus of jingles. Eyes widening, I run hands through my dark hair. It's matted and damp, but as I follow each clump to its end I find small Christmas bells tightly woven in. One, then two, three, then more and more.

It's me... I'm ringing.

Latching onto one, I try to pull it free. Locks of hair are interwoven within the tiny bell's metal casing, and it refuses to budge, jerking at my scalp. Gripping it harder, I try again, trembling from the pain. The quivering sets all the bells to ringing. There are so many, I can't believe it.

"Sound carries, Inuk," Ikiaq's words remind me. "Stay silent and downwind."

Letting go, I glance out my foot-wide opening. While Ikiaq had warned me so as not to scare away our prey, the same sound could alert predators. In Alaska, grizzly bears and wolves are always looking for an easy meal. If they're hungry enough, frozen human is better than a chocolate-covered ice cream. Thankfully, I don't hear anything approaching.

Where am I? I wonder again. *Why'd they leave me out here?*

In this enclosed space, I'm starting to warm up... a little. As a result, the fuzziness shrouding my mind seems to be falling away. Night owls hoot outside as I consider my situation. I was selected, chosen. My life is the village's gift to the Saumen Kar, our great beast and protector. And then I found myself here, no clothes or weapons, my hair braided with bells. The only explanation I can find comes from the old-timers who fish the local rivers. Some use fake bugs or minnows that make sounds to lure the fish in.

What if that's what I am, bait, and these bells are lures? But for what exactly? As panic seeps into my thoughts for a second time this holiday, Ikiaq's words come back to me again and I regulate my breathing. *In, out. In, out.*

The calming mantra helps, and I still myself against it from happening again. But that's when I notice something else. I'm thawing, the numbness from the cold that previously infused my body seeping away. What is left aches all over, from head to toes. The snow and dirt beneath me are uneven, rocks or roots digging into my side and butt. Even spots on my arms flare up. Placing my left forearm under the opening, there's just enough light to see slices of red skin periodically spaced up and down it. The sliced spots aren't bleeding, but the skin is inflamed from what appears to be cauterization marks. Testing one red spot with a finger, I feel a hard lump beneath the skin. Pushing it ever so slightly to try and break the sealed burn and force the object out, a small jingle echoes from within my arm. Astonished, I quickly check the other spots. They all match, as do small incisions in my chest, stomach, and legs. Giving my arm a shake, all the inserted bells rattle together.

"Oh God!" I whisper. "What did they do to me?"

Gazing at my pained body through the dim light filtering between tree limbs, a thought strikes. *If they inserted them in every part of my body all the way to my feet, why stop there?* Hesitantly, I feel my neck, cheeks, and forehead, halting each time I come across a tender spot. Bells had been inserted in my neck and forehead. "The cheeks must be a little difficult for surgery," I mumble, "even for them." Then it occurs to me that the tender bumps digging into my butt and side from the ground probably aren't roots or rocks. "Guess those cheeks are simple enough." Sadly, a part of me wants to laugh at the epiphany, while everything else just makes me want tear up and cry.

Taking a deep breath, I turn my attention back to the raw, sealed wound on my arm. The bell is the size of a nickel between my fingers. Shoving it toward the original insertion point with a thumb, I wince but keep going, attempting to force the wound open and eject the damnable bell. The wound opens, sending streams of blood pouring out, along with the bell, but the pain is so intense that I can barely see through the tears.

"Shit, shit, shit!" I can't help but say. Grabbing the damnable thing, I try to send it flying out the opening, anywhere away from me, but the force of my throw jerks both arms forward and causes my eyes to bulge from the pain. "Jesus!" I cry, sucking in a deep breath and cradling my further injured arm. Amidst the bloody mess, four threads of filament still tether the damned bell to me somewhere within the wound. "Really? They seriously attached it inside? Fuck! And with fishing line. Who does that?"

After I regain my composure, I scour my small shelter for a severed limb or rock with a sharp edge, something to cut the lines. After a few minutes, I dig up a rock from the snow and hack at the lines of filament until they finally give way. Rolling onto my back, I hold my arm close. Throbbing pain from tender wounds in my back remind me of how many times I will have to attempt this and how many awkward places on my body the bells have been imbedded.

Really? I wonder silently. *This is hopeless.* I close my eyes and as my breathing returns to normal, I can't help but drift back into nothingness.

A minute later, or hours for all I know, I'm jolted awake by an ungodly howl more like a guttural scream than any sound a wolf would make. As it echoes across the snow-covered trees and mountains, I scuttle further into my shelter. I've never heard such a noise before. Unsure exactly where it originated from, I decide to remain where I am for now. *Maybe it'll pass me by or go the other way,* I hope. Knowledge that such a creature is out prowling the forest does not motivate me to venture out into the night--far from it.

I remain still, waiting for further sounds of the creature's location, but nothing comes. Unfortunately, the natural sounds of the night do not return either. Aside from limbs periodically dumping overloaded piles of snow to the ground floor, silence permeates the air.

What to do? I ask myself. *Can I wait here till daybreak?*

While the idea of remaining in the shelter is much more attractive than venturing into the night of biting wind, the fact of the matter is that I'm freezing. Some sensations have returned without the wind making matters simply intolerable, but the cold will get to me eventually. The only way I have a chance to survive is if I leave the shelter and head back for town.

But what's waiting for me there? I argue. *They'll probably throw me back into the forest if they find me.*

What else can I do though? The nearest town is over a hundred miles away and I've got on nothing but a shift.

Memories of this day's events return: the look in my pa's eyes, the fact that he couldn't even look at me as he handed me off to that bastard Chokoteh. Anger fills my stomach, seeming to form a rock the size of a bowling ball, while more tears threaten to come every time I remember the shamed look on Pa's face. "No matter what, I'm getting out of this," I promise myself, needing to hear the words. "And Chokoteh, you've made my naughty list." Saying it felt good.

Summoning my courage and working the knots that formed in my legs and back out, I crawl back into the howling wind. Casting around the sky overhead for the subtle glow of lights illuminating my village, I can barely see them amidst the distracting Northern Lights. As soon as I do though, a large weight lifts from my shoulders. Ikiaq taught me to track and navigate through the woods but primarily during the day, not at night or during a heavy snow such as this. Finding the right direction is the first step in my journey. With that done, it's time to go home.

The journey starts with difficulty, and more merrily than I would like with the sound of jingling bells ringing literally from inside my body, but soon my bare feet grow numb. This isn't good, for it is one of the major indications of frostbite, but there is no alternative.

An hour passes as I slog through, slowly closing the gap between the village and myself until another ungodly howl permeates the air, silencing every creature within miles. Swallowing the frog that crept into my throat at the startling sound, I continue onward. While closer, the creature is still quite a distance away. My path of deep tracks grows longer. I even notice streaks of red left in the snow from where my feet have been rubbed raw and cut, but without shoes or anything to wrap them in beyond the thin shift attempting to keep me warm, I have no choice but to plod onward.

The howl comes again another hour later, this time much closer, stopping me in my tracks. The beast is undoubtedly tracking me, the "bait". Determined to overcome whatever the night holds, I simply tell myself, *We'll see what kind of bait I really am.*

Stripping off the shift, I rip it in two and sit naked on the snow, wrapping my feet. At this point the garment is doing little to help my warmth and will be more help cushioning what remains of my feet. They are red, raw, and torn up in more than a dozen places. If I have any hope of salvaging them when this is over, it must be done. The abrupt immersion in snow should have set my teeth to chattering, but at this point the cold has suffused my bones. Standing, my trim body quivers as a blast of arctic wind tears through the trees, tossing snow and eating into every part of my bared body. Licking my chapped lips and firming my determination, I step forward with one thought, *At least the sound of my chattering teeth is drowning out the ringing bells.*

While I am making progress, it's slow and I can't feel my body. Slogging through the foot-deep snow pack, the next time the howl comes I'm forced to pick up the pace. It is far from a run, more of a drunken stumble than anything; the sound behind me is far too near. I can hardly keep my eyes open, and amidst the falling snow and coarse winds, I can barely make out trees within ten feet, but from behind comes the sound of heavy, plodding feet. A glance back ignites a fire deep in my gut. Out of the darkness what must be Saumen Kar strides, white fur covering its entire body and framing blue, hungry eyes.

The panic I've tried to stamp down for so long thrusts itself to the forefront of my mind. The creature is enormous, nearly ten feet tall with arms the size of tree trunks and two large canines that would intimidate a rottweiler. It seems to smile upon seeing me, wicked and looming. Falling forward onto its long arms and bulbous fists, the creature lets out a more impassioned howl than before. A split-second later it's charging on all fours, closing the short distance at a maddening rate.

"No, no, no! Please no!" I scream, scampering as far away as I can, but the deep snow drift absorbs every numb foot I place, sending me sprawling to the ground just as the giant creature pins me under its weight. The force bearing down is excruciating, along with its putrid breath. It snarls, its great yellow fangs engulfing my vision. For a second the weight shifts, until Saumen Kar grips my left leg and a narrow arm in each hand, lifting me with a shake as though I'm nothing more than a doll. The bells jingle, and the creature grins. It feels as though I'm about to be torn apart, pulling a gut-wrenching scream from the depths of my soul.

Saumen Kar gruffly mumbles, "Bow-bow," then shakes me again and again, each time grinning wider.

A bloodcurdling scream stretches from my lips as he lets go of my leg and swings me over his head like a giant child with a lasso. Tendons stretch and break instantly, suffusing me in a pain like no other. A moment later muscle and skin rip and I hurtle into the trees two dozen feet away. Tree limbs scour every part of me as I crash deeper into a large tree, barely conscious as I fall to the snow-laden ground below. As arterial flow gushes from my armless shoulder, staining the white floor crimson, I barely catch sight of Saumen Kar's angry snarl as he approaches. Thankfully, darkness is seeping into my vision too, overwhelming the vision with a growing black haze.

The last thought to cross my mind as the pain subsides is, *He doesn't look happy. I think he broke his toy.*

The morning of Christmas day, Umi Yazzie struggles from his lounge chair where he's sat all night. The limited belongings that had been arranged in the house are now strewn across the wood floors. Nothing went untouched. Everything in the Yazzie household had been turned upside down with the selection of Inuk the previous evening. Umi had lost his wife fourteen years before on that same very night, and now his daughter. Certain he can't take any more, a Colt 45 sits waiting on the side table, barely an inch from his hovering hand.

What about Miki? a voice inside his head asks.

Miki? He's better off without me. What've I ever done for him? he tells himself. Part of Umi's shame delves deeper with the realization, resignation gripping him tighter. Finally, he mumbles, "It's for the best."

Taking hold of the revolver, Umi lifts it to his temple. His hand trembles, wavering ever so slightly. Readjusting for just the right grip, a knock at the door startles him, his finger almost pulling the trigger. Glancing to the door, then back at the wood-paneled wall across the living room, Umi's curiosity wins out. Fear grips him for a moment, and his gaze steals to the mantle above the fireplace where an aged wooden box sits.

No, no one would be that cruel twice, he tells himself, setting the gun down and heading for the door. Opening it to find no one there, something pulls Umi's gaze down to his snow-covered doormat. Atop it sits a tented note. As Umi leans down to pick it up, the words "Merry Christmas" are clearly legible. He flips the note open, only to find it blank. Umi looks on the back but still finds nothing, no message, until something glints at his feet. Beneath the tented paper, four small bells sit, dirt encrusted and bloody.

Eyes widening, Umi scoops them up, slams the door shut and deposits the bells into the box on the mantle next to four more, although these are aged and rusting. "Why'd you leave me, Tikaani? You didn't have to volunteer. I would've gone. I really would've," he promised, but even now he knows it is a lie.

A moment later, a gunshot wakes the sleepy village to start Christmas morning.

Author's Bio:

Weston Kincade has helped invest in future writers for years while teaching. He also writes fantasy and horror novels which have hit Amazon's best seller lists. His non-fiction works have been published in the Ohio Journal of English Language Arts and Cleveland.com, his fiction published by Books of the Dead Press and in anthologies by Alucard Press and TPP Presents. When not writing, Weston makes time for his wife and Maine Coon cat Hermes, who talks so much he must be a speaker for the gods.

The End

Santa's Midnight Feast

By

J. L. Lane.

The sound of a creaking step seems heightened in the dead of the night, especially for a little girl creeping down to spy on Santa on a cold Christmas Eve.

It was nearing bedtime and Emily was helping her parents put up the last of the decorations for Christmas. She was rather sad it had taken so long for her mother to get a tree; it wasn't a very impressive tree, either. But, at least now it finally felt like Christmas; it should, it was Christmas Eve after all. She placed the last bauble on the tree and stepped back and awaited her father to switch the lights on. Finally, as all the lights illuminated, she felt a warm glow in her heart-it was perfect! She went to move the empty boxes into the hall, when she noticed one still felt quite heavy. Fumbling around, she pulled out a heavy wooden box; it felt like something was rattling inside. There was a message engraved into the front of it, saying "Do not open, Crampus resides!" She had never heard of Crampus, maybe it was a type of decoration.

"Mommy what's this?" she asked as she held it.

Her mother looked over, only half paying attention, "I don't know, Sweetie, a lot of these decorations were left here by the previous owners."

"Yes, but what does this name, Crampus, mean?" Emily persisted.

"Oh, sweetie, just some old legend about a creature the very opposite of Santa; nonsense, of course, so pay it no mind. Now we must get finished!"

Emily was very curious to see what was inside of the wooden box she had found...maybe it was treasure! As her mother left the room to check on the mince pies in the oven, Emily lifted the little latch keeping it closed. She was a little disappointed to find it was only a decoration- a glowing red bauble. Then as she reached up as high as she could to reach the bald patch on the tree, she tripped over the stand and dropped the decoration. It landed with a shattering smash and a puff of red smoke escaped the bauble. The lights flickered and Emily could have sworn she saw her mothers shadow grow up the wall, but as she quickly spun around, no one was there. Scared she would get into trouble for breaking an expensive-looking decoration, she quickly brushed it behind the tree; maybe once they finally found it whilst taking the tree down, they'd think the dog did it.

Emily helped her mother place a mince pie and glass of milk on the mantelpiece and kissed her parents goodnight before rushing up to bed. There was no way she would sleep though, not tonight. Tonight she would finally meet Santa!

Emily placed her tiny, slippered foot upon the top step trying not to wake her parents. Every year she snuck down to catch a glimpse of Santa, but by the time she made it down the stairs he was gone and left nothing but presents and crumbs in his absence. This year was going to be different. She had sat up and waited for him and the moment she heard the thud on the roof, she quickly stepped into her fluffy cat slippers and pulled on her robe. She could hear the jingling of bells as she crept out of her room with Mr Hops – her favourite plush toy – in hand.

Each step seemed to squeak louder than the last, almost as if little mice were being squished underneath them.

By the time she reached the bottom of the stairs, she was worried she had already missed the wonder that is Santa Claus, but when the Christmas tree rustled and shook, she knew she had finally caught him! For most of the eight years of her life on this earth and all those Christmas Eves missing her chance, finally she was going to meet the most magical person in the world!

She tiptoed slowly towards the tree, which was softly illuminating the room around it, grasping at Mr Hops and holding him close to her pounding heart.

The presents were already stacked high around the glowing tree and the stockings were stuffed full to their brims, so Santa must've been finishing up his snack before moving on to the neighbour's house; Emily had to hurry if she wanted to see him.

She shuffled around the tree and there he was! It was really him, knelt down on one knee stuffing his face with something, but that wasn't where she left the mince pie and milk.

She looked over at the mantlepiece, confused to see the refreshments indeed gone. So what was he eating?

"Santa?" she called out in a timid little voice.

Santa sprung up to his feet, as if surprised by the little girl's presence behind him.

"Santa, is that you?" she asked tremulously.

Slowly Santa began to turn around, and as he did, something caught Emily's eye. She looked down by his boots and noticed it: Santa's midnight snack lying there in a pool of red. She looked back up in horror to see his beard stained red. He had feasted upon Emily's dog, Patch; his blood-soaked collar still hanging from the old man's dripping mouth.

Emily couldn't believe her eyes, this *thing* was not Santa, it couldn't be! Its mouth snarled like a feral animal, revealing two rows of razor sharp, jagged teeth. Its long hooked nose scrunched tighter with every snarl and as she stared into its crimson eyes, she felt her legs tremble and knees buckle as her bladder gave way, releasing dark yellow urine all over the living room rug.

The creature stared at Emily with a wild look in its eyes and as the little girl screamed for her parents, the monster opened its jaws wider than seemed physically possible and pounced.

Emily's tiny body jerked and jolted as the creature clamped its teeth down, devouring her head in a single bite.

Mr and Mrs Milton thundered down the stairs at their daughter's shriek, but as they rushed into their living room, they couldn't have prepared themselves for the nightmare which stood before them.

It didn't take the creature long to notice them, as it sucked the last leg of the little girl into his mouth like it was a string of spaghetti before grinning at its next victims.

The screams of Emily's parents soon transformed into bubbling gurgles when the creature darted across the room and thrust its claws into the couple's stomachs, pulling out their intestines and shovelling them into its mouth.

When all of the snacks were gone, it climbed up the chimney and made its way to the next house; it was Christmas Eve and it still had a lot of stops before sunrise.

The End

The Christmas Spirit

By

Lisa Morton

"Merry Christmas, sweetheart."

Ray handed her a small package wrapped simply in tissue paper with a length of hemp cord wound around it.

Elise looked up in surprise; the clock on the mantel read just after four. "

Why so early?" She regretted the words as soon as she said them; she knew Ray would think she was refusing the gift. She tried to recover with a smile as she reached for the present.

He handed it over. "Just open it."

She did, with an odd knot of dread in her stomach. Things hadn't been good between them for a while, ever since the fertility experts had been unable to help them conceive. Elise had inherited Great Aunt Priscilla's house a month ago, and they'd decided to get out of the city, leave London and spend the holiday at the old country place before they put it on the market. It was an isolated cottage, situated near a peat bog in the Yorkshire countryside. Aunt Priscilla hadn't actually lived in it for years, having forsaken the isolation for the relative comforts of the city. It'd taken them six hours to negotiate the holiday traffic coming up from London, and the place was a slight let-down – neither old enough to be romantic and intriguing, nor nice enough to bring a decent price. "Dear God," Ray had said as he'd pulled their bags from the car, his feet crunching on ice and gravel, "someone actually lived out here?"

The inside was dusty and dim, with just enough furniture left behind to make it function as a residence. Elise had brought a few Christmas decorations along, but the strings of twinkling lights and fragrant green wreaths did little to enliven the gloom.

That arrival had been two days ago. They'd quarreled and retreated to silence since; today, the 24th, Ray had spent most of the day in the village while Elise had puttered in the kitchen with a roast and Christmas pudding. Now she tried to act happy as she unwrapped the gift, but she was imagining it as something sarcastic and cruel – a baby name book, perhaps.

It *was* a book, an old hardback bound in plain green cloth. She opened it and read the title page:

The Christmas Spirit

By

Mrs. H. Warren

Privately Printed by the Author

1895

"I found it in the antique store in the village," Ray said. "The proprietor thought the author might have lived around here."

Elise flipped forward a few pages, looking for a clue about why Ray had bought this, but she found only a first chapter about a young widow spending Christmas with an eccentric aunt. She looked up at Ray, trying to seem merely curious.

"Remember last week, we were talking about how people once read ghost stories to each other on Christmas Eve? I thought maybe we could read this aloud tonight. Might be fun."

"Oh, yes – of course." Elise closed the book and saw the author's name in gilt on the spine – Mrs. H. Warren. There was something vaguely familiar about the name, but she couldn't place it. "I wonder who she was, and why she had this privately printed…"

Ray laughed as he headed for the kitchen, going for the wine. "She probably wasn't good enough to sell to a real publisher. Nowadays she'd just put her self-published e-book online."

"Probably."

By the time Ray came back with a glass of Merlot, Elise had read the first two pages. "Actually, it's not bad."

He sipped the red wine, settled into the worn old green couch before the hearth, and said, "Read it to me."

"Now? Shouldn't we do it after dinner, when it's dark?"

Ray shrugged. After eight years of marriage, Elise knew that gesture meant he wasn't happy, but he didn't think it was worth fighting over. She relented. "Tell you what: Pour me a glass of that, and I'll start reading."

Smiling, Ray rose, heading to the kitchen.

The smell of the roasting meat filled the house, a small fire glowed from the hearth, and Elise tried to feel comfortable in the house, but she couldn't. She remembered visiting it once as a child. That had been in June, but even then the house had been chilly, and there was something Elise could only describe as "oppressive" about its atmosphere. Her Great Aunt Priscilla had lived here then, surrounded by frilly pieces of the past – ceramic dog figures, tatted doilies, ruffled pillows, framed photographs of other people's children – but Elise wondered if all the manufactured cheeriness had been her aunt's attempt at covering up the essential gloom of the house.

There'd been something else on that visit, something Elise had never confessed to her skeptical husband: She'd been playing outside, alone, in a small out-building that served as a combination storage shed/garage. She'd felt an odd sensation, like a chill without a cold temperature, and had turned to see a man watching her. He was inside the garage, in the farthest, darkest corner. Even shadowed as he was, she saw quite plainly his old-fashioned suit, his handsome face, his large hands. "Hello," she said.

He didn't answer.

"Do you know my aunt?"

He continued to stare.

Eight-year-old Elise felt another chill, and turned to race back to the house. She bounded into the kitchen, where her mother and aunt were preparing tea. "Aunty Priscilla, who's that man in the garage?"

"What man, dear?"

"He wouldn't tell me his name, but he's wearing very old clothes, like something from an a black and white movie."

Priscilla, already a pale, older woman, had gone completely white. Elise's mum had noticed, grabbing at Priscilla's arm in concern. "Are you all right? What is it?"

"Oh, it's..." Priscilla shook her head before continuing, "...there's no one there, dear. Just a pile of old cans with some towels draped over them. You're not the first one to see something there."

"But I *did* see a man." Elise turned to her mother. "Mummy, there *is* a man out there, come see –"

Mum had cast a quick look at Priscilla, whose expression remained carefully blank. "I'll be right back."

Priscilla just nodded.

Elise led her mother across the yard to the outbuilding. She raised her hand to point. "He's back –"

She broke off as she realized they were alone. No man in an antiquated suit; just what Priscilla had described, a stack of containers and cleaning cloths.

"There, darling, you see? Aunty Priscilla was right. There's no one there."

Elise hadn't openly protested, but she knew what she'd seen. A man.

Or...something that was not a man.

That'd been nearly thirty years ago. Not long after that, Priscilla had moved and the house had been forgotten, until a few weeks ago when Elise had been shocked to find that

Priscilla had died with no other kin and had left her estate to her grand-niece. There wasn't much – a small bank account, some old belongings, a family album that Elise found fascinating – and Elise doubted the old cottage would be worth much. Unless it could save her marriage.

She heard footsteps overhead, and wondered why Ray had gone upstairs. Perhaps he'd forgotten something –

Ray returned from the kitchen, extending a full glass to her. She took it, puzzled. "Were you just upstairs?"

"No. Why?"

"Odd. I heard footsteps."

Ray set the rest of the wine bottle on the table near the couch and resumed his seat there. "Ooh, that sounds like the beginning of the ghost story right there."

"Hardly." Elise sipped her wine, then picked up Mrs. Warren's book. "This was written in 1895, so don't expect CGI effects."

"Just read."

Elise cleared her throat and began. "Chapter One…"

The Christmas Spirit

By

Mrs. H. Warren

Chapter One

At twenty-three, I was too young to be a widow, or at least that's what everyone told me.

But accidents don't care who's too young or too old; they're impartial when it comes to age. Otherwise, my Henry would still be alive, instead of moldering in a grave at the age of twenty-four.

"A freak accident", they called it. No one could have foreseen the machinery blowing apart in quite so spectacular a fashion at the exact instant that the factory foreman – Henry – was walking past. A plate-sized cog wheel caught him in the head. They said the machinery could never have been expected to do that, that it was really quite safe. They told me it had been instantaneous, that he hadn't suffered.

I, on the other hand, certainly had.

Henry and I had been married for two years. At the time we were wed, I had no family to speak of except dear old Aunt Vanessa; Henry, on the other hand, had family, but despised them all and invited none of them to the wedding. Until we could start our own family, we were really all each other had.

But we hadn't been blessed with children yet. We'd bought a lovely little place just outside Manchester; it had enough room for the son and daughter we hoped for. We clung to the notion that my own mother had had me late in her life – she'd been in her thirties – so perhaps ours would simply arrive later.

Then my world was taken from me. Henry was dead. There would be no children.

He'd left me with enough money to survive on for the immediate future, but when he died it was two weeks before Christmas, and I was quite naturally devastated, to the point where Aunt Vanessa feared I might attempt something foolish. She wrote me letters daily, urging me to join her for Christmas. "Dearest Jane," the letters would say, "you know how I care for you and worry about your future, because you're really all I have left." She even suggested that I might consider a permanent move.

I wasn't ready yet to give up our little Manchester home, but the idea of spending Christmas alone also held no appeal to me, so on the 21st of December I wrote her back to tell her I was coming. It took me a day to make arrangements, and I was off.

The train north was decent, but finding transportation from the station to Aunty's cottage proved more difficult – Carlton Abbey, the village where I disembarked, had no regular cab service. I finally found a man who agreed to drive me out in his open hay wagon, but because it was now late in the day, we'd have to wait until tomorrow morning.

"Nobody goes out that way towards dark," he muttered, in the thick local accent.

Luckily the village inn had a room to let; it was clean and quite tolerable. The bartender's wife was a kindly middle-aged woman named Sarah who had broad hips and vivid red cheeks. She brought me a bowl of savory stew once my bags had been taken upstairs and surprised me by asking if she could sit with me and talk for a few minutes. "Of course," I answered.

She pulled out one of the sturdy pub chairs and addressed me with a serious tone. "I don't mean to pry, miss, but…how much do you know about that old house and your aunt?"

The question surprised me. "Not much about the house, and only a little more about Aunt Vanessa."

"Have you visited these parts before?"

I shook my head. "No. I've only met my aunt a few times, and those were always when she visited my family. We never came to see her."

Sarah thought for a moment, and then said, "The house is not right."

"Whatever do you mean? Is it unsafe?"

"In a manner of speaking. And your aunt – she's not a bad sort, but there are things about her you don't know."

"Such as…?"

Sarah caught her husband watching her from behind the bar as he polished glasses with a towel. She lowered her eyes, pulling away from the table. "It's not my place to say more. Just…be cautious, miss."

She left, returning to the kitchen. After a few moments her husband followed, and I heard a muffled conversation occur between them.

I finished the excellent stew and returned to my upstairs room without seeing them again. The bed was comfortable enough, the fireplace kept the temperature at an adequate level, but sleep eluded me. I kept going over Sarah's words in my head. Something was wrong with the house? And my aunt apparently possessed – what, disturbing qualities she'd kept hidden from the rest of her family?

I would find out the answers to these questions soon enough.

###

Elise lowered the book. "And that's the end of Chapter One."

Smirking, Ray said, "I think I've seen this movie before. It's not exactly wildly original, is it?"

"It does feel a bit like a Hammer horror movie. Still, I like its earnest tone. Shall I keep going?"

Ray poured himself another glass of wine, and Elise realized he was already drunk. "Why not? Let's hear all about Aunty."

Elise returned to the book. "Chapter Two…"

###

The next morning – the 23rd – dawned chilly and gray. Outside, snow was falling; it had already piled up against the sides of Carlton Abbey's few buildings. I wondered if my trip to the house would be delayed, but Mr. Murphy, the wagon driver, appeared at the inn at exactly 8 a.m. He handed me a rough woolen blanket. "Here, miss – you'll need that for the trip."

We loaded my bags onto his buckboard wagon. The two horses drawing the contraption stamped in the cold, their breath coming in cloudy snorts. Finally we took our places on the open driver's bench, tugging hats and cuffs and blankets into place. Mr. Murphy gave the reins a little flip, and off we went.

It's possible that, at some point in my life, I've been colder, but if so I have no memory of it. I wondered if we wouldn't have been better off in a sleigh, but the snow hadn't built up much yet and the simple but tough wagon served fine. Mr. Murphy wasn't a loquacious companion, but I did learn that he made this trip once a week, bringing food and supplies to my aunt. Occasionally he brought her into the village so she could tend to various matters, but I was the first visitor he'd brought out to her.

The trip took about an hour. By the time we passed the peat bog and the cottage appeared behind a whitened hedge, I wondered if I might have frostbite. I was moving stiffly as I stepped down from the wagon and heard a voice from the house: "Oh my dear, my Jane, come inside at once!"

I hadn't seen my Aunt in twenty years, and my memories of her were colored by childhood's perceptions. I remembered her as a small, neat, very pretty woman with a sweeping mass of dark hair. Now she was mostly silver-haired, prematurely bent and slightly pudgy. The lines of her face were still clear and striking, though, and she moved easily, without the stiffness I was currently conveying. She rushed out, took my arm, and led me into the cottage. Mr. Murphy followed behind with my bags.

Aunt Vanessa took me into her parlour and gave me the seat of honor closest to the fireplace, which was currently blazing. I let her remove the heavy blanket and my outer wraps, and hand me a cup of steaming tea. Seeing me settled, she went outside again with Murphy. They returned a few moments later with several boxes of supplies. Mr. Murphy hastily gulped a cup down, accepted payment, doffed his hat once, and then turned to go. "Merry Christmas to you and your family, Mr. Murphy," she called after him.

When he was gone she closed the door behind him before joining me in the parlour. "Now, darling Jane, tell me how you are."

"Thawing," I said, my teeth still chattering.

We chatted amiably for a bit, about the dreadful weather, and my train trip, and the world outside Carlton Abbey. Finally I seemed to have reached room temperature, and Aunt Vanessa showed me to my room. Mr. Murphy had already carried my bags there.

It was charming, with a large, fluffy bed, a small fireplace, dresser, basin, mirror, rocker, window seat. The decorations were warm and comforting. Aunt Vanessa suggested I take a rest before supper, and I agreed. I'd slept little at the inn; now that I was here and warm again, I was surprisingly drowsy. I lay down on the bed, thinking merely to test it, and drifted off almost instantly.

I awoke when someone came into the room.

I was half-asleep when I heard the footsteps. Thinking it was my aunt peeking in to check on me, I opted for a few more minutes of sleep and didn't open my eyes. But then I had the sensation of someone standing over me, and so I did force myself awake. I looked up to see that the light in the room had dimmed – the fire had gone out, the light spilling in through the window was less – and it took a few seconds for me to make out anything. Then I saw: A silhouetted figure at the foot of the bed. A large figure, with broad shoulders. A man, in other words.

I tried to call out, but couldn't seem to move, to even force sounds from my throat. My limbs were equally unresponsive, my heart hammered but uselessly. I was paralyzed.

He stood there for some time, not moving, not speaking. I couldn't make out his face or any particulars about him.

I finally closed my eyes, tightly, as if I could somehow make him vanish by refusing to see him. Almost immediately, I felt something in the room change – it lightened again, a crushing sense of essential *wrongness* gone. I opened my eyes.

He was gone.

I took a few moments to collect myself – to let my heartbeat return to its usual pace – before I rose and left the room behind. I found my aunt in the kitchen, sipping tea and writing in a journal which she closed as I entered. "Ah, there you are. Did you nap well, dear?"

"Aunt Vanessa, who is the man I saw in my room?"

Her polite smile disappeared instantly, her shoulders slumped, she set the tea cup down, rattling it in the saucer. "Oh. Oh dear. I'd hoped this wouldn't happen…"

"That what wouldn't happen?" I sat down across from her and poured myself a cup of tea from the pot in the center of the table.

"That you wouldn't meet Joe."

"Who's Joe?"

"Our ghost, dear."

I set the cup down and stared at her, incredulous. "Ghost? But surely…"

"Oh, please, dear Jane, don't tell me there are no such things, or that you don't believe in them." She stood, pumped more water into the tea kettle, and hung it over the kitchen fire.

"Aunty, do you mean to say that you think your house is *haunted*?"

She returned, sat across from me, and fixed me with a resolute stare. "I don't 'think' it, dear – I *know* it. Joe, you see, is a man named Joseph Hood, and he died here under rather tragic circumstances thirty-six years ago." She broke off as her eyes took on a distant look, then she continued. "In fact it will be exactly thirty-six years ago tomorrow."

"He died on Christmas Eve?"

Aunt Vanessa nodded. "He was intoxicated. He came into the living room, dropped something near the hearth, tried to reach for it but tripped and fell into the fire."

I realized she was referring to the same hearth I'd warmed myself before just a short time earlier, and I shuddered. "How horrible."

"They said he at least didn't suffer – he knocked himself out when he fell."

"Who was he? Did you know him?"

My aunt looked away, and I had the distinct sense that she was covering something up, or being less than completely forthcoming. "Yes. He…worked for me. Just a local fellow. I was the one who found him, in fact."

The way she choked up on the last bit seemed authentic, and I had a rush of sympathy for her. I stood and moved behind her so I could rest my hands on her shoulders in an empathetic way. "Oh, Aunt Vanessa, I'm so sorry."

She reached up and patted my hands with hers. "It's really quite all right, dear – it was such a long time ago. And frankly, having Joe around since has frequently been…well, interesting."

I resumed my seat and decided to humor her. "What does he do?"

"Oh, he's quite harmless. He might slam a cabinet door, or knock on a wall. He must be quite impressed with you – I don't actually see him all that often."

After that, we talked about other things. I told Vanessa about my life with Henry, and she told me about her family growing up. They were an intriguing group of people, this part of my family I didn't know at all – a collection of eccentrics that included a tea trader who'd sold opium in China, a madwoman who'd died in an asylum, and a professional street mummer.

We chattered away through the late afternoon, past sunset, and well into the night. Finally Aunt Vanessa yawned and said she needed to seek the solace of her bed. I was initially uncomfortable with the thought of returning to my room, but I soon convinced myself that whatever trick of light and shadow I'd seen couldn't possibly exist at night, and so I retired as well, taking a book with me. I stoked the little fire and slid under the blankets, convinced that sleep would elude me…but after an hour of wading through the sadly-dull book, my eyes became heavy and I slid into a deep and dreamless slumber.

###

Elise lowered the book and looked around the house. Ray poured more wine for both of them. "Was that the end of the chapter?"

"Yes," Elise said, distractedly. After a few seconds, she added, "You know what's odd? The house in this book could be the very one we're in."

Ray followed her gaze around the room. "True, but I would imagine that most of the old country houses were built like this."

"I suppose so…still…"

Ray smiled. "It's more fun to believe it's the *same* house, is that it?"

"You caught me."

He laughed and toasted her. "Please continue. This is so much more entertaining than watching another Fanny Cradock re-run on the telly."

Elise – who loved cooking shows – shot her husband a vicious look before raising the book again. "Chapter Three…"

###

I awoke in the morning surprisingly refreshed and happy to be where I was. Yesterday's storm had passed, and the day was bright, with just the occasional puffy white cloud scudding past the sun.

Aunt Vanessa and I spent the day like two old sisters, nattering about in the kitchen preparing foods for a Christmas dinner that could have fed ten. We fixed goose and mince meat and puddings and popcorn; we even made a wassail bowl, although there were only two of us and we had no intentions of going wassailing come evening. The lovely scent of the wassail – cider, cinnamon, nutmeg – mixed with the other food smells to fill the house with a cheerful holiday scent.

Day passed into evening. We laid out our merry feast and indulged ourselves. We were soon both quite besotted from the wassail. I'd never been much for drink; even a small amount went straight to my head. By midnight we were both reeling and stumbling as we wished each other a Merry Christmas and made our way to our rooms.

I undressed and crawled beneath the covers, warm from the drink and the food and the pleasant evening. The little fire began to die down as I headed into sleep.

At some point in the night I became aware of a dream I was having. I was still disoriented from the wassail, and unsure where I was. I felt another in bed beside me, felt the firm muscles of a man, and thought I must be dreaming of Henry. It would only be later on that I would realize how odd it was – if not close to impossible – to be so self-aware during a dream that you *knew* you were dreaming.

I shan't describe the dream in detail here, for it progressed in an extremely intimate fashion. Suffice to say I was ecstatic to give myself over to it, to have my Henry for one more evening. Even though he was somewhat rougher, more impassioned, than I recalled him having ever been, I considered this dream of Henry to be the most cherished Christmas gift imaginable.

A terrible headache awoke me in the morning, the after-effects of my wassail consumption. For a few seconds, I felt only the grinding pain in my temples, ears, and just above my teeth. Then I realized I was unclothed beneath the blankets, although I'd gone to bed in my usual proper nightgown, which lay discarded on the floor beside the bed. Increasingly alarmed, I drew back the covers, and saw small red splotches dotting the white linen. I looked down at myself, and saw the blood had come from crescent-shaped marks on my shoulders and bosom. They were unquestionably bite marks, and their pain was a large part of my headache.

I bit back a scream and leapt from the bed. That was when I saw it – red marks dabbed on the pillow that had just been beneath my head, marks that formed seven letters. The letters read:

LOVE JOE

I did cry out then, not so much a scream as a sort of prolonged sob. It was enough to rouse my aunt, who proceeded to bang against my door, calling my name. She asked me why I'd locked the door, and I realized I *hadn't*. I went to it and turned the lock, and she entered.

When she saw me, she gasped loudly. She was asking what happened when she saw the bed – or, more specifically, the pillow.

Her expression went cold, and she said, "You need to leave here. Today. NOW."

I didn't argue. I requested only the time it would take for me to attend to my wounds and gather my things.

She waited for me in the living room. When I came in, struggling with my bags, she told me to leave them, that she'd have them sent later. She had a neighbor less than a quarter-mile distant who had a horse and carriage; he could take me back to the village.

She offered no kind word of sympathy, no apology or explanation. Nor did I ask for any.

Together, we walked out into the chilly Christmas morn. It was overcast again, though not snowing yet. Our breath came out in opaque puffs as we trudged along the lane. We finally reached her neighbors, the Lees. They were a family of five, simple farmers with generous dispositions, who rushed to my side in concern when Aunty told them I'd fallen ill and needed immediate transportation to the village. They agreed instantly; the father, George, went out to hitch the horses to their carriage.

Aunt Vanessa gave me a rather cool embrace, muttered something about being sorry our Christmas had ended so poorly, and then left.

Once she was gone, I asked George's wife Annie who Joe Hood was. She gaped for a second, and then bade me sit down as she made a hot cup of tea for me. She sat beside me as I sipped the good, strong tea, and she told me the story of Joe.

"You may believe your aunt to be a lifelong spinster, but the truth of the matter is that she was married once – to Joe Hood. She was twenty, and although you might not know it now, she was considered a beauty among the local folk. She wasn't rich, but she'd been left enough money to live comfortably for the rest of her life.

"Because of all that she had any number of suitors, but only one caught her fancy: Joseph Hood was a young man who'd come up from the south – some said he'd been run off after a scandal with a society lady – and he was very comely. He saw an easy life with your aunt, so he wooed her. They were married just three months after they met, and Joe moved into the cottage with your aunt.

"That's when she found out what kind of man Joe Hood really was: He drank, he cursed if asked to work, but worst of all, he chased after every young lady in the county – including myself. I wanted nothing to do with him, but there were others who gave in to his tender words and caresses.

"Vanessa was hardly blind; she saw how Joe flirted with all the others, and it turned out she possessed something of a temper. They'd have terrible fights, and Joe would take off for the village pub again on their one horse.

"Well, on the first Christmas Eve after they were married, Joe came home late from the pub, drunk as usual. Later on the story was that he'd fallen in front of the hearth, hit his head, didn't even know as he was burned alive. But there were many of us who thought otherwise: That your aunt had surely had enough, hit him on the head with something like an andiron, and put him in the fire to concoct that story.

"It worked, too – they couldn't prove a thing against her. Plus, Joe was hardly well liked hereabouts, so the constabulary didn't exactly exert much effort on proving he'd been murdered."

I felt a chill despite the hot tea. My aunt was a murderess? And the crime had taken place in a house I'd been invited to share for the rest of my life? "The house…"

Annie reached out and touched my hand for support. "Did something happen to you there?"

I nodded, ashamed to admit the full truth. "Last night…I was – attacked."

Annie exhaled sharply before saying, "Your aunt was wrong to invite you, and on the very night of the murder, no less. She must have thought she could control him, or that he was weak –"

George entered then, saying he had the carriage ready; he told me he'd come back later in the day with my bags. I thanked the two of them for the great kindness they'd shown me.

Now that I look back on it, I think I can say in all truthfulness that I owe my life – or whatever is left of it – to them.

###

Elise looked up from the book, dazed. "My God. Well, I suppose we know now why she had to self-publish this. Sex with a ghost simply wasn't done in 1895."

Ray, who had already broken open a second bottle, laughed and added, "I'm still not clear on whether we're supposed to take this as fact or fiction."

"Oh, Ray, surely…" Elise broke off. She'd been about to say, "It *must* be fiction," but then she realized she wasn't so sure. A memoir about hysteria, perhaps? Wasn't the spiritualist movement in full swing when this written? Perhaps Mrs. Warren had been more deeply influenced by all the stories of ghostly contact than she'd been aware of.

Ray gestured at the book. "Is there more?"

Elise flipped through it. "One more chapter. The rest of the pages are blank – I guess to give it enough heft for the binder."

"Well, let's finish it out, then."

Elise turned the page. "Chapter Four…"

###

George was as good as his word, and arrived later on Christmas Day with my two bags. There was no train back to Manchester until the 27th, so I spent a quiet Boxing Day in the pub, letting Annie tend gently to my injuries.

A day later I was home again, determined to put it all out of my mind.

A month later I found employment working for an elderly solicitor. The work involved mainly writing letters and keeping accounts, and my employer was benevolent and thoughtful.

In March, I was finally sure: I was with child.

I sat up late into the nights, working out timelines: It *could* be Henry's. We'd been together as man and wife the night before he'd died. I tried over and over to tell myself that was the only logical explanation. Of *course* it was Henry's.

But the pregnancy became increasingly difficult. I knew, of course, about morning sicknesses and the usual little traumas, but that was nothing like what I was going through. Everything, even water, made me violently ill. I was constantly besieged by excruciating abdominal pains. Blood trickled frequently from my womb, staining my undergarments.

My employer not only gave me time away from the job, but provided the best medical care. The doctors were puzzled; they'd never seen such a condition. They asked me if there was any history of problematic pregnancy in my family. I told them I knew very little about my family.

I never confessed what I knew about the father.

At five months, I looked (and felt) ready to burst. I was completely bed-ridden by then, and I'd taken to biting a rolled piece of cloth to prevent shrieking in agony.

Finally, one night in early June, the pain peaked. It was midnight, and I was alone in my bed chambers. I felt a shudder take me, a great deal of warm fluid gushed from between my legs, and the sensation of ten-thousand glass shards piercing me caused me to (thankfully) lose consciousness.

I awoke several hours later, weak but at last out of pain. I struggled to a sitting position, looked down and saw –

I shall never describe what I saw, what had passed from my body as I'd lain unconscious. I was too spent to move, so I waited. The doctor who arrived to check on me in the morning saw the dead thing on the bed and promptly sicked up his breakfast. After, he assured me that he would dispose of it in fire and tell no one what he'd seen.

I was four weeks recovering. Thanks to the careful attentions of my doctors, I did regain my strength. I returned to my work and to my life.

That was some time ago now. I've done my best to put the whole experience behind me, but I've been unable to. I still bear semi-circular scars on the upper part of my body, and I will never conceive again. There've been men who've shown me attention, but I've fled in terror from them. I've never heard from my aunt, although the lovely Lees have corresponded with me throughout the years, bless them. We never speak of Vanessa or of that Christmas.

I know that as much as I try to forget, the rest of my life will be spent re-living that terrible night I spent in the house by the bog, a house where a sprightly yellow paint job and pillows quaintly embroidered with nature scenes couldn't hide a hideous crime and the undying nightmare it had spawned.

###

Elise closed the book and set it on the table beside the couch. Neither she nor Ray spoke for several seconds.

At last Elise said, "My God."

Ray could only shake his head and gulp wine.

Elise looked down – and her eyes widened at what she saw. "Ray…" She pointed at something beside him on the couch. He picked it up.

It was an ancient satin couch pillow, its sheen faded but still in good condition, hand-embroidered with an image of birds flying over snowy trees.

"This is the house."

Ray picked up the pillow and squinted at it before tossing it aside. "Coincidence…"

"The yellow paint job? The bog? The pillows? Ray, this is *the* house. The one in the story. I'm sure of it."

"That's it – no more ghost stories for you, my darling –"

Elise abruptly stood and went to one of her bags. She'd brought Aunt Priscilla's old family album with her, since she'd thought going through it in her aunt's old home might be a nice small tribute. She found the old, velvet-covered album, stuffed so full of pictures that it bulged out, and carried it back to the light by the hearth. She'd remembered something she'd seen in there, tucked in among all the photos of distant relatives she didn't know –

There. It was a large photo, showing around two-dozen people, dressed in the fashion of the 1930s, three lines on a short flight of steps. There was writing on the back – "*Family Reunion 1935*" – followed by names.

The third name from the right in the top row was "Aunt Jane".

Elise flipped the photo over and peered at the named woman. She was in her sixties, with short gray hair and a flower-print dress. Her expression was the oddest among the group: She seemed to be trying to smile, with a slight tilt to her lips, but her eyes were serious.

Elise showed the writing on the back of the photo to Ray. "There, I knew it: Ray, she's a relative."

Peering at the writing, then the photo, Ray asked (slurring his words), "Who is?"

"Jane – Mrs. H. Warren. The woman who wrote this book."

Ray hiccoughed as he tossed the photo aside. "Don't be absurd, Elise. I'm sure every family in England has an Aunt Jane."

"But I'm sure I've seen mentions of 'Warren' in Priscilla's things, too. We could probably track down the deed history of this cottage to be sure."

"And then what?" Ray staggered to his feet and threw an arm out at the hearth, in an overly-dramatic gesture. "'Ladies and gentlemen, step right up and see where the ghost was murdered'? Shall we charge a pound a ticket, sell souvenir shirts?"

This happened more often than not when they were together: They drank too much until the alcohol led to a fight. Elise hadn't wanted to argue on Christmas Eve, but now there was no escaping it. "Why don't you want to acknowledge that it's at least a possibility? Didn't you say that the man who sold you the book said it was written by a woman who'd lived around here? It's not exactly a heavily-populated region, is it?"

Ray raised his arms over his head. Wiggling his fingers, he began to utter a ghostly wail.

Elise was done. She stormed out of the room, heading down a short hall to the first room she found with a locking door. She entered, flipped a light switch, slammed the door, turned the lock. Outside, she heard Ray continue to utter his ridiculous moans. She regretted having left her phone outside; she could've at least plugged in the earbuds and drowned him out with music. Not Christmas carols, though; she'd had enough of the holiday.

He finally went silent, and she waited. Would he come knocking on the door, drunkenly taunting her? She didn't expect an apology, or even an offer at compromise. That wasn't Ray's style.

She turned to examine the room. It had a soft bed, a fireplace, a small dresser, a rocking chair. The bed covers were only slightly dusty. She pulled them back and saw that the bed was made beneath and seemed surprisingly clean. Outside the room, full night had fallen; she had no idea what time it was.

She turned on a bedside lamp, turned off the overhead, removed her shoes, and fell into the bed. The room spun; she'd had too much wine. She knew the sensation would pass soon, so she waited.

While she waited, she thought about the story. She was sure Jane Warren was family, and that this was the house. At that thought, her heart skipped a beat.

Because if this was the house, then this bedroom…

She started to sit up, but the room whirled around harder. She was afraid she'd be sick, so she forced herself back down. Besides, if she came out of the room now, what would Ray say? He'd surely launch into a fresh round of mockery. No, she wouldn't give him the pleasure.

She waited. The spinning slowed. Time passed. Her thoughts grew muddled. The temperature dropped as night set in; she pulled the musty blankets up over herself, enjoying the warmth they brought.

And sleep arrived.

###

At some point she was dimly aware that he'd entered the room and settled into the bed beside her. He'd come to apologize after all. He'd realized that he'd been wrong.

He reached for her. His touch was cold. Had he been outside? She wanted to ask him, but she couldn't speak. She was incapable of movement.

His frigid hand pulled her shoulder, hard.

Elise knew, then: The door was still locked. It wasn't Ray.

She struggled against whatever force held her, but it was immovable. Weight settled around her. The bed springs creaked.

No.

She wouldn't let this happen.

Elise gathered every ounce of will power she possessed, forced her mouth open…and screamed.

The power holding her evaporated. She was alone in the bed.

She leapt from it and stumbled up. She heard Ray outside, running to her door, calling her name. She reached the lock, twisted it. The door flew open and Ray stumbled in. “Elise – !”

“Ray.” She embraced him, the fight forgotten. She didn’t know if they could save their marriage, but right then she knew he was human and real and that she wanted to try.

She hung onto him, looking over his shoulder, wondering if Joe even knew he’d lost, or who exactly had defeated him. Elise didn’t believe – *couldn’t* believe – that *The Christmas Spirit* had come to her by happenstance.

“Thank you, Jane,” she whispered to the woman who had just given her the best Christmas gift of her life.

The End

Thy Will Be Done

By

J. C. Michael

On the morning of the 28th of December Patrick and Colletta Swift took their dog, Percival, for a walk. They found this letter blowing along the side of the street, the envelope addressed to "God, Our Father, Who Art In Heaven". Police are still looking for the author and although they accept it could be a hoax, they are treating it as genuine:

Dear Father,

Forgive them, for they have sinned. On this, the most holy of days, the day we celebrate the gift of your Son, bestowed upon our unworthy world, my family indulged in such wicked behaviour that it left me appalled at their debasement.

From the moment they awoke, my children, baptised into your family yet so clearly inadequate in their virtue, displayed such avarice, such envy, that it took all of my restraint not to cast them out as the innkeeper rejected the Blessed Mary when she arrived in Bethlehem bearing our Saviour. Their presents opened, their material desires partially appeased, they argued and bickered over what they had received, before progressing on their conveyor-belt of sin - with greed the next in line. My wife sat alongside them as they gorged themselves on sweets and chocolate, despite their full awareness of the feast that awaited them at lunchtime. For my part, my stomach churned with sickness, and I ate naught.

And so to the feast: a gluttons paradise. The traditional Christmas meal with all the trimmings. How the three of them had their fill like pigs at the trough! Father, it made me retch, and all they did was laugh at my discomfort. As children starve throughout the world, my family forced such volumes of food into themselves that it left them close to vomit. Yet still they ate more: turkey, roast and mashed potatoes, carrots, swede, peas, sausages, bacon, parsnip, Yorkshire puddings, gravy, bread sauce, cranberry sauce. Ha! I need not list the rest. You see it all don't you, Father? You do, don't You? You viewed their sin so You understand: what happened had to happen. It was Your will wasn't it? Forgive me, for I, too, sinned, but it was Thy will to be done, Lord. I was your instrument, the implement of Your fury at the parody the festival of Your Son's birth has become.

I rebelled Lord, leaving the table mid-meal and stinging the pride of my wife who, system already awash with wine, berated me as a demon would torment the damned denizens of Hell. Her anger unleashed, she ranted and cursed; her lack of respect for me as head of the household, setting such a vile example to our children, I could have torn out her throat. As her wrath was unleashed, so I controlled mine and I took my leave, demonstrating the kind of restraint she had so willingly abandoned. I sought refuge in my beloved garden.

Once outside, I allowed myself to appreciate the natural beauty of the world of Your creation; yet it only served to highlight the poison which had infected my home and my family. Perhaps that was when I realised what had to be done. I didn't hear You speak, Lord, but I am secure in the belief that You guided me to that decision: that point of no return. If I am mistaken, and the seeds of the deeds to come were planted by Satan, and not Your divine Self, then I throw myself upon Your mercy, for I have been deceived. I shall know soon enough, Lord. My time of judgment is at hand.

Back in the house, the checklist of the seven deadly sins continued to be ticked off one by one. The dominant mood now was one of sloth. The three of them unable to move from in front of the television. I joined them, but I was not slovenly. My mind was active; I knew the what, yet I needed the how. You did not guide me Lord, but I can see that was part of Your test to prove my worth: to exercise the self-determination that would realise Your heavenly instruction.

By nightfall I still had no plan, but as it turned out one was not needed. The kids in bed, my wife came to me, lust on her mind as she pulled me toward her. She backed up to the table and swept the detritus of the day to one side before perching herself upon it. I was weak, my body responding to hers as she pushed herself against me. Her legs were around my waist, her skirt around hers. I felt her unzip my trousers. "Stuff me, hon," she said. What a crude and common thing to say! She had no shame. The woman I had loved and taken as mine in Your House all those years ago was gone; replaced by a drunken harridan who needed to be cleansed from the Earth. As her hand grasped me, my own hand grasped the carving knife that still lay on the table by the carcass of the partially-devoured turkey. She tried to place me inside her but I pulled back. She wanted me to thrust into her, but there was a different type of thrust in our future…sharper, deeper, as I plunged the knife between her ribs. Oh, it felt good Lord, and that first stab was for You, the Father. My other hand went over her mouth to suppress her screams as I stabbed again in the name of the Son, Your Son. The warm blood ran over my fingers as I delivered the third strike in the name of the Holy Ghost, pushing and twisting until eventually she fell still. I had delivered the whore to You, Lord. I hope she gives you less trouble!

My two children looked so angelic as they slept, but I could see the demons writhing within them; taunting me that the sin of my flesh had created such beasts. I suffocated them; it was easy.

So now. One final sin. This letter is composed as I stand here in my garden, surrounded by Creation, the noose around my neck. I hope the short drop snaps my neck; though I fear not death, strangulation seems such an unpleasant way to go. I love my family Lord; I hope You can forgive them, I hope You can forgive me. 'Our Father, who art in heaven, hallowed be Thy name--I hope to meet you soon; my sin is done-- Thy will be done.'

The End

Psychopath Remix

By

J. C. Michael

On the first day of Christmas,
The Devil sent to me
A message through my Sony T.V.

On the second day of Christmas,
The Devil sent to me
Two leather gloves,
And a message through my Sony T.V.

On the third day of Christmas,
The Devil sent to me
Three beaten kids,
Two leather gloves,
And a message through my Sony T.V.

On the fourth day of Christmas,
The Devil sent to me
Four sharp knives,
Three beaten kids,
Two leather gloves,
And a message through my Sony T.V.

On the fifth day of Christmas,
The Devil sent to me
Five split personalities,
Four sharp knives,
Three beaten kids,
Two leather gloves,
And a message through my Sony T.V.
On the sixth day of Christmas,
The Devil sent to me
Six whores to cut,
Five split personalities,
Four sharp knives,
Three beaten kids,
Two leather gloves,
And a message through my Sony T.V.

On the seventh day of Christmas,
The Devil sent to me
Seven feet of rope,
Six whores to cut,
Five split personalities,
Four sharp knives,
Three beaten kids,
Two leather gloves,
And a message through my Sony T.V.

On the eighth day of Christmas,
The Devil sent to me
Eight women to strangle,
Seven feet of rope,
Six whores to cut,
Five split personalities,
Four sharp knives,
Three beaten kids,

Two leather gloves,
And a message through my Sony T.V.

On the ninth day of Christmas,
The Devil sent to me
A nine mil Beretta,
Eight women to strangle,
Seven feet of rope,
Six whores to cut,
Five split personalities,
Four sharp knives,
Three beaten kids,
Two leather gloves,
And a message through my Sony T.V.

On the tenth day of Christmas,
The Devil sent to me
A ten-gauge sawn-off,
A nine mil Beretta,
Eight women to strangle,
Seven feet of rope,
Six whores to cut,
Five split personalities,
Four sharp knives,
Three beaten kids,
Two leather gloves,
And a message through my Sony T.V.

On the eleventh day of Christmas,
The Devil sent to me
Eleven men to shoot,
A ten-gauge sawn-off,
A nine mil Beretta,
Eight women to strangle,

Seven feet of rope,
Six whores to cut,
Five split personalities,
Four sharp knives,
Three beaten kids,
Two leather gloves,
And a message through my Sony T.V.

On the twelfth day of Christmas,
The Devil sent to me
Twelve final victims,
Eleven men to shoot,
A ten-gauge sawn-off,
A nine mil Beretta,
Eight women to strangle,
Seven feet of rope,
Six whores to cut,
Five split personalities,
Four sharp knives,
Three beaten kids,
Two leather gloves,
And a message through my Sony T.V!

A Tome of Bill Christmas Carol

By

Rick Gualtieri

This story takes place shortly after the events chronicled in *The Mourning Woods*. It contains spoilers for *Bill The Vampire*.

With many apologies to Charles Dickens...

Part 1

Home was finally within sight. I so hated racing the sunrise to get back to my apartment. Sometimes the goddamned subway system seemed like it was purposely timed to make one miss their connection. If that N-train hadn't been an express, I'd have probably been forced to spend all day down in the station – a prospect that was only marginally more pleasant than getting turned into a pile of ash by the sun. I swear, Sally must've gotten some perverse amusement keeping me stuck in Manhattan with her until the wee hours of the morning.

Wait. I'd been with her? What for? I skidded to a stop just as I reached the stairs of my building. What the hell was I even out for? That was odd. For some reason I couldn't remember what I'd been doing last night or why it had made me late. Sure, it was probably some coven-related bullshit. I mean, it seemed there were always forms to fill out, petty arguments to settle, judgement calls on what was cool and what wasn't when it came to killing people. Sometimes you'd think I was babysitter to a bunch of preteen girls instead of leader of a group of vampires. Oh well, what did it matter anyway? Same shit, different day and all that. I was probably tired that's all. I figured that maybe a good night's ... err day's ... sleep would jog my memory. Whatever urgent business had kept me out could wait. Yeah, a pint of blood and then maybe a couple hours of sleep would do me well.

It couldn't have been too important anyway, I mused, walking up to the front door. I dug out my key so I could let myself in. From there I'd head up to the top floor apartment I shared with my human roommates, Tom and Ed.

I was just about to put the key in the lock when ... HOLY SHIT! Caught by surprise, I backed up and fell ass over teakettle down the stairs. I landed hard, but thanks to my vampire physiology the only thing really wounded in the fall was my pride.

Either way, I barely felt it as my mind was instantly a million miles away. For a split second there, I'd have sworn I saw a face where the doorknob should have been. Not just any face, mind you, but *Jeff's* face. But that was impossible.

Jeff, AKA Night Razor – AKA douchebag – was the vampire who'd turned me, quite against my will I might add, about a year or so back. He was a big muscle-headed dickhead of a vamp, which was bad enough. What made it worse, was that he'd hated my guts from the get go, to the point of wanting to yank them out and play jump rope with them.

He'd come damn close, too. I'd gotten luckier on that front than I had any reason to expect. Not only had we managed to kill him, but I'd ended up taking over his position as master of a coven of vampires located in SoHo of all places.

As I said, he was dead, very dead, as in *Dust in The Wind* dead. Even if he hadn't been, why the fuck would he be doing an impersonation of my doorknob?

Whatever mission had gotten me out of my apartment was now the furthest thing from my mind. I got hold of myself best as I could, then raced back up the stairs to find ... well, nothing. The door was there just like it always was. The knob wasn't Jeff's face, much like it typically wasn't. I must've been more tired than I thought. I needed to seriously consider adding a couple of shots of Jim Beam to that pint of blood once I got inside.

Speaking of which, I was still reflecting on the benefits of a good stiff drink when I smelled something. Hmm, had a bit of a bacony aroma to it. I was just thinking that someone must be up and cooking breakfast when it started to burn. That's when I realized *I* was the bacon. My hallucination had caused me to hesitate just long enough for the first rays of sunshine to peek over the rooftops. Let me just say for the record, having your head spontaneously ignite is not a particularly fun way to start the day.

* * *

The apartment was dark when I got in, smoke still rising off me. I was amazed that the building's fire alarms hadn't gone off on my way up. Maybe our landlord being such a cheap fuck wasn't always a bad thing. Anyway, a quick check of things – right after dousing my head in the shower – showed that I was alone. I had assumed my roomies might still be sleeping, but they weren't home. I smiled a bit at that. I didn't have anything against them. They were my best buds in this world, after all. Even so, Tom's girlfriend had been sleeping over a lot as of late and that had been starting to irk me.

It was bad enough that he was getting some, while I slept *alone* just a few yards away in my own bedroom. Still, I could live with that. What really bothered the shit out of me, though, was that he was getting some from a witch who just happened to be from a coven that wanted me dead.

Tom had been dating Christy for several months now. She'd originally been sent to spy on me by an asshole wizard who moonlighted as a VP at the company I worked for. Yeah, definitely a long story.

Suffice it to say, despite her mission, Christy wound up developing real feelings for Tom and the two had been a couple ever since. Unfortunately, her coven hadn't forgotten their original mission, which meant things could be a little tense when she was around.

But that was neither here nor there. I had the apartment all to myself for the moment. So, I helped myself to a pint of chilled blood from the fridge and allowed myself a moment to enjoy the silence.

Clink

Or relative silence anyway.

Clink* *Clink

Okay, what the fuck was that? Were the pipes now rattling in this rundown hovel of a shit hole? I wouldn't have doubted it.

Clink

There it was again and this time it sounded like it was in the same room.

I turned, not really sure what to expect. I'd been thinking maybe something had come loose and fallen off the ceiling. Instead, my eyes popped wide open – the forgotten blood pack dropping to the floor, along with my jaw.

Jeff, the dead dickhead of a vampire who'd escorted me from my mortal coil, stood there facing me.

"Hello, meat."

* * *

I tried to form words, but the English language suddenly seemed beyond my grasp. What I was seeing was impossible – and trust me, over the past year I've had to raise the bar considerably on that note. Apparently, I hadn't raised it far enough.

"Happy to see me again, asshole?" Jeff asked with that same dickhead attitude I remembered, a grin spreading across his pale face – and pale he was, even by vampire standards. It was like he'd been rolled in talcum powder. He was also covered in chains. That was a new look for him, but who was I to judge someone's BDSM fetish?

"If we're being honest here, not particularly," I said, still in shock.

"I can assure you, the feeling is mutual."

"You're dead."

"So are you, *Dr. Death,*" he replied mockingly, using my old coven nickname. I guess he did have a point there, though.

"I meant really dead. I killed you."

"*You* killed me?"

"Fine. Sally helped ... a little."

"I'm well aware," he spat. "And believe me, as much as I'd like to rip both your fucking faces off for it, that's not why I'm here."

Yeah, right. Back when he'd been in charge of Village Coven, I hadn't known him to give me the time of day if it didn't include a punch to the face. "So, this is just a social visit?"

"Not quite. I'm here to tell you that tonight you will be visited by three spirits. They are here to show you..."

I raised an eyebrow. Really? We were going with *that* old cliche? "Let me guess. You're going to show me the error of my ways."

"More like what a fucking little prick you are."

Okay, that was new.

"Listen, Jeff," I replied, realizing that I was standing there talking to a vampire ghost. Yep, I must've been losing my fucking mind. "I'm tired and..."

"NIGHT RAZOR!"

"Fine, Night Razor. Whatever the fuck. I don't care. You're obviously just a figment of my imagination anyway. Maybe I sucked down some expired blood or..."

"Think whatever you want, you cockless dweeb. It doesn't change what's coming." He raised his arms, rattling the chains he wore for effect. "Beware, Freewill!" he howled. "The error of your ways will be laid bare."

Huh? "Wait, didn't you just say it had nothing to do with that?"

Before I could finish, Jeff became translucent. A mere moment later he completely faded away, just like, well, a ghost. Pretty fucking freaky, if you ask me. Then again, I'm a vampire. Freaky kind of comes with the territory.

I turned toward my bedroom, briefly considering popping a handful of Xanax and chasing it down with a fifth of tequila. That would be a lethal combo for a human, but all it would probably do to me is knock my ass out for a few hours. If indeed Jeff was right and I was in for a series of visitations – just like in that Bill Murray movie – how fucking hilarious would it be if they couldn't wake me up?

On the flipside, there was an equal chance that Jeff was as full of shit in death as he'd been in life. That was all assuming he wasn't just a hallucination to begin with, something I wasn't quite ready to rule out.

Ah fuck it. What's the worst that could happen? I had read that book in school and I knew how it went. Even better, I wasn't some sort of Scrooge. Sure, I might not be the most festive person on the planet come the holiday season, but it's not like I had my own personal

Bob Cratchit to kick around. Hell, if anything, Sally was the one more likely to be the *Bah Humbug bitch.*

Screw it. I decided it wasn't worth worrying about either way. At the end of the day, I really was too tired to give a shit. Bed was beckoning and I decided to heed its call.

Part 2

SMACK

What the fuck?!

"Wake up, pussy."

Again I was smacked in the face. I opened my eyes, but – judging by the voice – I already knew who would be there looking down at me.

"You again?"

"Yes, *me* again," Jeff replied before backhanding me across the face a third time.

"I'm awake!"

"I know. I just enjoy smacking the shit out of you."

I sat up and scuttled across the bed away from him. "What the fuck are you doing back here?"

"I am the ghost of Christmas past, Freewill."

"Whoa there just a fucking second, dude." I stood and walked up to him, poking a finger into his muscular chest. Hmm, for an incorporeal spirit he sure as shit felt solid enough. That was potentially worrisome. Still, I couldn't let him know that. "I thought you were supposed to be Jacob Marley here. You ain't no Patrick Stewart, so how the hell can you also be the ghost of Christmas..."

I didn't get a chance to finish as Jeff's response consisted of colliding his fist with my face. Blood exploded from my nose as I staggered back. Yep, he was definitely solid enough.

"I'm whoever the fuck I say I am!" he snapped. "Want to argue the point?"

"No, not particularly," I mumbled, still holding my smashed face.

"Good, then let's go. The less time I have to spend babysitting your nerdy ass, the better."

He grabbed hold of my arm and dragged me forward. I knew the size of my bedroom and we should have impacted with the wall, but didn't. We just kept walking. Somehow, I wasn't overly surprised.

"Let me guess, you're gonna take us back to the day I killed your ass and try to convince me it somehow made me into a bad person," I said, still trying to stem the flow of blood from my crushed nose. Goddamn, for a ghost, the douchebag hit really hard.

"Sorry, but that didn't happen at Christmas time. Rules are rules. Oh, but thanks for reminding me about that." His fist impacted with my stomach, driving the wind out of me.

Ouch.

I fell to my knees gasping. This was getting old real quickly. I balled my fist, ready to spring up and cock-punch the bastard, but that's when I heard a voice.

"I want a bike!"

It was a whiney, childish voice. It was also familiar, *very* familiar, namely because it was mine. I opened my eyes and found myself in my parents' living room, back in Scotch Plains, New Jersey. It was just as I remembered ... from fifteen years ago.

"Santa didn't bring you a bicycle, William," my father patiently explained to my younger self. Thinking back on things, it was obvious why. At that age, I had sucked at riding a bike. My first few forays on one, borrowing Tom's, had resulted in me crashing into a tree, then a bush, and finally the side of my father's car – scraping the shit out of it in the process. "Why don't you open the nice board games he brought you?"

One of the 'board games' I'd gotten that year had been a *Dungeons and Dragons* set. In the end, I had gotten a whole lot more use out it than any of my other presents, but that wouldn't start for at least a few weeks yet. At the time, I'd been too firmly fixated on the bike Santa had gypped me out of.

"But I was a good boy!" the nine year old version of me whined.

"I know, William, but..."

"SANTA SUCKS! I WANT A BIKE!" younger me screamed before bursting into tears.

"Why are you showing me this?" I asked Jeff, making sure to take a step back so as to be out of punching range. "I know how it played out. I bitched for half the day until I got sent to my room. A month later, my parents finally caved and got me the damn bike, which I promptly fell off of and broke my arm. Lesson learned."

"A shame it wasn't your neck."

"Yeah pity that. Then I couldn't have grown up, been turned into a vampire, and, oh yeah, taken over your coven."

Jeff turned toward me, burning hatred in his eyes. He looked as if he was about to pounce upon me, but somehow managed to restrain himself. I figured that probably meant we were done here and would be off to another stroll down memory lane. That's the way the story went. Instead, though, he asked, "Have you fucked any of them?

"Huh?" I asked, caught by surprise. "My *parents*?!"

"No, dickless. The coven ... the *women*."

"Oh. Um, no."

"I did – *all* of them. Hell, sometimes two or three at once. I used to make Sally scream like the traitorous little whore she is."

Okay, that kind of stung. I'll admit, when I took over from Jeff, I had a few fantasies about all the orgies I'd be having with the insanely hot females of the coven. Sadly for me, that hadn't happened. One day they were all slutting it up with Jeff, the next you'd have sworn I had taken over a convent instead. Don't get me wrong, I wasn't like him. I believed in treating women with at least a modicum of respect. Regardless, that little detail continued to irk me.

"And your point is?" I asked, trying not to sound annoyed.

"My *point* is that nothing has changed. You were a little pussy back then and you're an even bigger pussy today."

"Thanks for the insight, Doctor Freud. So, again, what exactly is this supposed to teach me?"

In the blink of an eye, Jeff was right in front of me. Vampires can move damn fast when they want to. Guess the same goes for ghost vamps. I'd have to make a note of that.

"Not a goddamn thing," he said, a predatory smile on his face. "I just wanted to remind you how pathetic you are. That's lesson enough for me." Once again, his fist flashed out and caught me square on the chin. This time when I fell back, darkness enveloped me.

Oh well, at least I didn't have to listen to him anymore.

* * *

Hangovers suck. They suck ten times as bad, though, when you haven't even been drinking. At least I didn't remember drinking. No, all I remembered was Jeff hitting my face like a runaway train.

Wait ... Jeff?! Wasn't he dead, as in permanently? Then how come...? Okay, that must have been a dream; a really bad dream. A painful one to be honest, but a dream nevertheless. Vampires didn't come back from being dusted.

Okay, I didn't know that for sure. I mean I guess it's possible. Still, it seemed a little petty to come back just long enough to kick the shit out of me before disappearing back into the ether for all of eternity. Of course, petty was a pretty good word to describe Jeff, although douchebag was a much better one. Hell, I could've spent the next several hours thinking up new and interesting...

"Are you gonna lie there playing with yourself all night? Because if so, I'm gonna get the fuck out of here."

I bolted straight up at the sound of the voice.

Fuck! My head didn't like that one bit. I put my hands on my temples to keep my frontal lobe from trying to escape. While I did so, I processed what I'd just heard. I knew that voice, in fact I knew it very well. It was a voice that had nagged, complained, and been a non-stop bitch to me ever since that fateful night when I woke up to find myself dead.

"Sally?" I cracked my eyes open a sliver. They didn't stay that way for long, though. One glimpse was enough for them to fly open wide enough that I was sure they'd pop out of my head.

"Hey, Bill."

"Holy shit!"

"Take a picture, asshole. It lasts longer. On second thought, don't. Try it and I'll tear your fucking arms off."

I had no answer for that. Hell, I barely even heard her. One-hundred and ten percent of my attention was centered on how she was dressed ... or undressed. Sally stood there in front of my bed, bathed in an eerie glow; however, that part barely even registered with me. What did, was that she was clad in nothing but festive ribbon, big red bows of it covering all of her good parts. If Jeff had been a nightmare, surely this was the wettest of dreams.

"I am the ghost of Christmas Present," she said, sounding bored.

"Why are you dressed like that?"

"Don't ask me. Apparently your subconscious is filling in some of the blanks here." She glanced down at herself and rolled her eyes. "Offhand, I'd say this is one-half bad pun with the rest being some sick fantasy on your part."

"So this is all a dream?" I asked, getting out of bed and approaching her.

"Not quite."

Whoa. My eyes drank her in like this was the Sahara and she the only glass of water in a hundred miles. This was a *hell* of a lot better than that shitty old bicycle. "Mind if I unwrap my Christmas present?" I reached out a tentative hand, grinning...

...and was immediately met by another punch to the face. Sally couldn't hit as hard as Jeff, but only a fool would discount her. She packed one hell of a mean right. If someone had told me at the start of this day that I'd be signing up for some makeshift rhinoplasty, I'd have stayed in bed.

"Try that again and the only Christmas gift you'll be looking forward to is doctor to reattach your dick."

"Point taken," I replied, checking to see if any teeth had been knocked loose.

"Good, then let's go." She turned and began walking, but I didn't move to follow. My feet were rooted in place as my eyes traveled down, noticing the Christmas ribbon thong that was, so far as I could tell, the only thing covering her ass.

No doubt sensing my wandering gaze, she turned and gave me a glare. "Eyes up here, mister, before I rip them out of your skull. Let's get this over with before you totally creep me the fuck out."

"I'm in no rush."

"I doubt that. Probably already shot a load in your pants."

That wasn't true ... well okay, it *almost* was. Sometimes having a vivid imagination is an awesome thing. Still...

"So what's the deal?" I asked, trying to focus. "Last time I checked, you weren't dead."

"That's okay, the last time I checked, you weren't a man. How the fuck should I know? All I know is that I'm here, I'm supposed to show you some bullshit that's probably going to fail to teach you a lesson, and I'm dressed like I'm about to star in a porno called Licking Santa's Candy Cane."

"That last part sounds pretty normal."

She turned and shot daggers at me with her eyes. "You can either walk or be dragged."

"Okay, I'm coming, I'm coming."

* * *

For the second time that night, I followed a *spirit* into the unknown. As before, I was led up to and then through my own bedroom wall, finding myself floating in misty darkness. At least this time my company was far more pleasant to look at.

"Behold," she said, her tone that of someone reading off a cue card, "the misery that abounds this Christmas season because of your misdeeds."

I tore my eyes off of her figure long enough to take a quick look and comment, "Um, I know Tom's kind of special, but I'm pretty sure Tiny Tim never had it this good."

She turned to survey the scene, apparently noticing it for the first time. We were in Christy's apartment, or at least I assumed we were. At the very least it was far more tastefully decorated than Tom's room at our place. Either way, she and my roommate were in the middle of a pretty heavy make-out session.

"I did not need to see this," Sally commented with a sigh.

"Not doing wonders for me either."

The couple started tearing at each other's clothes as we watched. Finally, Christy started unzipping Tom's pants. At that point Sally waved her hands in a panic, causing everything in our view to thankfully get all hazy. "We're out of here," she said. "If I have to see that fucktard's bony ass, I'm gonna be one cranky camper."

I didn't bother to point out that she wasn't too far from being one even when she was in what passed for a good mood. Nope, I just kept my mouth shut and continued to feast on the eye candy.

"Next stop..." She turned to fix me with another stony stare. I quickly brought my eyes up, not wanting to get decked again. "Let us visit your coven and see what horrors have befallen them as a result of your ... oh, Jesus Christ!"

I looked past her, my jaw dropping open yet again. "Whoa! Why the fuck wasn't I invited to this?" The scene before me was like some kind of Roman orgy, only bloodier. We were at the SoHo loft, home of most of the coven's social activities. A couple of dead bodies were splayed on the floor, a not too surprising occurrence when dealing with vamps. As for the members of the coven, they were in various states of doing ... *stuff*. Loud techno music blared as the surreal scene played out before us.

"This is what goes on when I'm not there?"

"Well, yeah," Sally commented.

"Fuck me!"

"Quite the opposite, I'd say."

As we watched, two of the women – Vanessa and Firebird – tore each other's bloody tops off and began wildly making out.

"Now we move on to see what other..."

"Hold on," I said. "I'd kinda like to stick around here a bit. You know, learn some more about my misdeeds."

"You'd die alone in a women's prison," she said with an eye roll. Another wave of her hands and we were once again surrounded by mist and darkness. Dammit, just when the show was getting good.

"Ah, here we are." she said at last. "Behold your friend Edward. Let us watch as he wallows in the suffering that has been brought upon him by... Ooh! Victoria's Secret is having a sale!"

We were in the Manhattan Mall from the look of things. Okay, I could dig this. If Ed was here during the holiday season then he sure as shit was suffering. I wouldn't wish this fate on my worst enemy. I'd sooner sunbath naked on my roof than be here at this time of year.

We spied him as he came out of a jewelry store on the second floor. What the hell? If he was miserable, he sure didn't show it. Hell, he almost looked happy. That might not sound like much, but it was about as close to jubilation as Ed got.

"What's he doing?"

"How the fuck am I supposed to know?" Sally replied. "Watch and learn."

Ed stepped over to the railing, away from the crowd of mall minions cascading in both directions. He pulled a small jewelry box out of his pocket and opened it to inspect the contents. Inside was a bracelet, a pricey one by the look of things. Why the hell was he buying jewelry, unless...

"Are those rubies?" Sally asked, suddenly interested. "They're my favorite."

I turned to face her, her body momentarily forgotten – but only momentarily. "Are we here just so we can watch Ed buy *you* a Christmas present?"

She adopted her best innocent face. It came across about as sincere as an apology from Charles Manson. "Don't look at me. I'm just the tour guide here."

"Then we must be visiting a farm because I smell a lot of bullshit. Either way, I'm failing to see the point here. I thought you said we were going to be viewing scenes of the misery I caused."

"Well..."

"As far as I can tell, the only miserable person I've seen so far tonight is myself. Double that after all the fun shit I've seen everyone else doing."

A thoughtful look crossed her face for a moment then she shrugged. "Good enough for the accounting I guess."

"No it's not..."

"Will you look at the time." She glanced down at a wristwatch that wasn't there. "I gotta get out of here. Places to be, bracelets to unwrap."

"You can't just..."

"Sorry, I don't make the rules. I just follow them." She began to turn away, but then stopped. "By the way, if I suspect for even a second that you've been jerking off to ... well, *this*..." she gestured down at her state of undress, "I will make a matching pair of earrings out of *these*."

Before I could react, her hand – claws extended – came up and locked onto my crotch. It would have been marvelous, had it not been so excruciating.

"Wouldn't dream of it," I squeaked.

"Didn't think so," she blithely replied. To help drive home the point, she gave one final squeeze – hard enough so that the world greyed out around me and I fell to my knees, unaware of anything save the screaming jingle bells between my legs.

Part 3

THUD

My head connected with the wooden floor of my bedroom. I sat up, wrapped in my sheets and covered in a thin sheen of sweat. Holy shit, what a dream!

Or was it?

I did the first thing that came to mind, reached down and checked on the boys. Whew! Thank goodness, they were still intact, although they were oddly tender, almost as if they had been...

Nah! It couldn't be. I had obviously gotten a hold of some tainted blood. Maybe it had been unwillingly donated by a crackhead or something. That had to be it. It definitely helped to explain the weirdness of the night.

I was almost ready to believe that, when a shadow fell over me. Vampires have excellent night vision, so it's not like I was at a disadvantage in the dark, but even so, when I looked up all I could see was a black void standing over me. No, that wasn't quite right. There was something in it. Whatever it was, it was draped in an unnatural shadow. As my eyes attempted to adjust to the supernatural darkness surrounding it, I saw that things weren't helped by the black clothing it wore – a hooded robe, the color of obsidian.

"Let me guess," I said, untangling myself from my bedclothes. "Ghost of Christmas Future, right?" Standing, I found myself looking down upon it. Hmm, awfully short for a ghost. I felt like I was standing there staring down a Jawa. Oh well, I guess the Grim Reaper didn't need to be seven feet tall to be intimidating.

The figure raised one arm, covered entirely in the sleeves of the robe, and pointed. What a surprise – I was supposed to follow it through my wall *again*. Jeez, didn't ghosts believe in doors or shit like that?

"Alright, let's get going. Show me my staking, my funeral, or whatever the fuck dog and pony show you've got in store so I can get back to bed. I'm tired and I figure it's only a matter of time before someone kills my ass anyway. Hell, barely a day goes by where I'm not surprised I lived to see the end of it."

The figure began walking and I found myself following it. "It's Sally, isn't it? She's the one who kills me, right? That's okay, you can tell me. I wouldn't be surprised."

The mists began to coalesce around us as we walked. Despite knowing what I'd be shown, I found myself rambling nevertheless. "The Draculas, it's gotta be them. They're all assholes anyway. I'm sure they'll sacrifice my ass whenever it suits their needs."

There was still no response from the figure.

"It's not Colin, right? Please tell me it's not him. That guy is an absolute weasel of a prick. I'd sooner be staked by..." I trailed off as the world began to take focus around us. Grey bleakness stretched toward the horizon. I found myself wondering when someone would hit the colorization button to fill things in, but then everything snapped into focus, sharp and crisp, but still drab in tone. This was how things looked? Kinda depressing if you ask me.

My attention was caught by something off in the distance. Squinting my eyes, I saw it was a great city or at least the remains of one. Broken buildings littered the landscape and random fires burned throughout. Damn, I guess some serious shit went down there.

The figure stopped and I almost bumped into the creepy little Oompa Loompa. It pointed again. I had been so focused on the *Mad Max* scenario playing out in the distance, that I'd missed a fairly large gathering of people off to the left of us.

We approached and I saw there was an order to the group. Several dozen people stood at attention in multiple columns. Though there seemed to be discipline in their actions, their method of dress varied. Some wore crisp suits while others were dressed in casual street attire. The spirit entered their ranks, and I followed. Passing the first few rows, I caught sight of several smiling faces, fangs protruding from them all. They weren't people, they were *vampires*.

Okay, so was this the vamp apocalypse everyone kept telling me about? It didn't look so bad. I could deal with...

"The last human city has fallen!" What the? I turned toward the front of the gathering, where the ghost was now heading. The voice had come from there. Once again, I knew it quite well.

I should have. It was *mine*.

"Even now, our brothers and sisters comb through the wreckage, picking off the last of their resistance," future me said from the head of the group. I was dressed ... well, damn. I looked fairly badass. I wore a long leather duster over a black uniform of sorts. Not to sound egomaniacal, but I apparently cleaned up pretty well when I put my mind to it. I'd have to remember that look. It might score me some points with the ladies.

I quickened my pace so as to catch up with the spirit. It was now approaching the head of the column, only a few feet from where I gave my victory rant. Don't get me wrong, I'm not particularly fond of the thought of becoming a genocidal nutcase. Still, I think there are few amongst us who haven't indulged in an evil overlord fantasy or three. Mine just happened to be somewhat more vivid than most.

"I have fulfilled my destiny," *Emperor* Bill continued, giving a psychotic monologue that would have made Ernst Blofeld proud. "The Icon is dead and my enemies lie crushed beneath my feet. We are now free to remake the world in our image. The vampire nation reigns supreme!"

A roar of approval rose up from amongst the assembled vamps. It was both disturbing and kind of flattering at the same time. I looked down at my tormenting spirit and remarked, "This isn't so bad. I mean there are worse fates than winding up in charge. I could have ended up..."

The figure silenced me by holding up its arm. The sleeve of its robe slipped down revealing a small pale hand. It then pointed back toward where I stood triumphant. Oh well, I guess it wouldn't hurt to hear what other kick-ass things my future-self had to say.

"We shall stride into this new age with our heads held high. Never again shall we hunt from the shadows. Together, I and my beautiful bride shall lead you to the glory our kind haven't known for far too many centuries."

Wait? Beautiful bride? Ooh, now this was getting interesting. Not only was I a kick-ass motherfucker, but I was apparently getting some too. I could dig this.

"Come here, my love, and share in our triumph." Badass Bill raised his hand and held it out in front of him, pointing it to the left of where I stood.

"Of course, beloved," came an eager reply from the crowd.

I knew that voice.

No fucking way!

Gansetseg, daughter of Ogedai Khan, strode forward. She was over three-hundred years old in my time, so who knew what age she was now. There was only one small problem – well, okay, a *lot* of small problems. For starters, Gan was batshit crazy. Under other circumstances, I could deal with that. The more pressing issue, though, was that she had been turned into a vampire shortly after her twelfth birthday. Physically, she had stayed that age ever since.

In short, she was the most psychotic munchkin to ever walk this Earth.

I blinked my eyes, not willing to believe it. Gan walked up to my future self and put her arms around me. He ... err ... *I* returned the affection. Ewww! That proved it. I was either in Hell or the vampire apocalypse was playing out in Arkansas. Neither was a particularly appealing proposition.

"Okay, you've got my undivided attention," I said to the spirit beside me, a feeling akin to panic starting to settle in. "I get it. I'm a horrible, evil person. Just tell me what I need to do to avoid this fate."

"Avoid it, my love?" the spirit replied, finding its voice at last.

Oh shit.

It reached up and removed the hood from its head. Gan's face peered up at me, a large grin spread across her prepubescent face, her green eyes sparkling with excitement. "This is your destiny. There is no avoiding it, although I cannot imagine why you would ever wish to. Is it not marvelous?"

It's about there that a lesser person would've probably cracked.

Oh who am I kidding? I *am* a lesser person. "Holy motherfucking shit!"

"I am pleased to see you too, beloved."

When confronted by the most horrific destiny that they can imagine, some people man up and charge headfirst into their fate. Others beg for mercy like the whiny little bitches they are. Me? I prefer to think I'm my own person, an independent thinker, a *free will* if you please. Thus I did neither. Instead, I took what seemed to be the most logical course of action.

I turned tail and ran off screaming.

Gan's voice followed after me as I entered the ether. "This is your future. You cannot escape your fate!" The last thing I heard as darkness closed around me was perhaps the most chilling of all. "By the way, our wedding was beautiful."

Well wasn't that just dandy like motherfucking candy? The world was in shambles, I was joined at the hip with the most dangerous pre-teen alive, but at least I knew how to throw a good reception.

Lucky me.

* * *

I'd like to tell you I woke up with some of my dignity intact, but let's not bullshit ourselves here. I bolted out of bed, sweat pouring off my brow and a scream escaping my lips.

Bright light streamed through the windows. It looked like it was morning. Had I slept through the entire day, then night again? It certainly seemed that way. Oh, who cared? I was back in my own bedroom and the nightmare was over. I was so happy that I would have even kissed Gan had she been there. But just for the record, I was glad she wasn't.

A sense of elation filled me. I had seen the very worst life had to offer me, including a nightmarish vision of the future, one that I would strive to avoid like the plague itself. Screw all that destroying mankind crap! If anything, I would embrace my humanity more tightly than ever before. There was no way I was going down that other path.

Oddly enough, that realization made me feel good, *really* good. I stood up, feeling light in my step. A smile on my face, I strode to the window and opened it, letting the cold morning air wash over me. I stuck my head out and surveyed the town ... *my* town.

"MERRY CHRISTMAS, BROOKLYN!" I shouted. Wait, was it Christmas yet? I couldn't quite remember.

Thinking quickly, I looked down and saw a teenager, gift in hand, ambling down the street. When in doubt, ask.

"You there, boy," I hailed him. "What day is ... OH FUCK!"

I began to sizzle as the rays of the morning sun hit me. I yanked my head inside as fast as I could and shut the drapes. Note to self: embracing my humanity was fine, I just needed to remember that there were still a few caveats attached to it.

Remembering that I had just exposed my vampiric nature to the world at large, I peeked through the curtains to see what was happening below. The kid I had yelled to was continuing on his merry way as if nothing out of the ordinary had just happened. Thank God for New Yorkers. This was the only place in the world where the heights of weirdness were barely worthy of a shrug.

Oh well. I stopped, dropped, and rolled to put myself out, then threw on a fresh – and unburnt – set of clothes. Slightly singed, but presentable, I opened my bedroom door and stepped out. Despite my little mishap of bursting aflame, my new outlook on life was still intact.

"Merry Christmas!" I shouted, spotting Ed in our kitchen nook, coffee cup in hand.

He took a sip and nonchalantly replied, "Christmas is tomorrow, Bill. I'm driving you to your parents, remember?"

"Of course I remember," I lied. "But just because it's tomorrow, doesn't mean we can't celebrate it today. Hell, we can celebrate it *every* day!" I turned and spied my other roommate, Tom. He was sitting on the couch with his lovely girlfriend Christy.

"Merry Christmas, you two!" I said, striding over. I gave him a hearty handshake, then pulled him to his feet and embraced him like a brother. I even bent down and gave Christy a little peck on the cheek.

"You're in a surprisingly good mood," Ed remarked, walking over. He raised one eyebrow quizzically and said, "I thought you weren't excited about the holidays."

"Not anymore, my friend. I've decided I need a whole new outlook on life. From here on in things will be different. No more moping and whining. I've been given a gift and, by God, I'm going to use it to make a difference in this world. Today is the first day of the rest of my life and it's going to be a long, fulfilling life. It's..."

"I knew it would work!" Tom cried, turning to Ed. "You owe me, dude."

Christy swatted his arm. "Shhhh. You're not supposed to say anything."

"Say anything?" I asked, confused, albeit still elated.

"It's nothing," Ed said.

Tom nodded and replied, "Ed's right, but he still owes me ten bucks."

Despite knowing that more important matters awaited me, I found my curiosity piqued. "Why do you owe Tom ten dollars?"

"Oh, no reason," he replied, sipping his coffee. I still had a grin on my face, but something about his tone bothered me. When you lived with people long enough you could practically smell when they're bullshitting you from a mile away. This whole place stank of it right then and it was causing my veneer of good cheer to start cracking.

I knew Ed was a tough nut to crack. Thus I turned to the weakest link in the room. "Tom, why does Ed owe you money?" Christy opened her mouth to say something, but I held up a hand to silence her. "Care to enlighten me?"

"You're probably gonna be pissed" he replied. Ed let out a sigh of disgust and walked back over to the kitchen. We could both tell when Tom was about to spill his guts. It wasn't particularly hard. The dude couldn't keep his mouth shut if it was Krazy-glued.

"I promise I will *not* be pissed." I held up a finger and crossed it over my non-beating heart.

"Well, you've been a little glum lately, what with all the shit going on."

"And," I prodded, keeping an overly-friendly smile plastered on my mug.

"And I remembered Christy mentioning a couple of weeks back that she knew this spell, something to do with using a person's subconscious to help perk them up. Right, hon?"

"Heh. It's a little more complicated than that," she replied, quickly stepping behind him, a sheepish grin on her face.

"How so?" I asked conversationally.

"You know, dimensional doors, linking of minds through the astral plane. Silly stuff like that."

"You don't say," I replied, feeling my smile falter as I gritted my teeth. "Truly fascinating."

"I thought it was an awesome idea," Tom continued, still oblivious to the hole he was digging himself, "but Ed told me it was all bullshit. We argued a bit until he bet me that Christy couldn't change your outlook on life."

"Let me get this straight," I said, walking over and putting an arm around his shoulders. "Ed bet you that Christy couldn't make me happy by fucking with my brain – all for the princely sum of ten dollars. And you accepted?" As I spoke, I slowly tightened my grip on him into a choke hold.

"Something like that," he sputtered.

"And you thought this was a good idea?!" I asked Ed, feeling my fangs involuntarily extend.

"I take it, then," he replied calmly, "that your outlook has not improved."

"What the fuck do you think?"

"What do I think?" He turned his attention back toward Tom. "I think that proves my point. Kindly fork over the cash."

I let go of Tom, feeling utterly exasperated. My God, what a bunch of pricks I lived with.

I turned toward my room, deciding that going back to sleep was my best course of action. Visions of Gan suddenly didn't sound so bad.

"No hard feelings, Bill?" Ed called after me. "It was all in good fun ... and a little easy money."

"Ask me that in about a hundred years," was my reply as I slammed the door shut behind me.

I took a step toward my bed, then had a thought. Didn't Christy say something about linking minds? Was it possible? Hmm. What the hell? It was worth a shot.

I stuck my head back out and said, "Oh, and just for your information, Sally hates rubies."

The last thing I saw before shutting the door again were Ed's eyes opening wide in genuine surprise.

It was only then that I allowed myself the ghost of a smile. Perhaps it was worth the ten bucks after all.

Bah Humbug indeed.

THE END

Christmas Market

By

Amy Cross

"How about now? Are you *finally* feeling Christmassy?"

It takes me a moment to answer. The Christmas market is so bright and busy and loud, and so beautiful all lit-up against the dark trees and the night sky beyond, that it feels curmudgeonly to not join in. I mean, it's not the market's fault that I'm not in the mood for Christmas, and it's not Jessie's fault either. It's no-one's fault but mine. So I do what I always do in these situations, which is that I turn to her and smile, and I tell her what she wants to hear.

"Sure, Jessie. You were right. It's kinda cool and -"

"Let me show you something!" she stammers, grabbing my hand and pulling me past several stalls, dragging me through the sea of thickly over-coated, scarf-wearing Christmas shoppers. "You're gonna love it!"

"If you say so," I mutter, almost tripping several times before slamming into her shoulder as she comes to a sudden halt ahead of me.

Feeling a little breathless, I look around at the stalls, and I have to admit that they look very warm and jolly. Tonight has been advertised as a special food extravaganza, *The Gobblin' Market*, which means every stall is selling some variation of cake, pies, puddings and glog. I swear, I can feel my waistline expanding simply from looking at the pile of chocolate logs on the stall next to me, and that's before I've even spotted the vast array of marzipan animals on another stall. Electric lights are shining so brightly all around me, and I can feel their warmth as I step over to take a closer look at the array of marzipan pigs, marzipan ladybugs and marzipan farm animals. One of the pigs, in particular, looks extremely happy with his little red scarf tucked tight around his neck.

For the first time in months, I actually smile a genuine smile. Mum and Dad would have loved a marzipan pig.

"Not that! This!" Jessie says suddenly, grabbing my arm and turning me around, before pulling me a few feet forward until we're right in front of a completely different stall. "Look at it!"

This time, I find myself staring at a stall filled with old-fashioned Christmas puddings, the kind I remember from when I was a kid. The kind you have to eat carefully, in case you get the slice with the penny. Stepping closer, I see that there are puddings of all shapes and sizes here, including one in the middle that's easily as big as Grandpa Joe's head. Grandpa Joe was known for having a very big head – big from the front and very long from the side – so a pudding of that size is quite an achievement. Not that anybody could ever eat such a thing, even if they had a huge family. Or am I underestimating the appetite of the modern British family?

"Aren't you gonna buy anything?" Jessie asks.

"Um -"

"I want one of those!"

She points at a medium-sized pudding near the front of the stall, while taking some crumpled banknotes from her pocket.

"I'm gonna wait and see what else there is first," I mutter, as the woman behind the stall reaches for the pudding and starts wrapping it, ready for Jessie to carry it away.

"What about that one?" a man says next to me.

I turn a little, not enough to look straight at them, just enough to see that he's admiring some brandy trifles.

"Are you kidding?" replies his companion, a middle-aged woman wearing earmuffs. "They look deadly."

"That's what Boxing Day's for," he tells her, and now I'm getting a really strong whiff of his bad, coffee-stained breath. "You sit around in your pants, trying to digest everything you ate the day before. It's all part of the fun."

"I'm just gonna take a look at some of the other stalls," I explain, nudging Jessie's arm.

"Just hang on a mo!"

"I won't go far. I just -"

Suddenly the whiff of the man's breath becomes really strong, and I almost gag.

"Catch up, yeah?" I tell Jessie, before turning and squeezing my way through the crowd. I swear, that guy's breath was the worst, and it's clear that Jessie's going to have to wait a few minutes for the stall-holder to finish wrapping that ginormous pudding. Besides, the market isn't too scary, and I think it might be good for me to spend a few minutes alone in the crowd.

After all, I'm getting better and better. Maybe Christmas isn't going to be so bad this year after all.

I glance over my shoulder and briefly spot Jessie's excited face, bathed in the stall's light as she waits for her pudding.

Wandering through the crowd, I take the path of least resistance whenever I come up against a wall of bodies. Instead of fighting my way to specific spots, I just let the currents of the crowd bump me this way and that, and for several minutes I don't get anywhere near any of the stalls. Instead, I'm kept more or less in the center line of the crowd that's flooding through the market, and that's absolutely fine. Stuffing my hands into my pockets, I crane my neck to catch passing glimpses of all the stalls I'm missing, and after a while I actually start to think that I wouldn't mind a biscuit or two, or maybe a slice of cake.

Of course, that would require wriggling through the crowd with some sense of purpose, and I'm not sure I can do that. I guess I'll just let the crowd carry me along, and I'll wait to see where I get spat out. I mean, I have to get spat out eventually.

Suddenly I'm squeezed between two passing freighter-like women, neither of whom seems to have noticed me. Just as I think I might be crushed to oblivion, one of the women shifts slightly and this allows the force from the other to shoot me out past a couple of boys and their mother, at which point I trip slightly and pull the other way. This, in turn, sends me bumping into a well-dressed man who mutters something – I think directed at me – as I stumble between a pair of very thin girls who look like they're heading to a club. After ricocheting against a few more people, and clattering into a wall of arms and elbows, the flow of the crowd briefly carries me around the far corner before finally – and very thankfully – I find myself dumped out at the crowd's edge, in a slightly darker part of the market to which everyone else seems to have their backs turned.

Well, at least I have survived so far.

Taking a deep breath, I can't help feeling slightly relieved. I know I should go back into the throng and find Jessie, but now I can't quite find a gap in the flow. I try to excuse myself and ask if I might nip into a few gaps, but the wall of bodies is resolute and after a moment I step back, figuring I should wait for things to die down slightly. The market is insanely busy tonight, and I honestly don't know how everybody else manages.

Turning, I look around and realize that I really *do* seem to be in an ignored corner of the market. At first, all I see is a dark, unlit patch of ground, but after a moment I see that there's actually one stall here, albeit one with no lights and no attention. In fact, this particular stall is not only set well back from the crowd, it also seems to be turned the wrong way, with the serving platform facing the crowd and the display section – where it would have all its wares for sale, if it *had* any wares at all – facing out toward the dark forest.

Stepping closer, I hold my mittened hands up to my mouth and blow on my exposed finger-tips, just to get a little warmth.

The ground beneath my feet is slightly muddy here, less even, and a little soggy. The air is noticeably colder.

When I reach the darkened stall, I find that there's definitely nothing on display. I guess this stall must have been left over when all the others were rented out, so the market's organizers simply dumped it here so it was out of the way. I can't help feeling a little sorry for the poor stall, since all the others have been dressed up so nicely whereas this one was unceremoniously pushed aside. As I get closer, I peer through the open rectangular frame and try to imagine what it would be like to sell something to a customer, but all I see are the cold, naked trees at the far edge of the park. Reaching down, I place my bare finger-tips against the stall's cold, wrinkled wood. This stall isn't quite like any of the others. It's a little more battered, as if it's from an earlier time.

"What's up?" I mutter. "Too old and ugly for anyone to rent you, huh? Well, *I'd* rent you, if I had anything to sell."

I pause for a moment, before realizing that I'm getting unbearably maudlin and sentimental. Stuffing my hands back into my pockets, I take one final look through to the stall's dark other side, and then I turn and head back toward the bright crowd.

"What about that one?" a voice suddenly asks behind me. "The one in the green coat?"

Turning, I'm startled to see a man and a woman standing on the other side of the neglected stall. The man is pointing toward the crowd, but the woman next to him is already furrowing her brow as if she's deeply unimpressed. There was no sign of them a moment ago, and I have no idea where they came from, but they're definitely here now.

"No?" the man mutters, as he continues to look past me. "What's wrong? Too short? Too round?"

"I don't like the head much," the woman replies, squinting now as if she's having trouble seeing the crowd properly at all.

"What about the one in the brown coat, then?" the man asks. "I know it's a man, but he might be okay with that. After all, variety is the spice of life. Maybe he's sick of girls."

Looking over my shoulder, I see that there's a man in a brown coat not too far away, with his back turned to us. There's a woman in a green coat, too, but everyone is looking at the other stalls. Nobody else seems to have noticed this dark, out-of-the-way stall at all.

"It's not a very enticing mix this year, is it?" the man continues as I turn back to look at them. "It's usually a lot better than this."

As they continue to discuss the matter between themselves, I can't help noticing that while I can just about make out their faces in the low light, I can't see their eyes very well. Not that I *need* to see their eyes, of course, but something about not being *able* to see them makes me curious, so I take a cautious step forward, heading back toward the abandoned stall.

"That one in the orange might do," the woman murmurs, although she still doesn't sound too keen. "Emphasis on the *might.*"

"Well we can always try somewhere else," the man tells her. "It's only the twenty-third. We've got the rest of tonight, and then tomorrow night too, before -"

"What about her?" the woman asks suddenly, pointing straight at me. "Look! Her in the red coat!"

The man looks at me, although he doesn't seem too interested.

"I know she's not perfect," the woman continues, "but for God's sake, Julian, do we really want to go traipsing around every Christmas market in the country, hunting for perfection? She looks perfectly fine to me, and you know the red will go down well!"

"I suppose so," the man mutters, eyeing me up and down. "Still, we shouldn't be too hasty. She looks a little... Well, you know."

Taking another step toward the stall, I can't help smiling slightly. These two people seem so utterly strange, and so lost in their conversation, that I find myself wondering if they're quite alright in the head. They're dressed rather formally, and in fact they even appear a little old-fashioned, but evidently they're quite happy to discuss my various merits and failings without worrying one jot that I can hear them. The way they're talking about me, it's as if they view me as some kind of inanimate object. A cake, perhaps. Or a bun that didn't come out quite right.

"My legs ache," the woman groans as I get closer, adding an elaborate, slightly theatrical sigh. "Julian, can we *please* just settle? There's nothing wrong with her, at least not that I can see, and it's not as if we have to achieve absolute perfection. Maybe this can be a lesson for you. Next year, you can jolly well agree to start Christmas shopping with me a little earlier, instead of always rushing at the last minute!"

"Come on, Agnes, don't take pot-shots," he replies. "Let's try one more market and -"

"We've found what we came for," she says firmly. "Julian, honestly, will you just be told?"

The man stares at me for a moment, and it's clear that he's not entirely convinced. I can see his eyes now, but they're very dark, with no hint of white at all. Finally, he shrugs his shoulders.

"Okay, fine," he mutters, with a resigned air. "Where's the little man, then? Let's get it all sorted and paid for, and then we can go home to the fire."

"Can I help you?" I ask, raising a quizzical eyebrow. "Do you need something?"

I wait for a reply, but the woman simply continues to watch me with a critical eye, while the man turns and looks around as if he's waiting for somebody else to arrive.

"Where the bloody hell is he?" he asks after a moment, sounding annoyed. "You'd think these people would bother to stay put, so they can take our money. This is no way to run a business, Agnes. I'm telling you, these stall-holders have no work ethic whatsoever!"

"Oh, do be quiet, Julian," she replies. "He'll be along in a minute."

"What exactly is it that you're after?" I ask as I reach the stall again. "I don't think anyone's running this one. I think it's just been dumped here. The actual market's just over there, where all the lights are."

Again, I wait for a reply.

"I think this is a sign," the man grumbles finally, ignoring every word I just said. "We should just keep looking."

"We've found one that'll do, Julian!" the woman groans, rolling her eyes. "Now make yourself useful and locate the little man who runs the stall. It's cold out tonight, and I want to get this over with. Don't forget, we've got a nice bottle of mulled wine waiting for us at home."

Mumbling something under his breath, the man turns and walks away, quickly disappearing into the darkness. Left alone, facing the woman as she waits on the other side of the stall, I can't help thinking that I've wandered into something rather surreal. The woman seems completely uninterested in listening to me or making conversation, and she doesn't even seem to think it's worth acknowledging me at all. At the same time, she has no problem staring straight at me, watching me as if she thinks I'm just a *thing*.

"Can I ask you a question?" I say finally. "What are you... I mean, I don't quite get what you're doing here."

She maintains eye contact with me, but she doesn't say a word.

"I'm not the stall-holder," I continue. "If that's what you think, I... I really don't think this stall is selling anything. I think it's just been dumped here."

Again, she doesn't reply.

"Emma!" a voice calls out suddenly, far behind me. "Where are you?"

"That's my friend," I tell the woman, recognizing Jessie's cry. "I should probably go to her, but I don't think anyone's going to come to this stall and sell you anything. You need to go to the main part of the market, just over there. Do you see all the lights?"

"Emma! Come on, dude, where are you?"

I wait for the woman to acknowledge me, before finally figuring that there's nothing more I can do here. Turning, I keep my hands in my coat pockets as I head back to the crowd, and fortunately the market seems to be just a tad less busy now. Slipping into the sea of bodies, I quickly spot Jessie waving at me, and I wave back at her before glancing over my shoulder toward the stall. The man has returned, standing next to the woman, and he seems to be taking some money from his wallet. He's speaking, too, although I can't imagine what he thinks he's going to achieve, and then a moment later he holds the money out across the stall.

Suddenly I spot a dark figure, standing pretty much exactly where I was standing just a moment ago. Tall but hunched, the figure takes the money, at which point the man looks this way and points straight at me.

Before I can reach, the dark figure turns and looks at me, and I'm shocked to see two pitch-black pits where it should have eyes. Its limbs are mostly long, thin, very straight black lines, with occasional sharp bends, like the branches of the dead trees in the distance, while its torso is plump and rounded at the bottom. There seems to be a kind of shell-like arch to its back, as if the guy is wearing some kind of old, tattered insect-style Halloween costume. The sight is creepy as hell, and yet I can't look away. For a couple of seconds, I feel as if this *thing* is staring straight into my mind.

"There you are!"

Jessie grabs my arm. Startled, I turn to her, and then I look back toward the stall, only for the crowd to bump me along until all I can see are all the other, more colorful stalls. I crane my neck, trying to peer back toward the strange couple and the dark figure, but they're completely out of view now and I can already tell that there's no point trying to fight the crowd's momentum.

"Where'd you go?" Jessie asks excitedly, clutching her packaged pudding. "Are you having fun yet?"

"Did you see that?" I stammer.

"See what? Come on!"

As we make our way around the rest of the market, I try telling her about the strange experience with the couple and the abandoned stall, but she's not really paying attention and finally I more or less give up. That doesn't mean I think I imagined the whole thing, of course, although Jessie keeps laughing at the parts of the story that she actually hears, and she's clearly far more interested in all the other stalls. My mind's really not on the market any longer, and I keep trying to figure out if we're getting closer again to the weird stall, although the layout of the place seems somewhat haphazard.

Finally, with no warning, I find that we've suddenly reached the entrance, where people are excitedly piling in and out of the market.

"Bloody hell, I'm knackered!" Jessie sighs. "Wanna go to the pub? Selina and Tim are gonna be there!"

I try to tell her that I'm too tired, but she's typically persistent and by the time we're out past the market's main gate I've already agreed to follow her to Jekyll's for just one drink. Of course, one drink with Jessie always turns into two or three, but I've already factored that into my decision-making process, and I figure I can handle a mild, short night out. Maybe some socializing would even do me good. It's been a long time since I really went anywhere.

"Where the hell's my pudding?" she says suddenly, sounding panicked as she looks down at the various packages and boxes she accumulated while we were in the market. "Damn it! I must've left it at that last stall!"

"Well -"

"Back in a minute! Don't go anywhere!"

With that, she turns and hurries back into the market, while muttering loudly about how some "thieving buggers" had better not have taken her pudding and done a runner.

I almost go with her, before realizing that the idea of going back into the surging mass of the market really isn't a very appealing prospect. Crowds are definitely not my thing.

"I'll just wait here, then," I mutter under my breath.

I didn't even buy anything in the end, which feels vaguely anticlimactic, but I guess it's not as if I have many people to buy gifts *for*. Or much money to buy gifts *with*. I'm spending Christmas with Jessie and her family, and I know they feel sorry for me, but I also know it's really nice of them to invite me. There's still a part of me that wants to just make an excuse and go back to my flat, and spend the entire holiday period alone. I could be perfectly happy with Christmas dinner for one, and a copy of the bumper *Radio Times*, and some books and maybe just one little box of candy. I've always been the kind of person who doesn't mind being alone, but Jessie has already shouted down all my attempts to slip out of this big Christmas visit. I guess I should be grateful that I have such a good friend.

"Stephen, can you please stop complaining?" a woman says suddenly, marching a little boy out of the market. "I told you, we can't afford any more. You got the one you wanted, didn't you?"

"I changed my mind!" he hisses angrily, holding a slice of cake. "I want chocolate now!"

"Well, I'm sure the carrot cake is still nice. If -"

"I don't want it!" he yells, turning and throwing the cake with such force that it splats against the boundary fence that marks the edge of the market.

"Stephen!" his mother shouts. "What did you do that for?"

"Why can't I have chocolate?" he screams, starting to pull a full-on tantrum. "I want chocolate!"

"Okay," she mutters, pulling him along faster, toward the distant lights of the parking lot. "That's it! If you can't be grateful for anything you get, then why should I bother? We're going straight home!"

"I hate you!" he shouts as they get further and further away. "And I hate everything you give me! You never get it right!"

I can't help watching their silhouettes as they reach the parking lot. A kid like that is my absolute worst nightmare, and I feel sorry for the mother. If the kid behaves that way with everything she gets for him, then frankly I feel like she should stop buying him gifts at all. When I was that age, I was always grateful for anything I received, and I understood that my parents barely had enough money for us to get by. Some years, we couldn't even afford crackers.

"Emma?" a familiar voice calls out suddenly, over my shoulder. "Are you ready to go?"

Turning, I see that Jessie has retrieved her pudding, although she also seems to have picked up two toffee apples on sticks. She's licking one of the apples as she comes back out from the market, while holding the other apple and balancing her various packages and parcels.

"Hey," I say with a faint smile. "You won't believe the kid who just came by here a moment ago."

"Emma?" She takes another lick, silhouetted against the lights of the market as she looks around. Since she came back out, she hasn't quite made eye contact with me once. "Where are you, babe?"

"Right here," I reply, holding up a hand and waving at her, even though she's only a few feet away.

She continues to look around. "Emma?"

"Shall we get to the pub, then?" I ask. "Sorry if I didn't seem enthusiastic earlier. I was just in a weird place. I'll perk up, I promise."

She turns and looks back into the market for a moment, before taking her phone from her pocket and tapping at the screen. I hear a faint ringing sound coming from her phone's speaker, but to my surprise my own phone doesn't react at all. When I pull it from my pocket, I see that I have no signal at all.

"Seriously?" Jessie says with a sigh, tapping at the screen again, and this time she seems to be typing out a message. "Come on, Emma. Don't do this to me. Not after everything I've put up with from you."

"Put up with?" I reply, startled. "What do you mean?"

She stares at her phone for a moment longer, before tapping again and then holding it at the side of her face.

"It's me," she says with another sigh. "Hey, Selina, I'm two minutes away, but Emma's vanished. She didn't seem very into the market, I think she might have just gone home without saying anything."

She hesitates, listening to a voice on the other end, and then she starts wandering toward the road.

"I know," she continues. "I've texted her to say where we'll be, but I'm not standing around waiting in the cold. I swear to God, I actually think I'd prefer it if she went home. She's being such a downer."

"Sorry?" I stammer, hurrying after her. "Jessie -"

"I know!" she adds, still acting as if she can't hear me. "Frankly, I'm starting to think she's a stuck-up bitch. I dragged her to the Christmas market, but she had a face like a wet weekend the whole time. I get it's sad that her parents died in a car crash, but that was three months ago! She should be starting to pick herself up by now!"

"You think I'm a bitch?" I ask incredulously.

She laughs at something.

"Yeah," she continues. "Maybe. You're right, screw her. If she shows up at the pub, she shows up. If she doesn't, it's her loss. Snooty cow."

Stopping, I watch as she makes her way to the crossing, and then she heads across the road. She's still talking to someone on the phone, and I can hear her laughing, but I feel genuinely hurt by everything she just said. Even if she was joking, she took it way too far, and I'm not in the mood to be called a bitch or a snooty cow.

"Fine, then!" I mutter, even though I know she can't hear me anymore. "I'd rather spend Christmas alone, anyway!"

I watch as her silhouette disappears around the corner, and then I turn and start heading back past the market, toward the path that leads home. Stuffing my hands into my pockets for warmth, I tell myself that I'll be much better off just staying in my flat and keeping myself company. There'll be loads of films to watch, and I can pick up some books, and I'll have a quiet, un-rushed Christmas. Maybe I'll take some flowers to the grave on Sunday morning and spend some time up there. Jessie told me it'd be maudlin and depressing to do something like that, but I actually think I'd rather see whether -

Suddenly I'm grabbed from behind and a black sack is placed snuggly over my head. I try to cry out, but a hand clamps tightly over the front of the bag, forcing my mouth shut, and ropes are quickly wrapped around my chest. A moment later, someone grabs my legs and I'm swung around. I tell myself this is all a joke, that Jessie is staging some kind of dumb, elaborate prank, but I can hear whispering voices nearby as I'm carried across uneven ground. I try to twist free, but I'm being held far too securely.

A moment later the bag is yanked off of my head as I'm dropped into some kind of empty space. Immediately, a piece of cloth is shoved into my mouth, pushed far down my throat before something is tied over my lips. I manage a few muffled groans as I try to climb out, but I'm quickly forced back down as the bag is once again roughly yanked down over my head. Panicking, I try to kick out at my attackers, but something slams into my chest, momentarily blasting the air from my lungs.

"Wait!" a familiar voice hisses. It's the man from earlier, from the weird, dark stall. "Let me get a proper look at her before we leave!"

"Oh, Julian," the woman replies, sounding exhausted. "We've already paid! He said no refunds, remember? You never get refunds from the market."

"Take the bag off," he continues. "I want to be sure he'll like her. The last thing we need is to spend the whole of Christmas dealing with another of Leonard's tantrums."

Suddenly the bag is pulled from my head, and I'm shocked to find myself staring up at the man and the woman. I seem to be in some kind of trunk, maybe in the back of a car, and I quickly try once more to climb out. Suddenly the man pushes the tip of a walking cane against my chest, and I feel a burst of pain that sends me slumping back down into the trunk.

"I suppose she'll do," he mutters, as I try to call for help despite the gag over my mouth. "I think I really need to see her properly, though."

Reaching up, he starts digging a fingernail into his own flesh, at the edge of his left eye. Staring in horror, I see that he's carefully pulling loose a flap of skin, and then he starts slowly peeling a section of flesh away.

"These things always itch so much," he complains. "You'd think we'd have something better by now, for our jaunts out into the world."

With that, he pulls the fake skin aside, revealing his real eyes. Large, baseball-sized black orbs stare down at me from an otherwise human-looking face, and I meet his gaze with a growing sense of dread as I see my own terrified features reflected back at me.

"Fine," he mutters, followed by an approving grunt. "She's better than last year's, at least. She'll do."

Behind him, the woman peels the fake flesh from around her eyes too, revealing similar large, black balls that take up almost half her face.

"I'm glad you approve," she says with a sigh. "I'm sure Leonard will enjoy her, and that's what really matters. He always breaks them after a few days, anyway."

They stare at me for a moment longer, with those horrific, unblinking eyes, before suddenly the man reaches up and slams the trunk's lid down, plunging me into darkness.

I try to scream, but the gag over my mouth is too tight. I try to pull my hands free, but the ropes are holding my arms firmly at my sides. I try to wriggle around so I can force my shoulder against the top of the trunk, but a moment later there's a shudder that briefly shakes the dark space. I think I'm in some kind of old-fashioned carriage, and the man and woman just sat on seats directly above me.

"Get on with it!" the man calls out, and I hear the sound of horses whinnying before the trunk starts shaking again.

We're moving.

"I'll be glad to get home and back into the warm," the woman says calmly. "All this cold air is no good for my angina, you know."

As the carriage rolls over the bumpy ground, I turn and start furiously kicking the side of the trunk, trying desperately to get somebody's attention. There have to be people out there, people who can hear me, but I'm sobbing frantically now and no matter how hard I kick the trunk, I don't hear any sound of help coming. Someone has to have seen me being abducted, though. There's no way I could have been dragged away without *someone* noticing. Help's going to come. It has to.

"And for pity's sake, Julian," the woman continues above me, as the carriage rumbles along and I keep kicking the trunk's side, "next year, can we *please* not leave it to the last minute before we come out to buy the poor child's Christmas gift?"

The End

Deck the Halls

By

Xtina Marie

He dons the red suit
with the big black buckle,
humming 'Jingle Bells'
with a hearty chuckle.

Lacing the tall boots
With a flick of his wrist,
He glances out the window
As the snow begins to mist.

The radio plays softly:
'Silent Night' and 'Deck The Halls',
As he combs through his beard
While around him, darkness falls.

He throws the burlap sack
Over his strong shoulder,
Then leaves his quiet home
As the temperature gets colder.

"Ho, ho, ho!" he bellows
In a jolly voice.
People stop what they are doing

And smile as they rejoice.

Through the back door he creeps;
Smells the holiday cheer and
Sees confusion in her eyes
As she looks at him with fear.

Brandishing his knife
He hums 'Oh Christmas Tree'
Then shivers in delight
As she fights to get free.

She begs for her life
While he hacks her to pieces.
Blood splatters on the nativity
And defiles baby Jesus.

Her feet thrash and kick
In stockings of green and red.
She lies in a pool now
And knows soon, she'll be dead.

The colorful lights blink
And cast shadows on the walls;
Her screams die down
As he whispers 'Deck the Halls'.

Merry Fuckin' Christmas

By

Kevin J. Kennedy

Christmas Eve is a time for joy, a time to celebrate, to relax with your family, to drink and be merry. It's a time of year when very few people walk the streets, snow falls from the sky and the drab greys are lost to the beauty of a glistening white landscape. Re-runs of old movies take over the television, Christmas songs filter out from every store you pass, colourful lights sparkle in the windows of every house. It's a time to forget about life's troubles if only for a day and look forward to the Christmas dinner.

Christmas dinner was Alec's favourite dinner of the year. He got up first thing in the morning, often before even the kids were awake, to start preparing. The turkey was covered in bacon, and apples were sliced and placed around it for flavour, the stock later being used to make a mouth-watering gravy. He would cut the vegetables and place them into separate bowls to cook later. Next he would set the table. Christmas was the one and only day of the year they used a table cloth. It was white with little bits of red and green trim. Pauline, Alec's wife had bought the table cloth a few years ago and they had used it every year since. It looked nice adorned with the silverware that they also only used for Christmas. The family wasn't religious but Christmas wasn't really a religious holiday anymore. The retail chains owned Christmas now. The 1st of October this year, the stores filled with Christmas decorations, the same day they put out the Halloween decorations. It made no sense, and Alec felt it ruined it all a bit, but at least by Christmas Eve he was home with his family and he could shut out all the world's problems, if only for twenty-four hours.

Alec finished setting the table by placing a few Christmas crackers between the plates. He could smell the turkey cooking, the smell wafting in from the kitchen. It made his mouth water. He always cooked little sausages in with the turkey and by the time it was ready, they fell apart in your mouth. They were his favourite part; the kids loved them too. Christmas had been all about the kids the last few years: seeing their little faces light up with joy as they tore the paper from their presents, only to fling them aside and grab the next one. They were spoiled, Alec knew, but he just couldn't help himself, he would have spent his last penny on them just to see they were happy.

Walking into the kitchen, Alec opened the oven, then stepped back as the heat spilled out, he grabbed a fork from the shelf and speared three of the little sausages. He closed the oven door then began carefully nibbling on the piping hot sausages stacked on his fork. He leaned against the kitchen unit, staring into space as he finished them off, then threw the fork in the sink. The house was eerily quiet, something Alec wasn't used to. You didn't get a lot of quiet time with a wife and two kids. Sarah, who was the older of the two, was reasonably manageable, but his five year old son, Sammy, was a lunatic. The boy only seemed to need occasional small naps, then wake up with a whirlwind of energy. He could tire out both Alec and Pauline in a matter of an hour, however, he was a good boy overall, just noisy and energetic. Alec walked over to the unit on the wall just to the side of the kitchen window, opened it and slipped out a bottle of whiskey. He took his glass from beside the sink and filled it with three fingers then knocked it back in one shot. The burn going down his throat felt good. '*Daddy*' he heard, but only in his head; there would be no one shouting at him as they came running down the stairs, sounding like a heard of wild elephants, no wife to kiss his cheek and wish him a Merry Christmas, no one to sit at the table with and share his meal, no one to look at and feel filled with love just because they are part of his life. No...fucking...one!

Alec launched the glass across the kitchen, smashing it into a million tiny fragments. He picked up the bottle and upended it, taking several gulps before thumping it back down onto the work top. His throat was on fire but it felt good. It felt like the anger that was buzzing around in his head was somewhere else, if only momentarily. Alec knew he would never have a good Christmas ever again. His family had been taken from him, stolen by a scummy drunk driver that had walked free, all because the law was a fucking joke. His lawyer had told him in layman's terms that the police had fucked up, it was that simple. His family was gone and the guy got off. No justice, no retribution, just a big 'fuck you'. Alec lifted the bottle and took another drink of the whiskey; it was having little effect. He had been drinking pretty heavily for weeks now ,and it was taking more and more to have any effect. No matter how much Alec tried to move on, he knew he couldn't; there was nothing to move on to. His wife and his children had been his life, his sole purpose for living; without them he was nothing and had no reason to go on living. For him, Christmas wasn't a time for joy, for family, for forgetting about life's miseries. Instead, It was a time for giving up, self-loathing, pity, anger, hatred, and…revenge! Alec knew what he had to do, knew what this Christmas Eve was for. It was God's gift to him. The God that no one feared or celebrated anymore and had been replaced by Santa Claus. Alec thought about Christmas and all its modern traditions and smiled to himself. It had all been fun and games while he had a family but now that they were gone he could see how stupid it all was. It was just another distraction, given to the masses so they could be led like sheep through a life of pain by the few who held the power that those same masses gave them. People were weak and no longer fought for anything they believed; it was easier to go home and watch the TV and forget about it all. Not any fucking more, Alec thought to himself. *Tonight there will be consequences*, he thought, leaving the kitchen with the bottle still in hand.

***

The snow was falling heavily, there was already a good eight or nine inches on the ground. It was cold out but Alec felt nothing. The side of the drunk driver's house was pretty secluded by the high wooden fence, so that the only way he would be seen is if someone was walking by the front of the house and looked down, which was unlikely on a night like this. Alec didn't really give a fuck but he didn't want to get arrested before he got started; just like Santa Claus he had more than one person to visit tonight. Alec had half-expected to find the drunk driver sitting alone, in a pile of his own filth, feeling miserable. It was just the impression he had of drunk drivers but, looking through the small side window, he could see that, in fact, the man had a family just like the one Alec used to have. Two kids, and a wife..un-fucking-believable! It was too bad the family was here to witness what Alec had planned, but his mind was made up. Alec was left without a family, and now the driver's family would be left without a father/husband. *It's not a time of year for giving*, he thought, *it's a time of year for taking away.*

The snow crunched quietly underfoot as Alec made his way around the back of the house. It was a nice neighbourhood so Alec could only hope that the family didn't lock their doors. He couldn't believe the man who took his family lived on a nicer street than he could ever afford. He had to wonder if this man was somehow connected to someone in power, having seemingly gotten off so easily. Alec reached out and tried the handle and the door popped open. The houses in the street were pretty new and the door opened silently. Although he didn't want to alert the family to his arrival, he wasn't exactly going for a stealth job here. He would enter, take the man and leave. He walked through the kitchen and stopped behind the door, because he knew when he opened it he would be in the dining room where the family were sitting.

"Is it getting cold in here?" he heard come from through the door. He turned to see he had left the kitchen door open and the cold night air was spilling in. *Fuck it*, he thought to himself before pushing the door open and bursting in. Screams filled the air instantly. One of the little girls jumped up from her chair and ran to her mother's side. Alec pulled the large kitchen knife from the inside of his jacket.

"You! Cunt! Come with me or they all die. I'm not here to fuck about, I'm not here to argue with you or make a deal. You get up out of your chair and come with me if you want your family to live. You know who I am. You stood watching me in court, looking smug while getting your 'not guilty' verdict. Well you are guilty, and you will pay but your family doesn't have too." Alec said, pointing the knife straight at the driver.

"Okay, okay. Don't hurt them. I'll come." The drive replied.

"Barry!" the woman screamed, hugging the girl tight to her side and reaching over the table to grab his arm.

"It's okay, honey. I'm just going to go with the man and sort this out." Barry replied.

"Move!" Alec demanded.

Barry got up from his chair and slowly moved around the side of the table that was empty. He never took his eyes from Alec. Alec knew that most men would do whatever it took to protect their family, so had counted on the driver coming quietly. Alec kept the knife pointed at him as he passed into the kitchen then followed him out without looking back at the family. Scaring the two girls was a sad, unintentional consequence of today's events, and Alec knew they would always remember the bad man who took their father away. But really, what choice did he have when it was their father that caused all of this? And Alec would see to it… Barry had to pay!

***

Four hours later

Alec pulled his jeep into his driveway, groans coming from the backseat as he did. The snow was still coming down heavily, which had been a godsend in keeping his actions discreet throughout the evening. The roads were empty and no one was walking anywhere at this late hour. It was almost approaching midnight. The kiddies would be wrapped up in their beds to allow Santa to do his rounds and the parents would be trying to squeeze in some much needed rest before the big day. Alec turned and looked over the seat at the Chief of Police, tied up and gagged in the back of his car.

"Now we are going to go inside. I'm sure all my neighbours will be asleep and as you know it's a very important time of year. I would appreciate very much if you could keep the noise down as we go in. I could always just knock you out so you can't make a noise but I am affording you the opportunity to behave yourself. The downside being that if you don't behave things will be much worse for you. Do you understand?"

The Chief of Police nodded his head, sweat was running down his brow. It was clear he had been struggling but Alec knew he was going nowhere. Alec came round the side of the jeep and opened the door before pulling the Chief out into the snow. Not bothering to lift him into a standing position he dragged him through the snow to his door leaving a furrow behind them. He took his keys out quietly and unlocked the door. Taking one last look around his street and seeing it was deserted he dragged the Chief inside. Last year when he stood outside the front door having a smoke before he went to bed, he had never felt so good. Tonight though, the only positive feeling was that he had achieved what he had set out to do. The night was far from over, however.

***

Sweat dripped from Alec's head in the kitchen. It had taken him the last few hours to get everything prepared. The turkey had only needed warming up but he had to cook the vegetables and make the gravy. His kitchen was pretty small so the heat built up quickly. He removed the turkey from the cooking tray and settled it on the platter. Lifting it with care he walked back through into the living room and gently placed it in the middle of the still decorated table.

"Get anyone a drink?" he asked, looking around at his guests, before chuckling to himself.

The three men were tied securely to the hard backed dining chairs, their mouths tightly gagged. They looked from Alec to each other, their eyes filled with fear. Alec felt that people should pay for their transgressions on this most holy of evenings, and especially those he deemed responsible for the tragic loss of his family. Alec had spent the evening rounding them up. They were: the driver who had killed his family, the chief of the police station where the evidence was conveniently lost, and the local politician, primarily because he was a useless, corrupt fuck. Alec left and went back to the kitchen.

Twenty minutes later Alec had laid out all the food, the room smelled gorgeous. For a split second, as Alec left the kitchen for the last time that night, he saw his family sitting around the table, only for the briefest instant and then he was back with the three men--the three wrong doers who represented the problem with this world and the reason that Alec felt like he had no reason left to play the game of being a good guy anymore. His entire life he had questioned himself about the way things worked and often found that though he disagreed with the world on a basic moral level, it was never quite enough to do anything about it at the time. Now everything was different and he no longer felt the need to conform to society and it's ridiculous rules. The people in charge weren't looking out for his best interests so he would do it himself in any way he saw fit, and this was the start.

"Now gentleman, I know what you're all thinking. Yes, the food does smell delicious, and no, you wont be able to eat with the gags in your mouths. It's not for you. I just wanted to do this one last time." As he finished speaking, a single tear ran down Alec's cheek. "I loved my family you know, truly loved them. I suppose most people say that, but I really did. You don't know what you have until it's gone." As Alec stopped speaking again, instead of sinking into thoughtfulness, this time his face hardened and his brow furrowed. "But you! You cunts took everything from me! Every fucking thing! Look around this place. Does it look like a fucking bachelor pad?" he asked rhetorically. "No!" he answered himself and continued, "It It fuckin' doesn't! Do you know why? Because it was a family home, FAMILY! Do you know what I'm saying? A family home." Alec knew he was getting too worked up and didn't want any of his neighbours calling the cops before he was finished.

"I'm sorry gentlemen, my emotions got the better of me. One moment please." Alec got up and went back to the kitchen, returning with a new bottle of whiskey.

"I'd offer you a drink but.....well, you know." He snickered.

The three men could barely budge since their restraints were so tight. Their eyes flickered nervously from each other to Alec, knowing that the situation couldn't be much worse. The driver, Barry, knew his wife would have called the cops by now. The police chief lived alone, and, since having anyone else around was often someone who ended up knowing too much, so did the politician.

"Now. I've been drinking a lot, gents, and while this all seems to have gone rather smoothly, I didn't actually think it through a whole lot. You see, I want you all dead and while I am sure you all would strongly disagree, I truly believe the world will be a better place without the likes of you three." All three of the men were grunting through the gags now, obviously trying to explain their own reasons for past transgressions.

"I'm sorry guys. It's not an 'explain yourself and walk out of here' kind of night. You will all die at this very table. This will be the last Christmas dinner that any of us have—not that you will be eating much." Alec suddenly broke out in a crazy grin. "You have to admit I put on a great spread for you." The crazy grin disappeared as suddenly as it had appeared, and Alec grew somber once again as he continued, "My wife always used to say I loved Christmas more than the kids did; maybe she was right."

Leaning over the table Alec used the long, thin lighter to light the candles before getting up and dimming the lights. The snow continued falling outside as Alec started to speak again. "My wife liked to eat by candlelight, We probably didn't do it enough now that I think about it. I have a lot of regrets, if I'm honest. You always think there will be more time, but there wasn't… WAS THERE!?" Alex roared, standing up and flipping the table over, all the food flying everywhere. The turkey smashed against the wall and the three men and most of the living room were covered in vegetables. The gravy landed on the politicians lap, burning him, causing the man to reflexively kick his chair over, landing him on his back. Alec stormed out of the room and returned with a claw hammer. He walked over to the bottle of whiskey that lay on its side on the floor, spilling out some of its contents and picked it up. He took a large drink and, still clutching the bottle, dropped his arm back to his side. The men looked terrified, they both had their eyes glued to him while the politician stared at the ceiling. Alec sat the bottle in the middle of the floor and hoisted the politician back into an upright position, telling the man sarcastically. "Wouldn't want you to miss any of the fun now, would we?"

As Alec made his way over to his laptop, he smiled to himself as he heard at least one of the men crying; his wife had cried as she died in his arms, their two small children dead already in the backseat. The car had flipped several times after the collision, but landed upright. Alec had been the only one to survive; he wished he hadn't. After the laptop was fired up, he clicked into his Christmas music and played 'Santa Claus, You Cunt' by Kevin Bloody Wilson. He had always liked this one because it made him laugh, though his wife had warned him the kids had better not hear it. For this reason, he'd waited until the children were in bed before he'd played it.

'Santa Claus, you cunt! Where's me fuckin bike, I've opened all this other sh…..' drifted out from the speakers as Alec approached the men. "Okay gentlemen. I think we have wasted quite enough time." Then like lightening he swung the hammer above his head and brought it back down, blunt-side first, right into the politician's forehead. Before the man's head had even bounced back he let out a torrent of blows all over it. He quickly flipped the hammer over and brought the claw side down, sinking it right through the top of the politician's skull. When he let go of the hammer, it stayed in place. Blood started to run down the length of the handle and drip onto the carpet as the room filled with the scent of piss and shit. He looked at the mess of the skull. For the first time he realised the other two men were screaming through their gags; everything had gone silent while he worked. He realised he didn't even hear the music that had been playing. He admired his work for another few seconds and returned to the laptop to restart the song.

Santa Claus, you cunt! Where's me fuckin'…' started to play again. "You know I think as the years pass by, the world becomes a worse place. We move forward with technology and medicine and various other things but none of it's real; we are just mice in a cage. I've decided to get off the wheel now, guys, which means you are both pretty fucked. I'm sure you will now realise I am serious. I want you to think about this question: why shouldn't someone kill a policeman?" he asked staring at the police chief. "Because you spent a few months at police college? Because you are supposed to uphold the law? You are a bunch of corrupt, drug-taking pussies. A force filled with bully-victims turned bully that look the other way when they are needed. A joke!" Alec stopped his rant and walked over to the bottle of whiskey, lifted it and took two good swigs, then turned his attention to the other man. "And you!" he roared. "A fucking drunk driver who takes the lives of others because he is too much of a pussy to control his addiction. A man who has a family, though he has no care or consideration for others and their families. No!...I don't accept that either of you have a place on this earth." Alec glanced at the clock. "It's Christmas day you know. I should be getting up in a few hours to start making a lovely dinner for my family but instead I made one for you cunts-the people who took them. Not quite as pleasing I have to say. So! Who's next"

Both men started trying to plead through their gags, shaking their heads from side to side and nearly spilling their chairs over onto the floor. 'Silent Night' had clicked onto the laptop and Alec laughed. "It would be a silent night if it wasn't for you two," he said, grinning and looking between the two men. "What? That's fucking funny!" As he said it he stepped out and to the side and swung the biggest punch he had ever swung in his life. When his arm hit the cop in the side of the head, it felt like he had shattered every bone in his hand. The cop's lights went out and the chair flew onto its side onto the carpet. "Motherfucker!!" Alec raged, rubbing the hand that punched the cop with his other hand. "Ooohhhh, that felt good!" Alec now had a manic look in his eyes. He had drunk well over a bottle of whiskey today and for the first time all day, he was starting to feel drunk. "Let's wake him up. I've always heard people calling the cops, pigs or bacon. Let's see shall we?" and with that Alec left for the kitchen. He came back shortly after, still smiling. Barry thought Alec had truly lost it now. Earlier, when Alec broke into Barry's house and kidnapped him, Alec had looked ok at that point. Now he looked deranged, wild-eyed, his eyes constantly flicking from side to side, unable to settle. He marched across the living room and started dragging the unconscious cop across the floor. He yanked him upright before pulling him through the doorway. There were a few seconds of silence, then an ear-splitting scream, followed shortly after by the smell of charred flesh. Barry figured that Alec had pressed the police officer's face to the stove- there was no other explanation for what he was hearing and smelling. The cop's hands were tied by his sides and they hadn't been in the kitchen long enough for Alec to untie him. Barry knew he was going to die here tonight. He thought about his family and hoped they would be okay without him. He had had a drinking problem for a long time, and any mistakes he'd made, his wife did her best to cover for him, and his kids loved him. He couldn't deny that he was guilty for the death of this man's family but he didn't want to die, just like he hadn't wanted to go to prison. Money sorted most things out, but he doubted he could buy his way out of this one. Still, he hoped he would have enough time to try. The screams coming from the other room continued.

Surely the neighbours must have heard that, Barry thought to himself. Someone must have called the police. As Barry thought about rescue, Alec appeared in the doorway again, dragging the dead cop with him. The man's face was a mess of burnt tissue: bright red and bubbling with ring shapes imprinted on it. A knife was buried in his ear. "Making too much noise, so he was. I got a little carried away, but I can't go waking up the neighbours at this time on Christmas day." The smile was now pasted onto Alec's face; he really did look like he had lost it. He walked across the room, stopped in front of Barry and proceeded to untie the gag from the back of his head. "I don't suppose it matters if you scream now, does it? It's not like you will be any louder than the pig was. Oh, and by the way, he didn't smell like bacon. It's all bullshit." As Alec finished speaking, he remained standing in front of Barry but his mind seemed to wander off. Here was his opportunity, Barry thought.

"Alec, I have money, lots of it. You have seen my house, you know I'm well-off. You've already had your fun. Let me help make the pain go away; money can solve a lot of problems. By tomorrow you could be gone, sitting on a warm beach, sipping a cocktail. Fuck! You could start a new family with the kind of cash I could give you." As Barry finished his sentence he knew he had gone too far. He saw the smile slip from Alec's face.

"Oh! I could start a new family could I? Set me up with a new life, make me happy? Is that what you think you will do? How about this? I'll make you a deal. I'll untie you and let you walk out of here free if you can do one thing for me. Give me my family back-not a new one, the one I had before I crossed paths with you. Can you do that? Can you give me my fucking family back, Barry?!"

Barry didn't know what to say to save his life: no amount of pleading, or begging, or any type of bribe would sway this man. "You're not going to hurt my family are you?" was the only thing he could think to ask as he resigned himself to his fate.

"No Barry, I'm not. I'm not really a bad guy, truth be told. I doubt that sounds realistic to you under the current circumstances but I don't really give a fuck. I've spent a lifetime trying to be good while others do what they want, and life always seems to bite me in the arse anyway. Yet scum roam the earth, polluting it with their spawn…the next generation of shite who will ruin good people's lives. If it was up to me I'd put you all down, since most people are cunts. It's just the way of it; humans are selfish creatures who try to kid themselves that they are more important than they really are. Personally, I think most people just go along with the status quo for an easy ride. Why rock the boat? It doesn't really matter anymore. When I'm done with you, I will take my own life and join my family.

Barry squirmed in his chair. He already knew there was no way to escape but it was clear that Alec was coming to the end of the proceedings and if he was ever going to get out of here, it would have to be now. With one final burst of strength he flexed against the cords that tied him to the chair and broke down sobbing with the realisation that this was it, he was going to die very soon and no one was coming to rescue him.

"Alec, please! If not for me then for my daughters!" Barry begged.

"Sorry, mate. I need you. Look around you. What's missing? Yeh, that's right. You guessed it. A Christmas tree! That's where you come in, my friend." As Alex finished speaking, he put the gag back into Barry's mouth and tied it tight behind his head. He had heard enough, had toyed with him enough- it was time to end it all.

Alec marched back into the kitchen and reappeared almost immediately, dragging a large cardboard box with 'Tree decorations' scribbled on the side, and left it sitting next to Barry. "It looks like you will need to step in as our Christmas tree, mate." Alec made his way over to the laptop and after a minute 'Rockin' Around the Christmas Tree' started to play from the speakers. Alec smiled as it drowned out the sound of Barry sobbing through his gag. As far as Alec could tell, at least he had stopped trying to beg for his miserable life. Alec leaned down into the box, grabbed a long red piece of tinsel and started to wrap it around Barry, working from his feet up. The tinsel still had little tabs of tape stuck to it from last year; there wasn't much glue left on it, but enough that it hung around him as it would a tree. He leaned back in and this time grabbed a long green piece and repeated the procedure. Alec stepped back and took a look at Barry. Sitting in the chair he was wider at the bottom with his knees sticking out and thinner at the top; Alec thought it looked pretty good if a little sparse. He grabbed one more piece, silver this time and again wrapped it around his new 'Christmas tree'. His wife had always liked bobbles, and while he wasn't a fan, he believed you should keep the wife happy, so they'd always had them. For a split second Alec toyed with the idea of nailing them to his victim but he doubted Barry would last long enough. He grabbed a roll of tape that still lay in the box and started biting off little strips. When he had about twenty he started taping the bobbles all over Barry, some seemed to have trouble sticking so Alec was a little over excessive with the tape. When he was done with the bobbles, he reached into the box and grabbed a can of spray snow. “This is the part my kids used to love doing, “ he remarked to Barry as he began to cover him with the stuff. There was a little hitch in his voice as he said it. Once he had finished he disappeared into the kitchen again and came back with a box of Christmas lights. “Thought I’d forgotten, didn’t you?” he asked, knowing there would be no answer. “Normally we use the same old lights, but who can be bothered untangling them all? It’s not like I need to watch my money carefully now, anyway.” Alec ripped the box open, tossed it aside and started to wrap them around Barry. The spray snow seemed to have gotten into Barry's eyes because it didn't look like he could see very well anymore. Alec was a little disappointed that Barry wouldn’t see how good he looked. Alec walked over to the wall and plugged the lights in, then flipped the switch so they would flicker and change colour. He stood back admiring his work; he had done a good job, but it needed just one last touch. He went to the box again and retrieved the Christmas star that he had jammed down onto a tent spike so it would work. He stepped up and in front of Barry, raised it high above his head and slammed it down, double handed with all the force he could muster. The peg pierced Barry’s skull and sank in, his body going into such spasms, Alec had to grab the chair to keep it from tipping over. Barry died quickly and Alec again stepped back to admire his work. His ‘tree’ looked much better with the star, and though it did hang to one side, the star had always been too heavy and caused the tops of their trees to hang sideways. Blood was running from the peg down Barry’s face but as it was red, it didn’t look too out of place with the decorations wrapped around him.

Alec stood in front of Barry for a few minutes, not really paying any attention to his creation, his mind just wandering through previous Christmases with his family. The sirens coming from somewhere not too far in the distance was what snapped Alec back to reality. With no more than an accepting nod, Alec went back into the kitchen and returned carrying his nail gun. He sat in the chair facing his new tree and pulled out a picture of Pauline, Sarah and Sammy that he had taken a few days before he lost them. He sat looking at it, nail gun hanging at his side. He could hear the sirens getting closer as a tear dripped onto the photo. “I’m sorry I couldn't save you,” he whispered sadly. Alec raised the nail gun so that it was pointing upwards, then placed it under his chin and, clenching the picture tightly, his finger began to push against the trigger when he suddenly felt someone touch his shoulder. Whipping around quickly and finding no one there, he then heard his wife’s voice saying, “No, Alec, not yet. There are other bad men to punish. Go. Go now before they get here. Your job isn’t done yet.”

"Pauline..... baby" he responded tearfully, but she was gone and he knew it. Wasting no time, Alec was up and out of his chair, dropping the nail gun next to it. He went straight for the back door and left it wide open as he ran out into a bright Christmas morning. He couldn't get caught just yet. There *were* more bad men to punish. "Merry fuckin' Christmas!" he said to no one but himself as he disappeared out into the day, thinking that he wouldn't let his wife down this time.

The End

Santa Came

By

Peter Oliver Wonder

Just like every year, Missus Claus gave him a kiss on the cheek before he got into his magic sleigh. It was the most action he got from her. Her lady parts had dried up centuries ago and were left undesirable and unusable to Santa. The sexual frustration built up all year long. The night before Christmas was his one opportunity to get laid by a real woman.

He tossed his big, fluffy, red sack into the passenger seat and saddled up beside it. As he took the reins in his hand, the smell of reindeer farts filled his nose and lungs. The old hag always fed them a protein-rich meal the night before to ensure they had the strength to pull his lard ass around the entire world.

"Now Dasher! Now Dancer! Now Prancer and Vixen! On Comet! On Cupid! On Donner and Blitzen!" He shouted through the flurry of snow to the deer. Their hooves dug into the snow and the sleigh began to inch forward. Santa gave a quick snap of the reins and gave a loud "Heyah!" followed by another snap.

Speed began to build up and the bitter cold bit at Santa's exposed face. The breathing of the deer was already becoming labored, sending plumes of frozen breath into the air. "Mush!" he shouted as the lead deer began its ascent into the cold night sky. As the sleigh began to rise, he reached into his magic sack and pulled out some hot buttered rum to sip on as he made his way to his first stop.

Beside him on the bench sat the magical 'Naughty or Nice' list. He picked it up and flipped through the first few pages, underlining names he remembered from previous years—these were the children that were either incredibly nice or insufferably naughty. After he got through the children's last names that begin with 'Bi,' he sat the list down on the bench once more and returned the pen to his right hip pocket beside the pouch of forget dust. That's what he used on the rare occasion a child strayed from bed while he was delivering the presents.

Now, everyone knows Santa for his jolly demeanor around the holidays. What isn't known by many is from where this jolliness is derived. Once, there was a time when giving toys to children that had little was enough to keep the old man happy all the time. Bringing such joy to all the little boys and girls in the world made him feel good down to his very soul. As of late, children had become spoiled rotten. They no longer behaved like well-mannered children. They threw tantrums until they got what they wanted. Throughout the year they collected mounds of toys, video games, and all manner of wonderful things from the parents they tormented so. Worse yet, he had to continue to give them things on Christmas despite their actions. After all, the Christmas joy was the source of Santa's power. Without it, he'd wither up and die. The rotten vermin of the world got rewarded for their greed and there was nothing Santa could do to change it.

Just because he had to deliver sophisticated equipment to undeserving puke-sacks didn't mean he couldn't find some Christmas joy of his own. It all began innocently enough. One Christmas Eve night, before most children of the world had become the monsters we know today, but after the Missus' snatch had dried up, a downtrodden Santa was making his yearly trip around the globe to deliver joy, though he felt little of his own.

It was in Belgium, where it happened. He remembers it as though it were yesterday, despite it having transpired nearly two hundred years ago, now. There was an upstairs fireplace in the widow's house. Him going down that chimney was a mistake, but a very fortunate one. The young mother of four was having a sleepless night and thinking of how her husband used to put her to sleep when she was so restless. When Santa exited the fireplace, she was trying to recreate the moment by herself.

Her eyes were clenched shut as she neared climax. Her passionate moans enticed Santa, who walked silently to her bedside. "Are we being a naughty girl?" Santa asked.

The widow was more than willing to accept his gift that night, and it was a gift that was given year after year. It was what Santa looked forward to most every year. Fucking someone that wasn't several hundred years old was a gift he could never match. The arrangement lasted long after the widow's children had grown and moved out on their own.

One year, he came down the chimney with a rock hard erection to find a couple sleeping in the bed. The trouble was, Santa didn't notice anything different until it was too late. He stripped down silently in order to surprise the widow. He freed himself of his big red coat to expose his chest with sagging man-tits and a field of gray hair. He managed to get his belt undone and off without making a single jingle. As he slid his pants down, the pen from his pocket shook loose and dropped onto the wooden floorboards. The sound of the metal pen striking the planks caused what sounded like a deafening *BOOM* as it resonated throughout the silent house.

The bed began to show movement beneath the covers and Santa sat on the edge of the bed and looked down at the face on the pillow. The man's face startled him enough to cause him to fall forward and land face down on the floor, beside his pants.

"What the fuck is this?" grumbled the angry, half-asleep man. He looked down at the bare ass of the fat, old man and was instantly disgusted and filled with rage. "What the fuck is THIS!" he shouted again as the adrenaline began to wake him. He dropped his legs over the edge of the bed, stood to his feet and proceeded to kick Santa in the ribs.

Santa rolled to his side after the blow and found himself nose to nose with the pen that had fallen earlier. He was shaken and angered and confused because the widow was not there, waiting with her legs spread wide. As the anger coursed through him, he snatched up the pen and sprang to his feet.

"Who the fuck do you think you are?" shouted the homeowner at the naked intruder.

Without thinking, Santa swung the pen, stabbing the man in the jugular. Blood shot out all over the headboard and onto the sheets, as well as the face of the sleeping young woman who was still in bed. After the blood sprayed her face, her eyes shot open wide with terror as she stared up at the man that was stark naked, save for the red stocking cap atop his head. He pulled the pen from the man's throat and let him drop to the floor.

"S-S-S-S-Santa?" she stammered almost inaudibly.

Santa looked at her, down at his still-hard cock, and then down at his pants that were in a wad on the floor near a pool of blood. He said nothing as he reached down to pick up his pants. He did not put them on, but rather reached into his pocket and retrieved the small, yellow pouch within. He untied the ribbon that held it closed. His fat fingers entered the bag, retrieved a pinch of the dust, and tossed it into the face of the terrified young woman. Her eyes shut as she instantly fell back to sleep.

After retying the bag, he put it back in the pocket from whence it came, and put one foot into a pant leg before stopping. Killing the man that lay at his feet had been a rush like nothing he had before experienced. He still clutched the blood-covered pen and a menacing smile spread across his face. He dropped his pants and climbed on top of the woman who was sleeping comfortably beneath the sheets. He put his nose to her cheek and inhaled her scent. His right hand brought the pen up under her chin and slowly stuck it into her throat. The blood slowly dribbled from the hole and onto the bed sheets where it mixed with the blood of her husband. Santa's eyes rolled back in ecstasy.

Once he finished, Santa put his suit back on and went through the rest of the house to make it look like an actual home invasion had taken place. It was less work than leaving gifts for the children (who were most definitely on the naughty list). The milk and cookies looked awfully tempting, but he knew there would be more in the next house, and the house after that, and so on.

As soon as he was satisfied that he would not be incriminated in anything, he went on his merry way. Christmas could continue, now that Santa came.

The End

Hung With Care

By

Ty Schwamberger

The newly fallen snow crunched under his black boots as he walked towards the next house. This one, wasn't quite as nice looking as the previous residence he had visited, but he was sure there would still be some nice little boys, or maybe even girls, that had been good enough all year to deserve a bountiful helping of Christmas presents. He disappeared for a moment behind a large pine tree nestled beside the house and paused. He looked through the pointy, green needles of the tree and out into the street.

Not a creature is *stirring*... He smiled and then continued on his way.

Ducking into a deep shadow by the side of the house, he rose up on his tiptoes and looked through the snow-covered window. No, it wasn't real snow. He could tell that easily enough. It had come from one of those aerosol spray cans that contained that fake, white sticky stuff that clung to windows during the season of ever-lasting joy. At first it was hard for him to see in, so he took one gloved-hand off the big, red sack he was carrying on his back and gently placed it upon the window. He slid his hand back and forth a few times until the condensation on the outside of the window disappeared and he was able to gaze inside.

The stockings are *hung by the chimney with care*... He then repeated the next line, silently this time, deep inside his soul, then smiled. God, did he love this time of year.

As he pushed the window up into its frame, smiled, and wondered if it was a Christmas miracle that this particular house's window hadn't been secured as were all the others. Not that it really mattered; by chimney, by magic key through the front door, or climbing through an unlocked window he had never been denied getting into a house on the Eve of the most wondrous day of the year.

He flung the heavy sack off his back and tossed it through the open window.

He then pushed himself up and onto the window sill, then followed the sack full of goodies into the nice, warm house.

* * *

After struggling to pick his rotund self up off the floor, he huffed a few times, and went to the open window and dropped it back into place. He wasn't sure why he did it, but then reached up and slid the lock into place. He then turned around and took a nice, long look around the cozy living room.

The first thing he noticed was that the fireplace still had some glowing embers. He slowly walked over, bent down, and stuck his still-gloved hands over the hearth. Even though the fire wasn't roaring anymore with hot delight, it still provided enough warmth to seep through the heavy, black gloves and reach his almost-frostbit hands.

After all, it had been a hell of a long night already and just the thought that he was really just getting started made him feel exhausted. But, this was his chosen profession, one he had made many, many years ago, so he felt like cold or no cold, it was his duty to carry out what he promised himself oh-so-long ago.

After crouching by the almost-dead fire for a few minutes, he slowly stood up and stretched his red, fur covered arms over his stocking-covered head. He then turned around and took a long look at the rest of the room. The decorations included snowmen, igloos, polar bears, angels, and even a figurine of himself. Santa. His belly shook like a bowl full of jelly, but he didn't make a sound. He couldn't. Oh, no.

Not with *the children nestled all snug in their beds*...

He smiled, again. Then hoped against hope his hunch was right.

Leaving his already full sack on the floor, he proceeded out of the living room, towards the staircase leading upstairs to the family's bedrooms, but not before picking up a gingerbread cookie from a Christmas tree plate, and biting the little man's head off.

He wanted to laugh through his cookie filled teeth, but knew he couldn't.

He didn't want to wake anyone, especially the parents...

Who *had just settled* their *brains for a long winter's nap.*

The word 'nap' made him laugh, again, but this time he couldn't keep it in.

As pieces of cookie flew out of his snapping jaws and hit his boots, he started up the stairs.

He paused for a moment at the top, pulling out a long, curved knife from the sheath buckled to his wide, black belt and then started down the dark hallway.

His first stop was the parent's room.

Then, no matter if they had been good or bad, it was off to the kid's room to slice and dice them and make himself all glad.

* * *

"Jerry...Jerry. Wake up. I think I heard something."

The balding father rolled over onto his back, stifled a last snore and mumbled, "Huh. What. What did you say, dear?"

"I said, I think I heard something, or someone, downstairs."

"Ah geez, Helen. It's probably just the long limbs of the pine hitting the side of the house. I promise, first thing tomorrow morning after the kids have opened their presents that I'll bundle up and finally go out there and cut a few limbs back, ok? Now, please, let me get some more sleep. You know as well as I do that the kids will be up at the ass-crack of dawn and running in here to jump on the bed to wake us up." Then, still half asleep, the husband and father rolled back onto his side and started snoring, again.

The wife and mother mumbled, "But…" then stopped from saying anything else. Sure, her husband was a kind and loving man but even he had his limits. Especially if she woke him in the middle of the night, like she often did, for a noise that she 'heard' downstairs or outside the house. Each and every time in the past that she had nagged until he had gotten out of bed and went downstairs or out into the cold to investigate - it turned up nothing. So, this time, since it was Christmas Eve and all, she decided to keep her mouth shut.

After deciding not to bother her husband any longer, she lay back down onto her pillow and closed her eyes. She was about to drift off when she heard something, again, closer this time than before. For the life of her it had sounded like it was coming from the hallway outside their bedroom door. Helen knew if she didn't have her husband take a look, pissed as he might get, she would never be able to fall back asleep and it would ruin her chances of being rested enough for a day full of opening presents, the kids running this way and that around the house while playing with their multitude of new toys, or cooking their annual Christmas Day feast. Finally, after thinking about it for another minute or two, and 'hearing' another sound out in the hallway, she rolled onto her left side, placed a hand on her husband's shoulder and gave it a soft shake.

He rustled in his sleep but didn't wake.

She leaned over, knowing one sure-fire way to stir him whether he was sleeping or just acting dead, and started to nibble on his ear. Just as she expected, he let out a soft, low moan.

"*Hummm…* Well, now. I think I can be persuaded to *get up* for something like this, dear." He then rolled onto his back again and reached for Helen's…

He heard the creaking of the bedroom door being opened.

"Damn kids," he mumbled, giving his wife a quick kiss and then quickly sitting up in bed. Through the dark, he said in a deep voice, "I told you kids to stay in bed, if nothing else, until the sun is above the horizon." He paused, looking at the clock on his nightstand and seeing it wasn't even 3:00 am, yet. He then turned back to the fully-opened door and shouted, "Hey! What did I tell you damn kids, huh? I told you to…"

His words were cut short, as a sharp blade was quickly and precisely drawn across his neck. Blood spurted onto his attacker and his wife.

Helen began to scream, but it was only for a moment, as a giant shadow suddenly leapt through the air, smashing on top of her, making the air in her lungs burst out.

Helen lay under the rotund man and thrashed this way and that. She felt something poke in between her legs, but the thoughts of being raped quickly dissipated as she felt something cold and sharp against the side of her neck. She wanted to scream, again, but the large man had already placed a large, smothering glove over her mouth. Finally, not that she wanted to, but knowing she had to, she opened her eyes…

And said to herself, *Oh my God, it must be St. Nick!*

Helen started to repeat a line in the famous poem over and over again to herself, *Now dash away! Dash away!*

Above, she saw Santa start laughing, as he said, "Dash away all!"

Then quickly slashed Helen's throat and her fright was never more.

He next sawed off both the husband and wife's hands, stuffed them into the deep pockets of his big, red coat and walked out of the room, gently shutting the door behind him.

* * *

Walking down the hall towards the sleeping kids' room, his eyes twinkled with delight and he could feel his dimples, his cheeks full with merry. And, yes, his cheeks were like roses, his nose like a cherry, but that was from the blood that had splattered upon his face from Helen and Jerry (not that he knew or even cared to know their names). As he wiped the dripping knife blade off on his fur-covered right leg, he brought up his other arm and mopped off his face. He smiled, again, knowing he had just done the world some justice – teaching people, especially the ones that acted like good model citizens, with their expensive cars and homes (not that this particular family had either of those luxuries, but that really didn't matter in his faltering mind at this point), when they were anything but. Besides, he was St. Nick, Santa Claus, goddammit, and it was his job to check off on his list who was naughty or nice.

Coming up to the kids' room, he slid the now clean, shiny blade back into the sheath on his belt and then slowly reached out with the same hand and grasped the doorknob. He gave it a quick wiggle back and forth, making sure the door was indeed unlocked, then twisted it all the way to the left and slowly eased the door inward. He then tiptoed into the dark room, shutting the door behind him.

* * *

Dressed in his traditional holiday garb, he stood at the side of the kids' bunk beds, his head throbbing with naughty images and his mouth watering with want. No, he wasn't a pedophile, never even had the slightest inkling to be one. What he wanted, craved, more than anything was to teach all the bad boys and girls in the world - more realistically, the city he resided in - that no bad deed goes unpunished. Especially, when it was supposed to be the season of giving and all he ever felt like the world ever gave him every Christmas was a lump of coal in his stocking. But not this Christmas. Oh, no. This Christmas, he was going to show the world: house by house, adult by adult, child by child, that *this* old St. Nick was someone to not be fucked with any longer.

* * *

He took care of the first child, a girl, the one on the top bunk, with one quick slash of his knife. Blood squirted from her carotid onto his face, changing his snow white beard into a crimson mess and mess. It was quick and painless and she didn't scream. The blood from the girl ran down his chin to the end of the beard's now tangled mess and down the front of his plump belly.

He smiled and chuckled to himself, as he started to saw off the little girl's hands, knowing she would never open another Christmas present ever again.

* * *

After stuffing another set of hands into his pockets, he leaned down close to the older of the two kids and took a good look. If he had to guess; he'd say she was probably either a senior in high school or a freshman in college, home for winter break. At first, he got so close to her face that he felt the tip of the girl's cold nose against his. He lifted his head away a bit so they weren't touching any longer and then took his free, left hand, and slowly pulled the heated blanket off her body, piling it down by her feet.

Even though she was the older of the two girls, she was still dressed from neck to toe in long, green pajamas. He tried to think of the name of the new blanket-like invention where you could literally have your entire body zipped inside a blanket, however, at this very moment the name escaped him. But, it didn't matter. Not really. It would soon be off her, anyway. Then he would show her how people in the world--rich, spoiled people like her--always treated people like him.

The true outcasts, the *little* people, the elves of society.

* * *

Even though she was way past the age of believing in Santa Claus, Crystal had dreams of sugar plums dancing in her head as she slept. Sure, she kept up with the *myth* of Santa for her little sister, Susie, but she definitely didn't believe any more. But, in her dream world, where everything was always perfect, Santa did exist and he brought her, not a shiny sled or a new Barbie doll with long, golden locks, but the hot stud quarterback on her college's football team - and he was all tied up in a red bow, just for her. She had the wet dream of waking up Christmas morning and seeing that Santa had delivered her ultimate present, Jake, and he was waiting for her, only her, under her parent's Christmas tree. She would run over to him, throwing her little sister out of the way, and tackle him like a linebacker, wanting to plant his ass into the ground. Then, suddenly she was naked, except for a red stocking hat with a big, white fluffy ball at its end, and it kept hitting her in the sides of the face, as she rode him like a reindeer wearing a saddle.

As Crystal climaxed, she awoke.

At first the room was too dark for her eyes, but soon they adjusted to the dim light from the moon coming in through the curtained window.

Then she saw a man, a big man dressed all in red, leaning down only inches from her face. He looked like Santa, but since she didn't believe in St. Nick, she knew it wasn't the real McCoy. Besides, she didn't see a stump of a pipe held tight in his teeth nor the smoke that would be coming from it encircling his head like a wreath.

Her eyes shot open wide and she tried to scream. But, her cries of terror were cut off by the big man slamming a big, gloved hand down upon her face. She shook her head back and forth but it was no use. She tried to kick her legs this way and that, but they wouldn't move. She was stuck. Done for. And she didn't know what to do. She wasn't sure if it was the holiday spirit or a never-dying love in her heart, but all she cared about right now was to know her sister was ok. She didn't care what Santa (not that this fat man was the real deal), did or didn't do to her, as long as Susie was safe. Crystal wanted to ask, to beg, for 'Santa' to tell her that he hadn't harmed Susie, but she had no way of doing so. The fact of the matter was, if the big man kept the pressure over her mouth and nose any longer, she was going to pass out. Then she'd have no idea what ever happened to Susie, or even her parents for that matter, because the man would probably end up raping and killing her somewhere outside on top of a pile of cold, white snow. She could picture in her head the man raping her, then slipping a long, cold blade deep within her belly, until she couldn't plead or beg at all.

Crystal closed her eyes and waited for death. She knew she was done for and there was no reason to fight someone so much bigger and stronger than her, so she just gave up. Crystal felt a lone tear form in the corner of her closed, right eye, and felt it then run off her face, onto her pillow.

Then the pressure from the big man's hand disappeared.

After what seemed like forever, Crystal slowly opened her eyes and noticed that the big man was now gone like the last wisp of smoke from a snuffed candle.

She quickly climbed out of bed to check on her little sister.

And that's when she let out a blood-curdling scream.

* * *

He was already loading up gifts from under the twinkling tree and stuffing them into his already full sack when he heard a scream coming from upstairs.

Now I've got something to dread. He knew he should have finished the girl off, just like he had done to her parents and sister, but there was just something about her that he couldn't bring himself to slice and dice her like all the others, tonight. As he continued to load the last of the presents into the already bulging sack, he felt a stir in his heart. Something strange was happening, though he couldn't quite put a finger on it, nor did he have the time to do so.

The pounding of footsteps from above and another scream made him turn his head with a jerk towards the staircase. Yes, she would be coming downstairs next and that would probably mean she would run to the phone and call the police. He definitely didn't need that. Oh, no. Not on a night like tonight – the Eve of the happiest day of the year.

Jerking the rope on the sack to close it, he hurried over to the fireplace. He heard the girl start down the stairs and knew he had to work fast.

He pulled the knife from his belt with his right hand and reached under his heavy coat with his left. He pulled six nails off a chain that was hanging around his neck and placed them pointed end into his mouth. He looked through the near-darkness to the staircase and saw a blur jump from the third to last step, turn, and then race to the back of the house, towards the kitchen where he assumed the phone was located.

He quickly dug his free hand into his soggy, left pocket, and pulled out the first of the six hands he had stuffed inside.

As he heard the girl started screaming, presumably into the phone to the police, he pointed the handle side of the knife away from him, and used it to start hammering each hand to the mantle of the fireplace.

As he worked, he repeated the line he had said earlier, but changing the words a bit this time.

The hands *are hung by the chimney with care... in hopes that folks from everywhere far and wide will know that Christmas is the time to die!* He laughed.

He then raced to a window and threw up the sash and leaped into the night and was ready to run away fast...

When something that felt like a sheet of snow coming from the roof smashed him to the ground.

Suddenly, he was being pounded in the sides and back of his head by big, heavy fists. He was pinned to the ground by a great mass and the blows started to rock his head and jaw back and forth. He felt teeth begin to crack and his jaw begin to bust, as the onslaught continued, the bones in his head felt like they were going to turn to dust.

* * *

Crystal was wrapped in a large, Christmas tree-covered blanket, as the first of several police cruisers and other emergency personnel pulled up in front of the house and came running towards her. All at once they began shouting, "Did you see where he went?", "Are you ok, miss?", "What the hell happened here?" and the like and then they started to go about their business.

When she was finished being treated by one very calm, and very good-looking young EMT, she heard something coming from above – on the roof. Her heart began to pound in her chest, as she jumped off the porch and ran into the front yard screaming, "He's up there. He's on the roof. I hear him…I hear him, damnit!"

With a crime scene to secure, a killer on the loose and a growing crowd of neighbours coming out of their homes to see what was going on, no one seemed to be paying Crystal any attention.

But then, Crystal noticed two things at once – a figure on the ground outside her living room window, lying in the middle of a large patch of blood-soaked snow and a large, red figure standing up on the roof, waiving to her.

She lifted her hand from underneath the blanket to do the same, but quickly put it back under. She didn't want people to see her 'waving to someone on the roof' and think she was crazy, especially since that was probably what they were already thinking with her family being slaughtered and all. Besides, with everything that *did* happen she might very well be going crazy and seeing imaginary people, Santa Claus of *all* things, up on the roof.

Crystal then thought she heard a clatter on the roof and a shout into the night.

But, that was just another piece of the *myth* that she would keep inside, nice and tight, for the rest of her life.

The End

Killing Christmas

By

Andrew Lennon

"Oh the weather outside is frightful, and the fire is so delightful."

The music pounded through Jeff's head as he entered the discount shop. He looked around to see green and red and gold Christmas decorations hanging from every corner. An inflatable Santa stood guard in the doorway.

"Really?" Jeff said to the person walking by him. "It was Halloween just a few days ago. They're celebrating Christmas already?"

The person gave him an awkward, halfhearted smile and continued with their shopping.

"Well, at least it's filling people with Christmas spirit," Jeff mumbled to himself.

He made his way through the aisles, collecting his various items. When he reached for his normal packet of Maltesers, he noticed that the usual pouch had been replaced with a box. Upon inspection, he saw that the contents had dropped from one hundred grams to seventy-five, although the price remained the same.

"Bloody rip off, taking advantage of the holidays."

He walked to the till where a cashier stood wearing a green elf hat with a small bell on the end. "Still dressed for Halloween?" Jeff smiled.

"No." The cashier looked confused. "It's Christmas."

"Yes, I know that, but it was only Halloween a few days ago. Don't you think it's a little bit early to be dressed as Santa's little helper?"

"Oh, if I could celebrate Christmas all year round I would." She flashed a wide smile.

"Yeah, I'm sure you would." Jeff collected his items and left the shop.

Biting into his sandwich, Jeff searched the internet for his normal lunchtime reading. At first, he checked the news, then he logged into his Facebook account. The first post on his news feed was a picture of Will Ferrell dressed as 'Elf', with the caption, "Only 50 more days until Christmas!"

Jeff sighed. This bloody idiot hadn't even checked before sharing this picture, or checked to see whether it was correct or not. It was now fifty-three days until Christmas. Nearly two months, and people were celebrating it already.

"They'll be sick of it by the time it gets here," he mumbled.

"What was that?" Chris, his colleague, asked.

"Oh nothing. Just people celebrating Christmas already. Bit early, isn't it?"

"Come on, you're not a Grinch are you?'

"No. I like Christmas, but I like it at Christmas time. We've only just finished with Halloween, for God's sake."

"Come on, Jeff. Get into the spirit." Chris got up and walked out of the office while singing at the top of his voice. "Tis the season to be jolly. Fa la la la la, la la la la!"

"Are you frigging kidding' me?" Jeff exclaimed.

The nights had grown cold. It felt as if the temperature had plummeted overnight. Jeff walked home from his office while holding his coat around him to try to shield his body from the wind. The traffic along the road was stationary. A car blasted out the Band Aid song, 'Do They Know It's Christmas'. Jeff rolled his eyes and shook his head, accepting the fact that he was going to be subjected to this music for the next two months. He used to enjoy the Band Aid song. Between that, and 'Fairytale of New York', they were probably his favourites, but after years of being overplayed, Jeff had grown to hate them. In fact, he couldn't remember the last time he'd heard a Christmas song that he actually enjoyed. He ducked his head further down, in protection from the wind, and continued his walk.

Entering his flat, Jeff stood on a pile of envelopes that had been posted through the door. He sighed at the fact that the top letters were now wet and muddy from his boots. He collected them and walked into the kitchen. He was surprised at the amount of mail he had received. Usually, he would get one or two letters a week. In his hand, he now held about twenty. He opened the first one and saw the heading: 'Celebrate this Christmas by saving £10 when you spend over £100!'

"Okay, that's a shop I'll never spend a hundred quid in. That's going in the bin."

He opened the next one. 'You can save…'

Bin.

The next one: 'Please help us this Christmas by donating to…'

"Jesus, they start cashing in early, don't they?" he moaned.

The next letter felt stronger, stiffer. He tore the envelope open to find a Christmas card. The picture on the front was a perfect example of consumerism Christmas today. There was no nativity scene, no Father Christmas, and no Christmas tree. There wasn't even any snow. It was a picture of what looked like a spoiled, obese child, biting into a chocolate bar while tearing into another present. The other presents sat discarded, partly opened and neglected in a pile behind him. The look on the child's face did not represent joy, or excitement. It was a look of utter greed, the kid indulging himself while waiting for the next item on their spoiled list.

"We're living in a material world and that is a material little shit," Jeff muttered.

There were no words on the front of the card, just the picture of the grotesque child. Jeff opened it. The preprinted words read, "Warm Wishes." The rest of the inscription, as written by the sender, said: 'Dear Jeff, I hope you have a wonderful Christmas and it is full of joy and happiness. Love from Marcy and Gerald.'

Confused for a while, Jeff held the card in his hand, wondering who the hell Marcy and Gerald were. Eventually it came to him. Marcy and Gerald Walters. They were his parent's neighbours. He hadn't spoken to them in over twenty years.

"Okay. Nice thought, I guess. Still, a bit early."

After a quick scan of the other letters, it was clear that they were all from some company or charity trying to get money from him…in the natural Christmas way, of course. Now that the season had changed, it wasn't just normal shopping and begging, it was 'Christmas' shopping and begging...it had *meaning.*

After changing from his work clothes into his 'The Simpsons' pyjamas, Jeff made himself a microwave meal of chicken tikka masala and then sat in front of the TV. He grabbed the remote and started to flick through the channels. He always skipped channels one to five at this time of night because he didn't like the evening news, game shows or awful soap operas. He skipped straight to the movie channels.

"Oh, come on!" he shouted.

All of the movie channels had changed their names. It was now 'Christmas 24', 'Sky Movies Xmas', and 'The Christmas Network'. He turned the TV off and ate in silence. Usually, the silence made Jeff feel uncomfortable, but today it felt right to him. It matched his mood. As he was finishing his meal he could hear something coming from outside. It sounded like singing. He placed his dinner on the floor and walked over to the window. He tried to see along the road but his view was restricted. He opened the window and felt a blast of cold air caress his face from the strong wind outside. The wind brought in with it the voices from outside.

"Glory to the new born king!" they sang.

Jeff leaned out of the window. He could hear the singing so loudly it felt like it was the same room as him, but scanning the street up and down, he couldn't see the source.

"It's only the beginning of November!" He shouted. "Shut the hell up!"

The singing continued, not even missing a beat. Jeff felt angry, and although he knew that he shouldn't be letting it get to him as much as it was, it just seemed relentless. No matter where he looked, there were Christmas decorations and celebrations. From mid-

December, okay, even the first of December he could tolerate, but not this early. This was just stupid; carol singers in November, for God's sake. That topped the lot.

Choosing to separate himself from the world, Jeff decided to download a book to his Kindle, and go to read it in bed. When the current list of bestsellers loaded up on his screen, Jeff's anger grew. Once again, it was full of Christmas selections. Of course, the book at number one was 'A Christmas Carol'. A classic, it was; Jeff had read it a few times and enjoyed it thoroughly, but November is not the time for a Christmas story. He searched for horror books and felt enraged when the top result was 'A Christmas of Horror'.

"Can't even have a scary story without a fucking Christmas twist now!"

He threw his Kindle on the bedside cabinet, turned his lamp off, and turned over to go to sleep.

***

'Oh the weather outside is frightful, but the fire is so delightful. And since we've no place to go. Let it snow, let it snow, let it snow'.

Jeff slammed a fist on his alarm clock, which flashed 6:30, abruptly ending the irritating Christmas music. Then he fell back to sleep. When he opened his eyes again, the clock read 8:00.

"Shit, I'm late."

He fell out of bed and then rushed around his flat. Not bothering to wash, as there was not enough time, he tried brushing his teeth at the same time as buttoning his shirt. He spat and left them half brushed. Once dressed, Jeff rushed out of the door, his hair stood upright on top of his head. He pulled his beanie hat tight over it, hoping that by the time he got to work, the hat would have made his hair lay down a little.

He turned the corner of his street and fell over as he collided with a small child coming in the opposite direction. "Watch where you're going," said the child in a deep voice.

Jeff turned to look and noticed the little man; he was wearing a green elf outfit. He had a beard. He wasn't a child.

"Sorry, sorry..." Jeff said, while getting back to his feet. Then he carried on with his run to work.

"Don't worry about it, Jeff." He heard the elf call. "Merry Christmas!"

Jeff turned to see the elf waving to him.

'How does he know my name?' wondered Jeff.

Jeff didn't see any other people until he reached the high street. When he ran his gaze along it, taking in the busy shops and its smattering of people in the area, he almost fainted. Everywhere he looked, people were wearing the same green and red elf costume, and they were all so little!

"Merry Christmas, Jeff." A small woman smiled as she passed.

"Merry Christmas, Jeff." A short old man said.

"Merry Christmas, Jeff," called another woman.

"Merry Christmas, Jeff," said a woman who was pushing her pram. The baby sat up and smiled. "Merry Missmus, Heff."

"What the hell is going on?" muttered Jeff, grabbing his head.

He felt as though all the elves were circling him. He pushed his way through them, almost falling over again. Sprinting down the road towards his office, he told himself this was just a dream. It's all just part of his imagination. Any minute now, and he will wake up.

Throwing the doors open, he stormed into his office. His jaw dropped when he saw that his colleagues had all been replaced by tiny people.

"Merry Christmas, Jeff," they called in unison.

Jeff's legs gave 'way on him. He dropped to the floor, trying to control his shaking. The people in front of him all had the faces of his normal colleagues, but they were all elves.

'*This can't be happening!*' Jeff thought to himself, panic-stricken.

"Boss wants to see you," a voice said, coming from his side.

"Chris?" Jeff asked as he looked at the child-sized man.

"Yeah, you're late. Boss wants to see you," Chris answered.

Jeff pulled himself up from the floor and slowly made his way towards the boss's office. Jeff's boss, Frank, was six foot five. Jeff couldn't imagine the guy as an elf. He didn't think his mind would be able to process it. When he knocked on the door, he could see a large silhouette through the frosted glass.

"Finally! Someone who's not tiny," muttered Jeff to himself in relief.

The door swung open. Jeff's face was filled with the sight of red. His eyes were level with this man's chest. He slowly brought his stare up along the red suited chest, until he met a huge white beard. Then, above that, rosy red cheeks and a red nose. The eyes looked angry.

"Santa?" Jeff looked perplexed at the giant man, who must have been at least seven feet tall. "You've got to be shitting me."

"Jeff!' the voice bellowed. "You're late."

"Yeah, I'm s-s-sorry," he stuttered. "I'm not feeling too good. I think I'm tripping out or something."

"Not only that, but you've also been trying to kill the Christmas spirit," thundered the giant red man.

"Kill the Christmas ... what? It's only November!" Jeff protested, "this is all a weird dream. I'm going to wake up in a minute."

"We can't have you killing Christmas, Jeff." Santa smiled menacingly. "We'll have to kill you first."

"What the hell?" yelped Jeff, looking around wildly.

"Take him," Santa ordered, and then turned back to his office.

Jeff turned around to see that all the elves were now approaching. They each had wicked smiles on their faces, and large candy canes in their hands. The canes were sharpened at the end into spikes.

"Leave me alone," Jeff pleaded.

The elves slowly crowded around him. They began to sing in unison.

"Tis the season to be jolly."

"Leave me alone," he pleaded again.

"Fa la la la la."

"No, please."

"la la la la..."

He grabbed a chair and smacked it down on the nearest elf's head. The chair leg snapped in half. Collecting the sharp stick from the ground, Jeff started to stab it into the elves, one by one. First, he stuck one in the stomach. The stick felt as though it was stuck for a moment but then he yanked it out. He clubbed the next one across the head. Then he roared as he jumped on top of Chris, and stabbed the sharp stick into his eye. The screams from the elves filled the room. A group rushed Jeff and jumped onto him, tackling him to the ground.

"Quick, get something to tie his hands," one called.

"Grab some tinsel," another almost sang.

Moments later, he was lying on the floor with his arms bound behind his back. He tried to struggle free, but the elves sat on top of him so he couldn't move.

"Just stay still, you arsehole. The police will be here any minute," he heard a woman say.

Finally, the police arrived and carted him off. The newspaper headline the next day read, "Man kills colleagues in office massacre."

Behind bars, and awaiting trial, Jeff sat on the floor holding his arms around himself. He ignored the stares that were coming from the guard through the cell window. He rocked back and forth, singing to himself.

"Tis the season to be jolly."

The End

A Disappointed Shade of Blue

By

C.S. Anderson

A man walks merrily through the woods
Dragging behind him the traditional yule time log
Wondering perhaps if he should return to his family sooner
Take the short cut home through a dangerous bog
He stops at the edge and sadly looks down
Shaking his head ruefully at the sight he has found
All holiday cheer fleeing his mind
As he stares down at his grisly find

There is a beautiful girl drowned beneath the cold waters'
She was no one's wife but she was somebody's daughter
She had a fist full of promises
All of them broken
She had a heart full of dreams
That will never come true
She has a mouthful of words
Forever left unspoken
Her wide open eyes are a disappointed shade of blue..

The Present

By

Israel Finn

November 4, 1965

His fists rained down again and again, until she barely had any strength left to ward off the blows. Mary prayed to a god she'd long since stopped believing in that Rachel wouldn't come home from school just yet. Above the sink, the kitchen clock, an ugly yellow monstrosity shaped like a duck (a gift from Ted's mother), said 3:05 PM. That was about the time Rachel usually breezed through the kitchen door. Unless she decided to stop off at her best friend Amy's house. Occasionally she did.

"How many times have I told you to have supper on the goddamn table when I get home from work, *woman?"* Ted punctuated his question with a right cross, this one landing on the side of Mary's neck. It set her whole face on fire.

It wasn't as if Rachel never witnessed these beatings. She'd seen plenty. Still, it didn't prevent Mary from wanting to shield her daughter as much as possible from the horrors that took place in the Garver household, a place that Mary had come to think of as her prison.

Ted wouldn't allow Mary to work. This was partly because Ted's father, Hank (a real son of a bitch if there ever was one), believed that a woman's place was in the home, and Ted was a chip off the proverbial block. But the main reason Mary was forbidden to get a job was because Ted didn't want her turning up in public with fresh bruises every couple of weeks. Yet he knew that she couldn't very well live her entire life inside the house. So he was careful to administer his punishments below the neck, when he could. Only sometimes, he got carried away.

Like now.

"You don't appreciate how hard I work for this family"—Ted brought his fist down like a hammer on the top of Mary's head—"but by God, you *will*." He gathered a handful of her hair and began dragging her across the floor toward the stove. That last blow had felt like it almost broke her neck, and Mary cried out as fire rushed down her spine. Her yellow cotton dress rode up above her knees, which scudded painfully across the linoleum.

When they reached the stove Ted flipped on the burner. Mary realized what he intended and she screamed and thrashed wildly. Ted seized her right wrist in his left hand, then drove an elbow into her forehead. Motes exploded before Mary's eyes, expanding like a galaxy of tiny dying suns until there was nothing left but a thick gray haze blanketing her vision. She felt herself slipping away, all cares and concerns scattering, and she welcomed oblivion.

The flame brought her back, though. Mary shrieked. She bucked and flailed and tried desperately to jerk her hand away from the burner. But Ted was much stronger, and he held her fast, letting the bright blue flame lick the back of her hand.

He didn't hold it there for long, but it felt to Mary like an eternity. When he let her go she crumpled to the floor and cradled her blackened hand to her chest, hot tears streaming down her cheeks.

Ted gave an exasperated sigh. "Go to the bathroom and clean yourself up," he said, as if admonishing a child.

Mary lay there a little longer. Not too long, though. It wouldn't do to ignore her husband's wishes. At last, she rose and, still favoring her hand, moved like a ghost from the kitchen, down the hallway, and into the bathroom.

"And don't think this gets you out of fixing supper," Ted called after her.

Mary had tried to tell him why his supper was late—that the bus she usually caught to the grocery store had broken down, so the company had to send another one out—but it was no use. There were no excuses in Ted Garver's world.

Half an hour later, Mary was at the stove frying pork chops when Rachel walked in. The girl's smile collapsed when she saw her mother's bruised face and bandaged hand, and a small whimper escaped her lips. Mary cast an anxious glance down the hallway toward the living room where a football game blared on the TV, then turned back to her daughter. Mary shook her head slightly while meeting Rachel's gaze. *Don't say anything,* that look said. *It'll just set him off again.* Then she offered Rachel a hopeful smile and a nod, which said, *I'll be okay, don't worry.* Tears welled up in Rachel's eyes. She pressed the heels of her hands to her eyes, her chest hitching once, quietly. Her head bobbed as she swallowed the huge lump in her throat. Then she rubbed away the tears and wiped them on the front of her dress. The sad smile she returned to her mother broke Mary's heart. It was a heart that had been broken so many times it was a wonder it was still beating.

That night, in the darkness of their bedroom, Ted asked, "How's your hand?" Mary jumped. She thought he had been asleep.

"Not bad," she lied. It felt like fire ants were devouring her flesh. But Mary knew better than to complain too much. "I took some ibuprofen."

He was silent for so long that she thought he finally *had* fallen asleep. Then he spoke again. "You know I don't like hurting you."

"I know."

"Do you really?"

"Yes."

A pause. "I just get a little mad sometimes, that's all. Doesn't mean I don't love you."

"I know."

A longer pause. "Do you still love me?"

Here it comes, Mary thought. "Of course."

Ted heaved a deep sigh. "I'm glad," he said. "I don't like thinking about things like that, like you not loving me anymore, or you trying to leave me, and taking Rachel away from me."

"That won't ever happen," Mary said.

"But if it *did* happen," he said, "I just don't know what I'd do."

Mary waited.

"Probably something really bad," Ted said.

November 13, 1965

Saturday. Mary was making breakfast when Rachel cried out in the bathroom. Without thinking, Mary flipped the burner off and rushed down the hallway. She flung open the door. And there stood Rachel, still dripping wet from the bath, a towel held loosely against her body with one hand, her other hand held out in front of her, trembling and slick with blood. Mary's eyes were drawn to the other redness between her daughter's thin white thighs, and her first thought was, *Oh, God, I never talked with her about this.*

Rachel looked up with tear-filled eyes. "What's happening, Mama?"

At that moment, Ted appeared at Mary's back. "You okay, girl? You cut yourself?"

Mary turned and caught Ted's gaze…saw his expression slowly change, his face become wooden. "Oh," he said.

Mary returned her attention to Rachel, who had lifted the towel higher in a self-conscious effort to cover more of herself. Ted made a disgusted sound. "Take care of this," he growled, pushing Mary forward. He stomped away down the hall, cursing under his breath. Something about "another goddamn woman in the house."

Mary shut the bathroom door behind her.

November 28, 1965

"What the goddamn hell!" Ted's voice boomed from the bathroom. Both Mary and Rachel jumped, Rachel spilling some of her popcorn from its Tupperware bowl. They'd been sitting on the sofa watching the Ed Sullivan Show on television. Now they looked up as Ted stormed into the room holding a tube of red lipstick in his fist. He held it out before them.

"What is this?" he demanded.

Rachel's eyes went wide.

Mary opened her mouth to claim the lipstick belonged to her, even though she was perfectly aware of the consequences. Back when they were dating, she had worn makeup, and Ted never complained. Indeed, he seemed to like it. After she became pregnant with Rachel, however, his attitude began to change. He made snide remarks about her looks and her fragrance. Once they were married, he forbade her to use such things anymore, said she had no business tempting men, since she had already snagged one. And in his mind, that was what it all came down to, really. She had caught him with her feminine wiles just as surely as a hunter's prey is ensnared by the scent of bait. And when she went and "got herself" knocked up, he was truly and hopelessly had.

But Mary never got the words out, because Rachel volunteered, "I just wanted try it, Daddy. Just to see what it looked like."

Ted hurled the tube across the room, where it struck the wall, leaving a bright red smudge before clattering to the floor.

He turned on Rachel.

"You little whore."

Ted unbuckled his belt and drew the leather through the loops like he was unsheathing a sword.

Rachel bolted off the couch, popcorn exploding everywhere. She tried to run, but the living room was too small and Ted was too fast. He seized her by her wrist. Rachel cried out. Mary was up instantly, mindlessly charging to her daughter's defense. She lashed out, clawing at Ted's face, the first time she had ever retaliated against him. But again, Ted was too quick. He dodged the swipe of her hooked fingers by feinting back, then drove a battering ram of a fist into her right eye. Mary went down hard on her back, the world going gray around the edges, the light fading.

The last thing she heard was the sound of Ted's belt against Rachel's flesh (*thwack, thwack, thwack,* over and over again) and Rachel screaming, "No, Daddy, no no *noooooooooooo!"*

Then blackness.

December 3, 1965

Mary wandered along John F. Kennedy Drive, tugging her coat collar tight against the bitter cold and giving the store windows only desultory glances. Although the afternoon was gray and misty, she wore her big tortoise-shell sunglasses.

The street's Christmas decorations gleamed and twinkled in stark and colorful contrast to the gloomy backdrop of the day. People bustled to and fro, bright packages in their mittened hands, and Mary knew that the crowds would only get thicker, the streets and stores busier, between now and the big day. She looked at the people passing by, at their seemingly happy faces, and felt utterly alone.

Mary knew she should be home doing Friday's chores—Ted liked the house to be spick and span come the weekend—but the walls had started closing in on her, and she thought if she didn't get out for a while she would simply suffocate. So she'd thrown on her coat and dashed out the door, turning a deaf ear to the frightened voice in the back of her mind: *Ted won't like coming home to a dirty house, you know. Won't like it at all.* He'd most likely get upset and… well, she knew what would happen then, didn't she? But that didn't stop her. Because she was used to it by now. At least, that's what she tried to tell herself. Used to the pain. The fear. Deep down, she knew that wasn't true, of course. The real truth was that, sometimes, even fear was not enough to hold back the need to feel *free,* if only for a little while.

She started to feel dizzy, experienced a light, fluttering sensation in the pit of her stomach, like when you floated over a hill in a fast-moving car or plunged headlong toward the earth on a roller coaster. She braced her hand against the wall of a nearby building for support, her head spinning unpleasantly. When a man paused on the sidewalk and inquired in a far-away voice whether she was all right, Mary thought she answered yes, though she couldn't be sure.

She waited, nauseated, for the vertigo to ebb. It seemed interminable. Finally she gathered herself, took a deep breath, squared her shoulders, and resumed her trek down JFK Drive. Or what she had thought was JFK. But when Mary reached the intersection, she saw that she stood on the corner of Keeling Street and Fourth Avenue. She was confused. Fourth Avenue was right where it should be, but how had she gotten off of JFK Drive without being aware of it? Not only that, but she knew this part of town like the back of her hand, and she had never even *heard* of Keeling Street.

She stopped a young woman passing by with a toddler in tow.

"Excuse me. Isn't this John F. Kennedy Drive?"

The woman looked at Mary as if she thought she might be joking. Then she asked it out loud. "Are you kidding?"

"Um. No."

"Don't they usually wait until someone's dead before they name a street after them?" the woman asked. The toddler, a little boy, goggled up at Mary.

Mary stared at her. What in the world was this woman talking about?

The woman's expression went from amused to puzzled, then turned to concern. She searched Mary's face intently, tried to scan the eyes behind the dark sunglasses, and Mary felt her face flush despite the cold.

"Are you okay, honey?" the woman asked.

"Unee," the boy echoed.

"I'm fine," Mary muttered absently. "Thank you." She turned and stepped off the curb, and jumped at the sound of a blaring horn and screeching tires. She gaped at the wide-eyed man behind the wheel, her legs turning to water. The smell of burnt rubber filled her nostrils. The driver leaned out his window.

"Jeez Louise, lady! Watch where you're goin' why dont'cha!"

Mary stepped back up onto the curb and pressed her palm to her heaving chest in an effort to keep her heart from tearing itself loose and jumping out onto the sidewalk. She tried to say she was sorry to the irate man, but her lips couldn't form the words. He rolled on through the intersection, shaking his head. It was then that she noticed the make and model of the car. It was a white Ford Galaxie 500. She should know: Ted drove the exact same one.

Except there on the front quarter panel, where the chrome Galaxie 500 logo should be attached, it said Impel.

Ford Impel?

"Miss, are you sure you're okay?"

Mary turned and saw the woman with the toddler staring at her. The boy's mouth formed an O. Mary nodded, looked both ways on Fourth Avenue, then crossed and continued along Keeling Street.

Mary had read the phrase *her mind reeled* before, but never had she fully grasped it until now. As she walked along a street that should by all rights have been named after their slain president, Mary began searching for other incongruities. It didn't take long to spot one. In the window of a record shop, an album cover leaned against a portable record player. It showed the rock group, the Beatles, whose music Rachel was absolutely crazy about. Mary enjoyed their music too, though she would never admit it to Ted, a devout George Jones fan. She thought their songs were catchy and clever. She'd become familiar with their faces from the posters in Rachel's room, and had heard her daughter coo their names enough times, though the only one she could ever remember was Ringo.

The cover in the window was of the band's new album, *Rubber Soul*, released that very day. The Fab Four stared at the camera, the album title appearing above their heads in fat orange letters. Except Ringo was missing. In his place stood a young man Mary had never seen before, his hairstyle unlike his band mates' "mop tops." It looked more like Elvis's Pompadour. Their first names had been dashed off next to their faces. His simply said Pete.

Mary frowned at the cover for a long time.

Farther down the street she froze in front of a store called Dave's Fine Appliances. In the window were a trio of televisions displayed at different levels. All three were tuned to the same station, which showed footage of a man in a spacesuit hopping around on some dusty, desolate surface. A small tinny-sounding speaker was connected to the upper corner of the store's doorjamb so that passersby could hear, as well as watch, whatever was happening on those screens. Accompanying the footage of the spaceman was the familiar voice of Walter Cronkite:

"And here we see astronaut John Herman, the first man ever to walk on the surface of the moon. These images were captured only minutes after Scorpio Seven's historic landing four days ago, November twenty-ninth, Nineteen Sixty-five."

The scene switched to Cronkite himself, seated behind his desk. He was pinching the bridge of his nose, presumably wiping tears from the corners of his eyes. *"I never get tired of watching that,"* he said.

Mary was stunned.

She whirled around to share her excitement with someone, *anyone*.

But, of course, these people already knew.

We landed on the moon, she thought, astonished. *In this place, anyway. Wherever this place is.*

Her eyes were drawn to a man across the street. He was leaning in the open doorway of a building with the uninspiring name PAWN SHOP over the entrance. He was tall, thin, with skin so pale and hair so white/blond that he might have been an albino. He leaned in the doorway with his arms crossed, dressed in ragged blue jeans and a black t-shirt with the word NIRVANA across the chest in bold white letters. The man was completely out of place. Like a clown at a cocktail party. Yet no one else appeared to notice him at all.

He looked straight at her. The corners of his thin lips curled up in a smile, and his hand rose like the head of a cobra from a wicker basket. With a slim index finger he motioned for her to approach him.

She did, feeling almost as if she were floating across Keeling Street. When she stood before him, he said, "Hi, sweetness."

His irises were so pale blue they looked liked ice chips, and something indefinable moved (*writhed?*) behind them, stirring within Mary several different emotions at once. One of those stirrings found its insidious way between her legs, and Mary was mortified. Even more so when he gave her a knowing smile. Her face burned, and the fire spread down her neck to her torso.

"You looking for something?" His voice was like silk.

"I…that is…" Mary felt the same way she had as a school girl, tongue-tied with one of the cute boys or popular girls. But she was a grown woman, for heaven's sake. And this man wasn't even all that attractive. Odd, yes, but certainly not handsome. Still, she couldn't deny he possessed a kind of…quality. A strange magnetism. She felt that tickle down there again and thought her face would burst into flames at any moment.

"A Christmas gift for the hubby, perhaps?"

Mary gasped, and realized she had not been breathing. She exhaled the word, "Yes," in a relieved rush of air.

"I think I have just the thing." He gave her a sly, conspiratorial wink. "C'mon inside."

He turned and disappeared into the store. Mary followed, or at least started to. She halted just past the threshold, her eyes unable to penetrate the dimness of the interior.

"You're gonna have to take those shades off, you wanna see," he called from deeper inside the room.

Mary hesitated.

"It's okay," he said. "No judgment here."

How does he know? she wondered, her heart speeding up.

"I'm psychic," he said, as if indeed reading her mind.

Mary stayed where she was. She heard boots scuffing against a wooden floor as he moved across the room.

"Actually," he said, "I'm just not stupid. A woman sporting dark sunglasses on a day like today usually means, one) she's blind, which you ain't, two) she's got one humdinger of a hangover, which *could* be the case, but my spidey sense tells me otherwise, or three) somebody's been tuning up on her face. Number three's my guess."

Mary reached up and dragged the glasses off her face, revealing what she knew was an unlovely black and purple bruise around her right eye.

"Well now," the man said, and Mary heard a tightness in his voice, "give the man a cigar."

He stood behind a long counter in a room shaped like a boxcar. A dusty hardwood floor stretched away toward the rear. The place appeared to be cram-packed with every kind of knick-knack and gewgaw imaginable: antique lamps; clocks (one, a black and white cat whose golf ball eyes swiveled disturbingly back and forth, counting off the seconds); cheap artwork; record players and radios; guitars; various containers; watches and jewelry and pistols (behind a glass case under the counter), and a million sundry other items. On the wall behind the counter, like a formation of soldiers, stood a row of long guns.

"Step right up, little lady," the pale man invited.

Mary approached the counter.

He bent down and appeared to reach into a section under the counter where a sign that read WE BUY AND SELL leaned against the inside of the glass, obstructing her view. In that moment something told her she should leave. Right then. Get out and retrace her steps back along Keeling Street until it somehow, impossibly, became JFK Drive again. Get to the bus stop. Go home. And try to forget this upside down day ever happened.

Then something else told her no. She had to stay, *must* stay. It was that same feeling from before, the one that recognized her need to feel free, if only for a while. She didn't know why this should be, but then she didn't understand *anything* anymore.

The man stood up, and on the countertop he placed a simple wooden container the size and shape of a cigar box.

"I think this little item is just what ol' hubby needs," he said, smiling.

Mary looked curiously at the box.

"Yes," the man said, "I do believe it's just what he deserves."

Now the man's expression turned sober. His mouth formed a grim line.

"Now, whatever you do, Mary," he said. "Don't touch it."

"How do you know..." Mary's voice trailed off, because the pale man had opened the box.

And what was inside was the most terrible thing she had ever seen.

December 25, 1965

Mary set the stack of pancakes down on the kitchen table, then settled herself gingerly onto her chair. Her rear end still stung from Ted's belt. He'd taken her over his knee the night before because, according to him, Mary had "sassed" him when he came home from Mickey's Bar, spoiling his Christmas cheer. In truth, all she had done was ask him to take his slushy boots off at the front door so he wouldn't track the mess inside. It was Friday evening, after all, and she had waxed the floor that day, and cleaned the house within an inch of its life. Mary had made sure to do this every Friday since that particular Friday she visited the pawn shop with the mysterious pale man. Because that day she never got around to cleaning up, and Ted punished her severely for her laziness.

When Mary left the pawn shop that day, the wooden box poking from the top of her purse, she stepped out onto John F. Kennedy Drive. Across the street, Dave's Fine Appliances was once again the Soap-N-Suds Laundromat. And when she turned around, she wasn't at all surprised to see no pawn shop there. The entire building, in fact, was just...gone. In its place stood an empty lot. She went directly home and did what the pale man had told her to do.

Then she waited.

In a sudden motion, Ted reached across the table for the bottle of syrup. Rachel, who sat across from Mary, flinched. She did that a lot these days. Mary ate her breakfast silently, each bite slow and deliberate. It was the longest meal of her life.

But finally it was over, and following their tradition, carried over from Ted's childhood, they all repaired to the living room to gather around the fake tree, drink eggnog, and open their gifts, each in turn. Rachel was first. She received a pair of plaid skirts with complimentary tops, the Beatles' new *Rubber Soul* album (this one with Ringo's face on the cover), and a new record player to spin it on. Rachel squealed with delight over the record, and hugged both her parents. But Mary couldn't help noticing Rachel's lip curl in distaste while embracing her dad.

Next it was Mary's turn. She got a new iron, a Toastmaster toaster—"Maybe now you'll quit burning it," Ted told her—and some pots and pans.

"Last but not least," Mary said, reaching under the tree and retrieving a package wrapped in shiny red paper and topped with a green bow. Ted sat on the sofa, glassy-eyed from the splash of rum he'd added to his eggnog. She placed the present on the coffee table in front of her husband. It was about the size of a cigar box.

Ted gave her a look that contained one part appreciation and two parts warning. "You better not have spent too much on this."

"No, Ted." In truth, she hadn't paid a dime.

Ted's eyes gazed into hers with dark promise for another few seconds. Then he grinned.

"Well, all right then," Ted said, and began unwrapping his gift. While he was thus occupied, Mary looked from where she was seated on the floor up at Rachel, who sat on the footstool, her new album on her lap. Rachel looked back at her.

Mary gazed intently at Rachel for a long moment, turned her eyes away and fixed them on Ted's present, then looked back at her daughter once more. Mary gave a slight nod.

Realization dawned in Rachel's eyes. Her mouth became a grim line. She nodded back.

She understood. Maybe not everything. But enough.

"What have we here?" Ted said. Before him sat a simple wooden box.

"Merry Christmas, Ted," said Mary.

Ted opened the box.

"Wha—?"

Mary saw darkness gathering around the box. Heard a rush of air. She flinched when it exploded into splinters as the thing inside it expanded. It was a perfect black circle. A hole. And the light of day in its immediate vicinity was being sucked into it.

So was Ted.

He tried to rise, to tear himself away. But the hole was far too powerful. Far too hungry.

Like a mouth, Mary thought.

She stood up to get a better look, and from the corner of her eye saw that Rachel was also getting to her feet. They watched.

The noise of air rushing into opening was deafening, like a jet engine, and Mary felt her ears pop.

Ted screamed, but even the sound of that was being sucked down the hole. He braced his hands against the top of the coffee table on either side of the aperture, every muscle in his body straining in an effort to prevent being sucked in like a spider through a vacuum cleaner tube.

When Rachel started to take a step forward, Mary shouted at her to stop. She remembered the pale man saying not to get too close once the box was opened, that the hole was unbiased. Which was why he exhorted her to wrap the box the minute she arrived home with it, and by no means to open it.

The pall of darkness expanded around the hole as Ted battled for his life.

"Mary…please. Help me!" he shrieked, but the words were torn from his lips and swept away. Mary now fought to draw a breath. It was as if she were trying to suck the air into her lungs through a straw. She glanced over and saw that Rachel struggled as well. Her chest was heaving up and down.

The hole widened again, and Ted's left hand plunged inside. He tumbled into the darkness, but at the last second his right hand caught on the rim. He reached out and clawed at the coffee table, seized its edge. Mary didn't understand how the table could still be standing there, intact, despite being almost completely breached by the hole. It hurt her mind to look at it.

It was getting harder and harder to breathe, and the scream of rushing air was pressing painfully against her eardrums.

She looked at Rachel. "We've got to get out of here!" she yelled. "If we don't we're going to suffocate—"

"Mom, look!" Rachel pointed at the hole.

Mary looked. And saw another hand, mottled and gray, reaching out of the hole to grasp Ted's hand. It was twice a large as Ted's hand, however, and its fingers—all six of them—were tipped with sharp black claws. It enclosed Ted's hand, and then dragged it out of sight.

The hole began to shrink. It looked like a puddle of oil receding into sand. As it dwindled, the noise of surging air died with it, and that area of the room gradually brightened.

The hole disappeared with a *pop* and a belch of the most foul stench Mary had ever smelled before. She wanted to retch. Rachel, too, was wrinkling her nose. But after a short time, the odor was gone as well.

Mary took a deep breath, looked at her daughter, and smiled.

Rachel returned it.

Mary knew they'd have much to talk about over the coming days and weeks. Much to do.

But there would be time.

And maybe in time, even the pain would be gone.

The End

Christmas Carole

By

Lisa Vasquez

'Pon the wintry eve of December 23rd
There was a sound 'til then ne'er heard.
A scream more chillin' than ocean's depth,
It stole God's name from beneath the breath.

Carole fell asleep to the sound of a crackling fire and the warmth of it on her young cheeks, smiling with thoughts of Christmas morning dreams. Her room was already warm, but curling into her favorite afghan added an extra layer of comfort to her. It was not only Christmas in two days, it was her birthday and she'd turn seven this year.

The smells from the kitchen where her mother and grandmother were baking wafted upstairs until at last, her little mind went away to where little girls dream.

The frightful sounds to which she awoke is one that no child should ever have to wake to. The barely conscious girl was so frightened by the sounds of them she lost control of her bladder. A warm puddle formed between her legs but she could not move, only stare into darkness with eyes as large and as round as saucers.

She could feel her breath coming in short, quick bursts to allow her tiny lungs to fill with as much oxygen as possible. The fear was on her chest, forcing her into the mattress with the weight of it. There was nothing but screaming rising up the old wooden stairs, slithering across the walls and shaking the bed with its desperation.

When they stopped, the silence was just as painful to her ears. They continued to ring, disorienting her and when she sat up the entire room swayed around her.

"P-Pappa?"

In the room that suddenly became so much larger, her voice sounded small and frail. She listened but there was no response. Panic swelled up inside of her. Her blood rushed back to her frozen limbs and her tears felt cold against her flush cheeks.

"Pappa where are you? What's happening?"

There was nothing but silence looming in the open doorway with the shadows cast on the walls by flickering candlelight. The thought of her parents being harmed was the only source of courage strong enough to persuade her to move as she did now, swinging one leg off the bed until her toes touched the frigid floor.

She hesitated, praying for her father's voice to come back through the blackness before her she'd have to force her other leg to meet the first. Carole could feel the constriction of her throat when she tried to swallow and her teeth began to chatter. She was breathing so fast, her head began to feel faint. To steady herself, she reached out for her bedside table and flinched. Her fingers had touched the beads of her rosary.

A sense of hope came over her and she collected it into her palm, clutching it to her chest but the relief it offered was short-lived. From behind her, she heard the heavy fall of footsteps coming toward her. After so many years of hearing her father climb them to kiss her goodnight, Carole knew whomever they belonged to was not him.

The chill of the air reminded her that her nightdress was wet and the thin cloth was clinging to her thighs. Soaked in the smell of urine, she ran and hid behind a panel of thick curtains bunched together on either side of her window.

The heavy sound of the steps drew closer and she pressed her back against the wall. As was human nature, the girl had to see the face of the terror that woke her up that night. She had to see the explanation for the screams before her imagination sent her spiraling into madness. And so, as gently as she could, she leaned forward and peeked at the doorway. The rays of the moon shone down on it like a spotlight, waiting for the star to appear.

At first there were only long shadows stretching from the floor to the door. Carole shivered, not only from cold, but from anticipation of who, or what, the shadow belonged to. With each step the shadow grew closer, the girl's heart slammed against her ribs like a bird desperate to be free of its cage.

What appeared first was a hoof. A singular, thick hoof glistening with fresh snow.

Her feet had grown roots where she stood. Trailing her eyes up from the hoof was blonde fur covering legs like that of a lamb. The small girl's mind could barely process it and her lungs forced out a breath in shock. That minute whispered exhale drew the animal's attention.

Filling the doorway, a creature appeared: haunting and terrifying all at once. Her eyes glistened like father's whiskey, gold and unnatural. She could see Carole. Not only could she see Carole, she could see through her. The small girl could feel the creature's gaze penetrate her skin and touch everything inside her.

Upon the *thing's* head were horns like a ram that spiraled back into a curl against a mane of honey. She was dressed. Yes, dressed, in animal furs covered in more of the fresh snow, now melting into small gem-like beads and hypnotizing Carole from her hiding spot.

Against her own will, she came from behind the curtains and walked toward the beast. A scream was welling up in her lungs but could not find escape. She opened her mouth wide but felt as though something clutched her throat.

The beautiful terror leaned forward and Carole was able to see her features more clearly. Her face was bathed in blood, *Carole's mother's blood.* The girl fought to get free of the monstrous grasp holding her still when creature leaned forward to take a deep breath, inhaling Carole's scent.

When she drew back and smiled, Carole could see rows of jagged teeth and pieces of her mother's hair between them. The scream locked in her small throat began to fight for freedom with sounds of gagging and gurgling.

"Yesssss," the beast hissed, "Sssssscream!"

Like the sound that woke her to this nightmare, Carole was finally able to unleash the repulsion and shock. The force of her scream ripped at the delicate tissues in her throat, yet she continued despite the pain, until the air ran out of her lungs.

The monster's eyes closed, seduced by the sound of it, and when she opened her eyes again, Carole saw the hunger in them. All the girl had in defense was her rosary and prayer so she closed her eyes brought the beads to her lips then began to pray.

"Saint Michael the Archangel, defend us in the day of battle. Be our safeguard against the wickedness and the snares."

Before the final word could be spoken, Carole felt her body falling and her head collided heavily and painfully with the ground. She tried to sit up to see what happened, but the blow blurred her vision. She could make out only shapes. Someone else was there with her and the monster.

"Papa?"

Crawling on the floor toward the struggle, she was desperate to know if her father was there. She needed to know he was safe, and that he would protect her.

The figure saw Carole and threw the beast down to the floor, plunging something that looked like a sword into her chest before turning and running at Carole.

"Oh God! What's happened?" she cried, reaching out for him.

The figure leaned in showing his true face, pressing a single finger against his lips, "Shhhh."

Without another sound, Carole went limp.

###

No matter how many logs Carole put onto the fire, the heat would not penetrate her bones. Resignedly, she sat back releasing a deep sigh. A plume of condensation hung in the air in front of her. Tight, near-frozen fingers curled into the worn, old afghan her mother had made for her many years ago and she pulled it around her. Everything was so stiff.

Behind her, the wind howled against the oversized cathedral windows. The thin panes of glass rattled and shook in protest. There were no clouds in the sky where the bright moon stared back at her. The snowflakes were so enormous they seemed to float past like large sails topping ships on a midnight ocean.

"Grant me, O Lord, the strength to endure. Keep me warm in Your glory."

The prayer was offered despite knowing it would not be heard.

Taking her rosary from her lap, she brought it to her lips to kiss the frozen metal of the crucifix that dangled from the beads.

Carole had been known to carry the same rosary with her everywhere since she was a young girl. Children often teased her for her piety by calling her names and excluding her from play but it only made her convictions stronger. Despite their cruelty, she would include them in her prayers and in the small hours of the night, passers-by could see her silhouette behind the glow of a single candle in the second story window, until the night her parents were slaughtered and she disappeared.

Carole's eyes never recovered from the night she was assaulted as a child. The world was a mass of blurry, monochromatic shapes. Since that night when she was seven, Carole was never able to see properly again, until the 23rd of December. Looking down at the street below, she could see a figure staring up at her. It was the anniversary of that deadly night when he would appear and she could *see* him. The madness of the misshapen world would part and his face would come through in all his brilliance.

And she would relive it again.

Over and over, each year, for nearly a hundred years. The battle between the Beast and the figure would be replayed, keeping Carole's spirit locked here in limbo as their pawn and link to the material realm.

The children in town were brought to her home and the story was recited to warn them about staying up too late on Christmas Eve. To ward off the evil, they would gather and close their eyes while singing Christmas hymns by candlelight.

"Why do we have to keep our eyes closed?" one of children asked.

"The legend says that if you catch even the smallest glance of the creature you'll go blind," her mother explained.

"What creature, mummy?"

"The one with the hooves, Ivy. Now be a good girl and close your eyes. We'll light your candle for you. When you hear the others sing, you join in."

Ivy closed her eyes and felt a hand touch hers. Her brother, Eamon, who was blind since birth stood beside her.

"I know you can't see, Eamon, but keep your eyes closed, too." Ivy whispered.

The children could tell it was nearly time to start. The rustling of clothing had gone quiet and the talking had ceased. The bells from the church rang out announcing the time to begin and they all began.

The first notes carried up toward the window illuminated with an amber glow. Carole stood in front of the glass in silence, staring down at the only figure she could see. Tears fell from her eyes in anticipation of the anniversary of her eternal Hell.

The voice of the sopranos carried higher and louder than the others, triggering the memory of the screams of her mother on that tragic night. Carole clutched her rosary until her palm was bleeding. Behind her, the sounds of the hooved beast caused her to spin around. She tried to scream but her voice was lost behind the veil of the spirit world and instead the world outside heard only the sound of singing coming from the window.

The figure who Carole waited for every year walked toward the door and stopped. Turning slowly, he looked down at the boy, blind from birth, who could now see him through another's eyes . The Beast was watching him through the boy's eyes and the boy was seeing him too.

The Devil smiled at the boy, gave him a wink, and went to save Christmas Carole.

The End

Stuffed Pig

By

Steven Murray

The street was quiet. Each house, dotted tastefully with Christmas decorations, was trying to outdo the other in tasteful understatement. A dusting of white snow covered everything. Paw-prints and footprints crisscrossed each other down the flour-sifted street and across the large gardens. The tall wrought-iron security fences outside most driveways were thickly iced.

It was starting to snow as the taxi pulled up to the gates. "Mike, it's Ali and Mickey," Abi shouted into the intercom. Pretty lights lit up the windows of Sharon's large modern house, turning the white snow pink then green then blue. The automatic gates opened as Mike, the security guard, pressed the button to let them in. A small Christmas 'gathering' held by Sharon Edwards; former model, semi-famous, blonde and beautiful with a gap in her teeth. Now pregnant, engaged to her manager, Eric Roberts, and off the runway.

Inside was warmth, the smell of a real fire, mulled wine. Canapés, chilled champagne and finger-food all on the huge white table. The tree in the living room was 7 foot and all the white lights decorating it sparkled. Angel on top. There was a garland across the art deco fireplace and the cream leather sofa curved around in front of the patio doors which reflected the lights. Wonderland.

Two hours later - all were drunk, except for Sharon, and talking together on the floor near the fire. Mickey had his hands in Ali's dark brown hair. She leaned back onto him, cradling a glass of brandy. "So, decided what you're going to call the baby yet?" she asked Sharon.

"Uh, not really…I don't want to tempt fate."

"So how are you feeling anyway, you know, in yourself?"

"Like a stuffed pig," Sharon laughed. "But I can't wait. I'm so excited."

"Well, it's not long now,' said Ali, sipping her drink. 'What? One, two weeks? I'm so jealous; I can't wait to have children."

"Hey, we've got plenty of time!" Mickey said, and they all laughed. Sharon absent-mindedly chewed on her bottom lip. She had a nervous feeling in the pit of her gut; had had the entire evening, and it was getting worse.

She sat on the sofa next to Steve, a well-built man with curly, dirty- blonde, hair and ice-blue eyes. He was stroking her leg.

"Well, I for one think you look amazing," he said, his eyes staying on her for too long.

"Yeah, you're glowing," Ali said, suppressing a small burp.

"Oh, you were always full of shit," Sharon said and they all laughed.

"Are you sure you won't have any champagne?" Mickey asked, grabbing it from the ice bucket. Slush slid down the side of the bottle and plopped back in. He held it out towards her. "One drink won't hurt.' He stood up. 'We'll toast to the baby!"

"No, but thank you. Not until after the baby's born."

"Come on. One won't hurt!" Steve looked at Mickey, giving him a warning, but it seemed to go unnoticed. Ali rushed to her feet as Mickey poured a small glass. "Come on. To the baby! … Hey, I remember what a party girl you were."

"Leave it, Mickey," Ali said, trying to grab the glass from him.

"Oh, if it's going to be so much fuss," Sharon said, grabbing the glass from Mickey.

"To the baby," she said holding up the glass. They all clanked glasses and yelled "to the baby!" Sharon swigged it back, dozens of Christmas lights reflected in her glass.

Sharon stood in the kitchen waiting for the kettle to boil. She needed a strong black coffee. I can't give up everything for this pregnancy, she thought, slightly bitter that Steve hadn't come to her aid with Mickey. The kettle whistled. As she went to grab it, the phone rang on the wall behind her. She jumped, laughing at herself, and walked over to pick it up. "Hello?"

"Hi honey, it's Joan, just across from you – how are you?" Joan was a sweet older woman in her seventies with emphysema from smoking forty a day. She had a rough, throaty voice and had to take long pauses between words.

Sharon poured the hot water onto the coffee. "I'm fine, thank you." The rich scent filled her head.

"I'm sorry to bother you, it's just I noticed… somebody around the side of your house, lurking, about a minute ago….Just to say, make sure the doors… are locked….darling. Can't be too sure…..what with those burglaries….last Christmas." Sharon's anxiety came back with a thud, creeping up the back of her spine with cold fingers and letting butterflies loose in her belly, floating around her unborn.

"Well Joan, we've got pretty good security here this Christmas. I doubt that anyone would get past Mike. He was a police officer for ten years." She dropped four teaspoons of sugar into her coffee and stirred. "Plus, this isn't America." She laughed and it came out too loud.

"Well…I thought I'd call. Better safe… than sorry, that's what my Jerry always said."

“Thanks Joan, I appreciate it. I’ll call and tell Mike to keep a look out. Bye now Joan, and Merry Christmas!”

“Bye sweetheart … and good luck with the baby….Do let me know when it’s…..born.”

“Okay, bye.’ Sharon put the phone back on the hook. She felt sick with anxiety. It bubbled near the surface getting closer and closer to the top. Rich, pure white fear. She frowned and picked the phone back up. She dialled Mike.

Sharon paced the kitchen, phone ringing. It went dead. She imagined a gloved hand reaching into the fuse box outside and cutting a wire. Silly. That only happened in the films. The baby kicked hard, twice, and she thought how badly she needed to pee. She had the phone pressed so tight against her ear it was starting to hurt. Suddenly, a hand clasped her shoulder. She turned quickly, raising the phone to use as a weapon.

“Whoa! Calm down lady, it’s just me,” Steve said. The light bounced off his blonde curls. She stared at him, a perfect shade of pale.

“Jesus, Steve, you scared me!! Do you want me to go into labour?

“I’m sorry, darling; I never meant to scare you. I need to talk – Hey, what’s wrong?”

“Oh, nothing probably. I just got a call from my nosey neighbour. She’s alone and spies on us all with binoculars.” She laughed, pushing a strand of hair from her face. “Joan said she saw someone outside, lurking. Her exact word, ‘lurking’. And now the phone line’s dead.”

“Do you want me to go down and check on Mike?” Steve asked, taking her hand and squeezing it, the diamond band digging into their flesh.

“What do you think?” she asked, her green eyes glittering.

“I think I’d like to talk to you, so I’ll ask Mickey to go do it.”

Sharon grabbed her cup of cold coffee and laughed. Again, it sounded too loud in her ears. Like she was trying to reassure herself of something.

Some old crooner was still singing about ‘chestnuts roasting on an open fire.’ Ali and Mickey were lying on the sofa together. Mickey was watching Ali as she slept. Steve slapped his hands together, hard, grabbing both their attention. Ali jumped and sat up. “Steve! I was asleep.”

“Mickey! You need to go down and check that everything’s okay with security because the phone’s dead.”

“Why can’t you go?!” Mickey asked.

"Because I need to talk to Sharon," Steve said, winking.

"What's with the winking?" Ali asked.

"I'll tell you later," Mickey whispered.

"Fine!" Ali elbowed him in the side then grabbed his beer bottle. "Go on, it'll only take a minute."

"What if there's some psycho out there?"

"Well, it's more likely to be a chav trying to make off with Sharon's Faberge eggs," Ali said, pulling a mock-snooty face. "The undesirables must keep with their Christmas traditions, as well as the rest of us."

"The line's just probably down," said Steve. "Go check, Mickey! It'll help Sharon relax." Another wink.

Mickey begrudgingly got up from his comfy position and swung his leg over Ali. "Love you," he whispered to Ali, much to her surprise. She was just about to answer. In their five years of dating, he'd never said it before.

Steve smiled. "Thanks Mickey, I appreciate it."

"You wink one more time," she warned.

Mickey sighed as he pulled open the front door. He was met with a gust of wind that chilled his face. Snow was now falling heavily. Mickey gazed up into the fleecy night. He shivered and hugged himself, pulling his long black coat tighter. He could feel the warmth behind him. 'Santa Claus is Coming to Town' was playing. He closed the door on it and descended the front porch, looking around and shielding his eyes with his hand. The moonlight struggled through the snowstorm. His breath blasted out into the skin-numbing air. He blinked as the snow caressed his face with tiny little kisses of frost. He wanted to twirl like Wynona Ryder in 'Edward Scissorhands.' But Steve could be watching from the window for all he knew.

It was a long walk to the security guard's booth. The snow crunched under his boots. He started to sing to himself. "He sees you when you're sleeping, he knows when you're awake…." He sang softly and tentatively as if someone might hear him. "He knows when you've been bad or good so be good for goodness sake."

Soon he reached the booth. "Mike? Mike, you about?" His voice got lost in the howling wind, though he kept on walking. It was dark now, the snow making everything dreamier. He noticed fresh footprints in the snow, two sets, and in his murky, dreamy-drunk head, fear seized. He looked up, then spun around. He could barely see the house through the blizzard.

Mickey hesitated. Yes - definitely more than one set of footprints. Maybe Madeline and Scottie decided to come after all. But where were they? He was too scared to call out. The lights in the security booth were flickering. There's something wrong with the electric, Mickey told himself. The security booth door swung open on its hinges; squeaking in the breeze. I should go back, Mickey thought. He didn't.

"…Mike?" His voice got eaten up in the hungry air. He approached the flashing booth slowly, scared like a kid. The flashing was coming from inside the booth. He grabbed the swinging door and wiped crystals out of his eyes with numb fingers.

"Oh my God!"

Mike was limp in his chair, his body slumped back. He'd been tied up with Christmas lights. They flashed on and off: blood on the security panel-Mike's throat slashed-then darkness. Again: Mike's eyes cut out with Christmas lights in the empty, bloody sockets-his mouth open in an unending scream-darkness. A spray of blood all over the window-uniform soaked in blood-darkness. Blood, thick and dark, like treacle, dripping onto the crisp white snow. "Oh God, Mike…"

He gagged and turned, coming face to face with a man wearing a cheap Santa Claus outfit. Mickey staggered backwards, hiding behind the security door and staring through the glass. The man, his features dark, held his head up high, twin trails of white vapour drifting out of each nostril. The number 666 was daubed on his forehead with what looked like lumpy, congealed blood- Mike's blood. He pointed a gun at Mickey's terrified face.

"Don't say a fucking word or you'll end up like him." He nodded to Mike, still flashing gruesomely from his seat.

Mickey put both his pink hands up. "Don't shoot!"

A girl appeared - long fair hair in pigtails, a Santa hat and fake white beard. Thin, tall, attractive, bugging eyes, clown smile. 666 on her forehead. Almost lost in a mess of tacky green tinsel around her neck like a feather boa. If Mickey had to take a picture of insanity, he'd aim his camera at her. They looked high, he thought. Maybe they just wanted to steal some stuff so they could go out and buy more drugs.

In his gut he knew better.

"What do you want?"

"Shut your fuckin' mouth!" the girl screamed, right in Mickey's left ear. It was so loud he couldn't hear for a few seconds. They pushed Mickey towards the house. The young woman used a hand-knife, poking it into his back, and Santa kept the gun aimed on him. Mickey's bottom lip quivered so hard that he started to drool.

"You better keep quiet; else I'll cut you with this baby a thousand fuckin' times." Her voice was strangely high, like she'd been sucking helium. She dug the knife in his back, causing him to cry out in pain as they walked towards the house.

Sharon and Steve were in the brightly lit kitchen, drinking camomile tea and talking in hushed tones. "Listen, you know I care about you," Steve said.

Not this again, Sharon thought. One mistake and he won't let go. Why can't he leave me alone? "You know I think you're great, Steve…"

"But Sharon, you can't raise my child with another man. I want to be there for you, for the baby. I love you!"

"Oh Steve, I love you, too. You've been amazing with me and the baby. You know how much I appreciate you, but –"

"Sharon…" He had to make her understand. He had to. He took her hand in his as a scream rose up from the living room. Ali. Then some strange voices. Steve motioned to Sharon to keep quiet.

"Please don't hurt her!" Mickey said, kneeling on the floor with his hands on his head.

"Who the hell are you?" Ali asked, staring at the strange man in the Santa suit.

"You can call me Santa, and this beauty here, this is Santa's little helper."

The thin girl, who looked pretty but insane, twirled around holding a knife above her head. "Da-dah!" she said like a magician's assistant. "Now…GET UP BITCH! MOVE YOUR ARSE!" She fluttered her eyelashes coyly. Ali got up slowly and steadily, determined not to show how scared she was. The fact she was close to shitting herself was neither here nor there.

"Sharon, get in the bedroom and lock yourself in. These people are not messing around," he whispered.

They were crouched down behind the kitchen island. Steve was rubbing Sharon's arm. She looked terrified. He helped her up and edged her towards the door which led to the side of the house. He could see the way she kept rubbing her baby bump through her white silk dress.

"Do you have a gun?" he asked.

"No! I hate hunting. I'm a vegetarian for God's sake!" Sharon said.

"Well, right now, this minute, we're the hunted. Do you have a mobile phone?"

"Yes! Yeah, it's in the bedroom, charging."

"Get in the bedroom and call the police – don't come out 'till I say. Lock yourself in."

"Steve, be careful please."

"Sharon, hurry. You do your part, I'll do mine."

"Steve," she whispered. "I do love you."

He looked at her with glassy blue eyes. He kissed her, and she let him. He held her face in his hands momentarily. Then he got a chef's knife from the knife block and handed it to her.

"Hold it like this, so you don't get hurt, and if you get a chance – don't hold back. Stab with all of your might. Think of the baby."

"Yeah, sure." She walked awkwardly away towards the back of the house, cradling her swollen belly before giving him one last worried glance. Steve returned to the knife block and took out a boning knife. He headed for the living room. He pushed the door open gently and peeked around the corner, seeing the gun in Santa's hand. Gun beats knife, he thought, knowing he'd have to wait for his opportunity.

Santa's helper was sat next to Ali, looking at her, like a little girl in the playground who wants to make friends but doesn't know how. "Who else is in this house?" she asked.

Ali glanced at Mickey who was still on the floor with his hands on his head. "No one," she said innocently. Instantly, the girl had hold of her by the hair, pulling it hard. Ali refused to scream until the girl prodded her in the ribs with the knife.

"You liar!" the girl screamed, twisting Ali's hair. She pulled it sharply, exposing Ali's neck. The girl took the knife and gently caressed Ali's throat with it. "Just a little kiss from the knifie-wifie and – whoops!" Ali cried out, blood trickling down her neck. The girl had a firm grip on her. "It's only a little cut, we're sorry aren't we, Mr Knifie-Wifie?"

"Leave the bitch and check the rest of the house!" Santa yelled.

"No fair! You said I could play.' She stuck out her bottom lip. 'Let me cut her, Damian!"

"No fucking names you moronic bitch!"

"Oopsy,' said the girl.

"Please…leave me alone!" Ali said, finally breaking.

The girl laughed, high and nasal. "Pwease leave me alone," she mocked.

Ali narrowed her eyes. "You sound like a fucking chipmunk!"

"What did you say?" the girl screamed, twisting Ali's hair.

"Hey, bitch," Damian said. "Check the house! NOW!"

The girl pushed Ali down onto the ground and booted her in the stomach with her big Dr Martens. Ali cried out and then lay sobbing on the living room floor. This is bad, she thought, this is so bad. They hadn't asked for jewellery or money. The girl walked away begrudgingly, poking her tongue out at Damian as she left the living room. Ali, gasping, looked on in panic. What did they want except murder? Bing Crosby was dreaming about a white Christmas and the snow poured down.

Mickey waited until the girl was out of sight and then began his rehearsed speech. "Why are you doing this, Damian? We're people like you, we're humans, and –"

Damian dug the gun into his forehead, saying, "We're doing His work, pig." And then he squeezed the trigger and blew Mickey's brains out all over the Christmas tree. Ali screamed from the floor. She could feel blood and pulpy chunks of hot gunk on her face. Using the coffee table for support, she got up and ran for the front door, leaping over Mickey's body. Damian, laughing softly, took aim as she pulled the door open. He shot.

Ali stumbled forward, out into the freezing cold air - free. There was a searing, fiery explosion in her chest, and blood sprayed out all over the porch steps. She stumbled to one of the porch pillars. She haphazardly grabbed white fairy lights from the pillar. Two more bullets exploded out of her chest and she stumbled forward and dropped to the cold floor, lit up like a Christmas tree. He loved me, she thought, and knew. Then all went dark.

The master bedroom was on the bottom floor on the left side of the house. Sharon had picked it for its walk in wardrobe. It was also near the kitchen, for midnight snacks, though none of that seemed important now. All the doors, including the patio, were locked. She sat in near darkness by the side of the bed, hidden. She jumped at every gunshot going off in her home and thought that all three of her friends must be dead. Tears streamed down her face, taking black eyeliner with them in rivers of black. She was still holding her mobile phone to her ear. After several rings, there was a click.

"Hello?" Sharon said, waiting to give the operator an overwhelming amount of information.

“I’m sorry; all emergency services are currently busy. You are in a queue and an operator will deal with your emergency as soon as possible, we thank-you for your patience.”

“Oh for God’s sake,” she whispered. She paid her taxes for this? Suddenly, the door handle of the master bedroom started going up and down manically. The sound of metal and hinges straining filled the darkness. Sharon placed the mobile phone, still ringing, by her side and held the knife with two shaking hands. The door handle was going up and down frenziedly. Sharon looked on in fear, the knife feeling exceptionally heavy. She’d fight. She knew that much.

“Who the fuck’s in there?” a female voice shouted. “Let me in fucker, else we’ll slice up your piggy friends!” The voice sounded manic. Fists started pounding on the door; Sharon was convinced it would rattle its way out of its hinges if it continued. “Damian, there’s someone in this room!”

“I’ll see if there’s another way in,” said a man.

Sharon liked his voice even less than the manic girl’s. It was calm and confident. It belonged to a man who knew exactly what he was doing.

Damian pushed open the kitchen door quietly, seeing no one in sight, and walked through. Steve, sensing his moment, jumped on his back, jumping up from behind the kitchen island and stabbing Damian in the back. Damian bucked and gurgled up blood as the knife was pulled free. Steve stabbed again and again, splashing the toaster and coffee machine with ribbons of dark blood. Damian fell to the hard linoleum, taking Steve with him. Steve rolled to one side and for a moment they lay next to each other, weapons in hand, breathing heavily. Steve lurched to his feet. He kicked Damian in the kidneys, once, twice, three times, before falling over and landing in a messy sprawl next to Damian, who was curled up into a protective foetal position. Steve was taking no chances; he got up onto his knees, above him, and lifted the knife high, screaming, “Die!”

But Damian still had the gun.

He thrust his hand into the Santa suit pocket and managed to get a shot off. The bullet hit Steve in the shoulder, but through pure adrenal rage, Steve still plunged the knife down into Damian’s throat.

Damian’s eyes bulged in shock and his gloved hands flew to his neck. He gurgled fresh dark blood and it puddled on the pure white tiles.

Steve slumped backwards. Floating out from the lounge was 'I saw Mummy Kissing Santa Claus.' Lunacy, he thought. He examined the gun wound spilling blood through his top, coughing and grimacing in pain. It had been more difficult than he'd anticipated. All those hours at the gym and a quick, scrapping fight had reduced him to this – panting, weak, limbs like heavy metal, a mess. He just trusted the woman would be easier to stop. He pulled himself up using the kitchen island, leaving bloody hand smudges all over it. He hoped that Sharon had called the police.

The kitchen door flew open and the girl wearing the Santa hat and pig-tails came charging in, eyes bulging over her fake moustache and beard.

"What have you done? You fucking murderer!" she screamed, running at him, the hunting knife in her hand raised. She was next to him in an instant. She was fast. He put his hands up defensively but she was too quick. She stabbed him in the gut. He staggered backwards, holding his insides. It felt like his intestines were coursing out, and a mixture of acid and blood fell out of his mouth. Sharon's never going to get all this blood out, he thought. The girl came again. She stabbed him in the chest. He fell onto his hands and knees, gasping for air.

"Please…please stop..."

But she was just getting started. The last thing Steve heard as the life ebbed out of him was, "Such pretty blue eyes you have."

Sharon, phone in hand, slid open the patio doors that lead to the front of the house. She looked around through the swirling snow and walked quickly outside, her breath immediately turning to vapour. Her bare feet sank into the thick snow as she half-walked, half-ran down the driveway towards the main gate. Within seconds they were stinging. It was strange, she thought, how cold could burn. The wind howled in her ears, turning them pink. She could hardly see the white path beyond the blinding night. Looking back, the house, trees and potted plants would come into vision and then disappear, swallowed back inside the white snow storm.

The girl got up from her position on the floor. She looked at the bloody knife and grinned inanely at it. She licked the blood off the blade. She licked it clean.

She went over to Damian and kissed his cool forehead. 'Goodnight, sweet Damian Daddy,' she whispered.

She stood up and walked towards the bedrooms. Her face and clothes were saturated with dark, sticky gore. "Where are you, pregnant piggy?" she said to the empty house. "Don't hide. I just wanna make friends. I know you're here, we've been watching you all night."

Sharon stood next to the security booth; Mike's dead body behind her, his hollowed out eyes still twinkling with fairy light. She typed the security code into the small panel with numb fingers. A bleep sounded, too loudly, she thought, and the two huge black gates opened, even louder and with frustrating slowness. She dodged backwards, grabbing the security keys from their hook and starting to run. She nearly skidded trying to get to the gates and had to steady herself. You'll survive this, she told herself. The cold had already spread across her skin like a layer of lace. She shivered in her white dress. He feet were probably bleeding, there was blood in the snow.

"Hey Bitch!" Sharon heard from behind. A girl in a Santa suit and pigtails was standing by the front door. The manic voice she'd heard through the bedroom door. Sharon's mouth fell open in disbelief. The girl was holding Ali's lifeless body up for her to see. She had her arms wrapped round Ali's chest as if she was doing the Heimlich manoeuvre. No, it wasn't happening. Sharon closed her eyes instinctively.

"I'm a boring bitch, HO HO HO!" mocked the girl, bobbing Ali's body up and down. Sharon made herself open her eyes and keep moving. Ali's body fell to the ground with a thud and flakes of snow flew up around it. The girl started skipping down the driveway, kicking up snow. She was covered in some sort of black tar, Sharon thought at first, and then realized better.

Her bare feet were running again, crunching in fresh snow, a frustratingly pleasant sound. Sharon slid again, grabbing onto the opening gates but dropping the mobile. "Shit!" she cried. The gates were freezing to the touch, but strong and heavy. They never stopped moving, even with her weight against them. She reached through them for the phone. Nearly. They pushed her away. The girl's skipping turned into a full-on sprint. "Screw it!"

Sharon ran out into the street. Over the pavement and into the road. "Help me! Somebody, help me please!" The wind answered with a lonely howl. She pressed the button on the key-chain that caused the gates to start closing and started down Church View. The girl raced towards the gates, kicking up a furious storm of snow. She was almost there. Sharon could see the whites of her eyes.

And then the girl's feet went from under her and she landed on her arse. "No!" she screamed. As the gates closed.

Sharon turned and ran gracelessly down the street.

"Run bitch! I'm coming for you! You think I can't climb a teeny-weensy fucking gate? I'm going to rip you open, whore!"

Sharon jogged, trying not to slip. She could feel the baby kicking. Could it sense something? The nearest house was Joan's, which was just up the street from hers. Quite a way, but possible. She could just see the house through the haze of white, which had numbed her nose and quivering lips. She knew she was leaving footprints, maybe even bloody ones, but she just had to hope the blizzard covered them up before the girl got over the gate.

Finally, she reached Joan's home. She entered her fence through the side door panel, to which she knew the security code. "Help me! Joan! Joan are you there?" She ran to the house, slipping slightly in the snowfall. She reached the front door. Joan's Christmas lights were on. She pounded on the front door. "Joan!"

She could hear the girl's laughter a way back. She's coming. "Oh my God, Joan, please!" She pushed down on the door handle, and to her astonishment it swung open, leaving her ice cold hand empty. She didn't hesitate; she ran into Joan's house, slamming the door behind her and pulling across the latch. The house was dark but warm inside. Her numb feet were delighted to sense carpet. A few Christmas decorations were strung about and some fairy lights cast shadows around the large, seemingly deserted, home. All was silent. "Joan?" Sharon dared to whisper. Something was very wrong. Joan had been home a couple of hours ago. Where was she?

The house was large and old fashioned. The TV was on; silent and showing 'It's a wonderful life.' The stockings were hung by the chimney with care. Sharon looked for a phone, her numb hands out like a zombie's. She grabbed a brown blanket from the back of the sofa and wrapped it around her head and shoulders to calm her shaking. Her full lips were tinted porcelain blue.

Pans hung above a kitchen island in the galley. Towards the side of the back door stood a Christmas tree with lights on it and a star on top. The lighting in the home was dim and Sharon couldn't find the light-switch. She ran her hand along the wall, searching desperately for a phone. Behind her, Sharon heard a window smashing. The girl had arrived. She grabbed a kitchen knife from the block on the counter and turned to see a phone, lit by the moonlight and stars. She snatched it up quickly and dialled emergency services. She backed into the darkness behind a pottery cabinet and prayed.

This time an emergency operator answered after several rings. "Which emergency service do you need?" A calm Scottish woman asked politely.

"The police! Please hurry! I'm being attacked. They've attacked my friends, murdered them…" She cried. "Please hurry."

"And where are you now?" the operator asked.

"In my friend's house."

"Do you know the postcode?"

"No, but my postcode is CF5 3NP – please help us. I'm pregnant."

"Okay, sweetheart. The police and ambulance are on their way. Can you tell me are you safe?"

"I don't think so," she whispered. In the hallway she heard glass crushing. Sharon dropped the phone, letting it bob up and down on the cord. She held the knife tight. "Please God, for my baby," she prayed.

The girl walked along the hallway, towards the kitchen. Her head out, craning to see on her long neck. Big eyes reflecting the Christmas tree lights. "Don't worry, pregnant piggy, I'm not going to kill you straight out. I'll go nice and slow. I'm going to make you scream though." She giggled manically. "Scream, scream, scream!" She repeated the word over and over to herself in small whispers as she searched the dark house with her fairy-light eyes. The bloody numbers on her forehead had become so congealed they looked black rather than red. She tiptoed like a cartoon villain into the kitchen, grinning wildly, her eyes darting everywhere. She heard the noise coming from the phone, off the hook. She darted behind the cupboard, knife raised. No one there. She sighed.

Sharon appeared behind her silently, knife raised. The girl felt her presence and started to turn, but too late. She felt something strike her lower back, a punch or a kick. The knife slid in as far as it would go, scraping bone and Sharon stepped back, leaving the knife handle jutting out.

The girl whirled around, her knife slashing thin air with a whoosh, and then staggered backwards. The kitchen light started flickering. Warm blood ran down the girl's backside. Sharon turned her head, tears running down her face; unable to look at what she'd done. The girl twisted, grasping for the knife which she couldn't quite reach and stumbled into the

Christmas tree, taking it down with her. The Christmas lights decorating it all smashed out as it landed.

Sharon stepped backwards, away. She heard a great gong sound come from directly behind her and jumped. It was the grandfather clock chiming Midnight. She pressed her back against the cool wood and closed her eyes. She felt her baby's foot dig into her bladder and wondered when was the last time she'd used the toilet.

A hand around her foot. The girl had pulled herself across the carpet. She was looking up at her with snarled teeth. "Merry Christmas," she said. Her dirty fingers dug into Sharon's foot. There was a bloody trail in the carpet all the way from the felled Christmas tree. She had tinsel and dead fairy lights caught around her ankle. How was she still alive?

"Just die," Sharon said with a hatred like she'd never known before. She pulled her foot free of the girl's hand, stepped to the side and with a giant heave, pulled the grandfather clock down onto the girl.

"Merry Christmas," Sharon whispered, sliding her back down the wall. She watched the girl's legs spasm from out underneath the clock, and once they were still, she burst into sudden, harsh sobs. She let the tears flow, warm and bitter. Hysteria hit. She held her hand to her forehead and sobbed. She gasped for air, trying to breathe through the pain. She cried until she had unleashed enough emotion to breathe steadily; and then looked around in the darkness. She looked at the girl's still legs and wondered why. There was something hanging from the girl's cheap Santa belt. A present, hanging on with red ribbon. Sharon carefully undid the ribbon and pulled the small gift free. She read the gift card. "To Sharon, love Steve," Sharon mouthed. Then she tore open the paper and opened the small, pale blue, jewellery box. It was an engagement ring. She felt the baby kick. "You already gave me the best present," she whispered to Steve, and to herself.

"Oh, Steve," she said, looking upwards. "I did love you. Really, I did." She put the ring on her finger. Then lifted it, to see the diamonds glitter like stars.

"What the hell is this?"

Sharon jumped, her hand fluttering to her throat. It was Joan, standing in the hallway in a long white nightie. She had an eye mask pulled up over her forehead and ear plugs in her hand. Her lined old face was pale with worry. Her brown eyes were warm and worried.

"Thank God, Joan! I thought you were dead," Sharon exclaimed..

Joan bent down to help her up. "Come here dear…everything's going to be okay now." Police sirens could be heard outside and the blue and red flashing of the cars, lit up the downed Christmas tree. The star tree-topper sparkled.

The End

The Last Christmas Dinner

By

Christina Bergling

“Would you like some more egg nog, dear?” Susan said.

Susan shuffled out from the kitchen clinging to the hefty pitcher with both hands. The cream liquid sloshed threateningly at the rim with her uneven movement. The ache radiated up from the titanium joints in her replaced knees as she moved in deliberate out-toed steps on her ergonomic shoes, which seemed to do nothing after so many hours in the kitchen.

“Yeah, sure, Ma,” Jared said, holding out his glass.

Jared did not move from the couch to reduce his mother’s trek. He simply lifted his glass a little and kept his eyes committed to the tablet glowing in his lap. Susan waddled over to him slowly and filled his cup with the speckled mixture.

Snow fell softly and silently outside the large picture window of the living room, the flakes reflecting the Christmas tree’s twinkling glow cast through the pane. Susan had hung the heirloom ornaments in measured and perfect spacing, aligning each glass ball with a nearby lightbulb to amplify the glimmer. She had hand-strung the popcorn garland with her trembling arthritic fingers like every year. When she looked past her son’s suspended glass, she smiled to herself subtly at her festive masterpiece.

“Tastes different this year, Mom,” Samantha said from the opposing couch. “Stronger, maybe?”

The screen of Samantha’s smartphone reflected in her dead eyes, making her look hauntingly possessed. Her finger moved mechanically and repetitively across the screen in practiced patterns.

The fire crackled behind Samantha, warming the toes of the stockings hung high on the mantle above. The ancient CD player in the corner mumbled out Susan’s favorite holiday compilation album. The soundtrack of decades of Christmases spent just like this one—and some when her young, happy children tore through gifts so joyously it made Susan’s heart threaten to burst.

“Yes, darling,” Susan said, turning to pad over to Samantha’s outstretched glass. “I tried a new recipe this year after you and Derrick kept saying how much better Derrick’s mother’s homemade egg nog was last year.”

“Oh, don’t mention Derrick!”

Samantha flopped dramatically back onto the cushions, keeping her phone locked at the same distance from her face. The concentrated light exaggerated the pout on her features, elongating the creases in her face with unforgiving shadows.

"You sure know how to pick them, sis. Just a parade of jackasses. How many women did he screw before you figured it out?" Jared laughed, face half-buried in his glass, egg nog mustache blooming on his upper lip.

"Shut up, asshole. At least I can get a date to bring. You probably haven't been laid since college."

Susan took a deep breath and closed her eyes for a moment, holding the pitcher of egg nog like a statue.

"Wow, feisty, sis. The egg nog must be stronger this year, Ma."

"I'm just glad you both seem to like it," Susan said.

She smiled, forcing the expression up into her cheeks through the exhaustion, and topped off both her children's glasses again.

"Where's Dad?" Samantha asked from behind her phone.

"Yeah, we haven't seen him all day," Jared echoed from behind his tablet.

"He's just resting, but he's nearly ready for dinner," Susan said.

"Good, because I am starving. Feels like we've been waiting here forever. I've already beaten like ten levels on this game. Just since I've been here." Jared shook the tablet out in front of him.

"Dinner is almost ready, dear," Susan replied.

"Did you make the honey ham?" Samantha asked.

"Yes, dear."

"And the green bean casserole?"

"Yes."

"And the mashed potatoes with Grandma's gravy."

"Of course."

"And the rolls?"

"Yes, dear."

"And the pies?"

"Yes, dear."

"Tell me you didn't make that awful fruitcake."

"I always make fruitcake, dear."

"Ick. I don't know why. It's so terrible."

"Do you want some more egg nog, dear?"

"Sure, Mom."

By time Susan eased back toward the kitchen, she had drained most of the pitcher between Jared and Samantha's glasses. She left her adult children in the same positions she had found them, immobile zombies married to their devices, hardly speaking a word to each other though they had not been in the same room since this time the previous year. Even though the glass pitcher was less full, it somehow felt heavier as Susan walked.

Listening to the robotic chirps and relentless chimes dancing from the other room, Susan began to meticulously set the table. She took small half steps around the chairs to painstakingly spread the brightly embroidered tablecloth over the length of the table top, smoothing her hands over the raised texture of the poinsettia pattern.

The ache in her bones began to permeate through her muscles, radiating up to the skin, as she laid out each place setting. Placemat, plate, salad bowl, silverware. She folded the napkins against the protest of her fingertips. When the settings were placed perfectly like the stack of magazines she kept beside the recliner, she began making slow trips to place the food.

With everything except the main dish artfully positioned, Susan wiped the thin bead of sweat from her forehead and beckoned her children.

"Samantha, Jared, it's ready." Her voice sounded as tired as she felt in her very marrow.

"Great! Finally, Mom. I thought I was going to starve to death," Jared said as he shoved past his mother and dove toward the table.

"Oh my God! Me too!"

Samantha scurried past her mother as well. They abandoned their devices on the table beside their place settings long enough to both begin grabbing up serving spoons and heaving helpings onto their plates. The clanking of dishes was only matched by their selfish and ragged breathing.

Susan moved slowly and calmly to ease herself into the chair at the head of the table. The chair was always reserved for her husband, where he barked orders and dribbled complaints onto all her meals the entire forty years of their marriage. She folded her hands over the place setting and stoically watched her children splatter her perfect staging in their haste.

Jared wobbled up from his chair for a second and popped his eyes wide. He shook his head, somewhat befuddled, then continued scraping food from the dishes.

"What's the matter, Jared, honey? Are you feeling all right?" Susan asked, expressionless.

"Yeah, I think so." Jared paused and licked his lips clumsily. His gaze roved over the feast before him as his eyes dropped in and out of focus. He shook his head again in a small jerk. "Yeah, Ma, I'm totally fine."

"Are you sure? You look a little peaked."

"No, just hungry. Or that strong nog."

Jared pressed his hand to the tablecloth and lowered himself down gently into his chair, still attempting to fix his gaze. Yet he snatched up his fork just the same and began shoveling the food into his mouth.

"If you say so, dear."

Susan turned from watching Jared struggle and looked to her daughter. Samantha started to waver as well, focusing hard to gorge herself on the spread.

"Samantha, you look a bit flush as well."

Samantha froze with an oversized portion of mashed potatoes hovering on the spoon in front of her, dark circles sprouting under her floating eyes to glance at her mother. Her eyes bounced past her mother before snapping back to focus.

"No," Samantha crooned. "I'm fine. Wait, Mom, where's the ham?"

"And where's Dad?" Jared asked, chewing messily.

"Oh my goodness, you're right." Susan tossed her hands up mockingly. "How could I forget the main course? How ever could I forget the every desire of my two ungrateful children? I gave them the past thirty-seven years of my life, but they could not be troubled to even give me a grandchild. Or call me on my birthday. Or carry a dish from the kitchen after I cooked since dawn."

Samantha and Jared halted mid-pillage and both turned to finally look their mother in the eyes. Their expressions hung slack from their skulls with shock as a putrid pallor crept onto their cheeks. Chunks of food clung half masticated on their molars as their jaws dangled. Even as they stared blankly at their mother, their heads appeared to grow heavy and tug down toward their overflowing plates. Susan basked in their confused, falling expressions.

"I'll be right back." Susan smiled cheerily and popped up more quickly than she had moved all night.

Susan returned from the kitchen with a large serving dish stretched between her hands. Her entire day, all her preparation had been leading up to this reveal. She clung to the platter lovingly, feeling an unfamiliar sense of freedom spiral out into her fingertips. She practically beamed as she heaved the dish up to place it at the climax of the feast between her children.

"Oh my God," Samantha breathed, pressing a hand to her mouth.

Samantha had started to sweat and glistened under the low lighting. The terror momentarily snapped her back, and her eyes began to well with fat tears. Her lips twitched and wiggled in unformed words.

“Mom, what is that?” Jared gaped.

Jared leaned forward to try and see through his failing eyes then slammed himself back in the chair in horror. Susan could hear him gulping in breaths as he struggled to speak. He stuttered sloppily before finding the words.

“It’s a heart! Oh my God, it’s a heart. Mom, whose heart is that?”

Samantha began to tremble. The quivering began at the fingertips over her mouth then reverberated down her arm into her trunk. Her entire body shook in subtle, frozen panic. Jared looked down at the roasted, bloody flesh. His eyes went wide before falling distant again. He began to heave, his whole body contracting down around the reflex.

“Your father finally decided to help with dinner this year,” Susan said calmly.

Susan’s smile illuminated her entire face. She seemed to float on her aching and exhausted joints. Samantha managed to turn her face up to her mother in sheer dismay before her eyes involuntarily rolled back into her head. Her traumatic shaking ascended into a violent seizure. When her body fell limp, it dropped her face squarely into her heaping plate. Blood poured out of her mouth and nose, spreading rivers of red through the gravied-mountains of mashed potatoes.

Jared’s face grew more pale. His eyes sunk deeper into his cheeks, flitting between his mother’s sneering grin and his immobile sister. His fork clanked against his oversized plate as the tremor started to vibrate in his hand, eerily tapping in time with the Christmas carols still floating on the air around them.

“Would you like some more egg nog, dear?” Susan said with the most genuine smile he had ever seen on her lips.

The End

The Veil

By

Rose Garnett

"Deck my balls with boughs of holly," sang a leering passerby to his ugly female companion as he brushed past me in the crowd, gripping the body part in question. Bloody disgusting if you asked me - she looked old enough to be his grandmother.

I had made the mistake of going to Edinburgh's Christmas market on the Mound in Princes Street and was hating every seasonal second. The press and crush of the drunken, jovial mob was doing my head in -and that was the best I could say about the whole hellish experience. The stalls, smothered in strings of lights and intricately crafted crap destined to be bought for Christmas and binned by Boxing Day, covered the city centre like a vivid rash. Worse, it had begun to snow; big fat, fan-dancing flakes that froze my face and flattened my hair.

Sour violated sweet as the stench of fried food dry-humped the sugary taint of candy floss into submission, overpowering my stomach in the process - although to be fair, the nine pints I'd sunk last night might have had a little something to do with that. The barrage of noise from different fairground rides fought an ear-bleeding battle with a maudlin, yet top-volume, medley of eighties Christmas 'classics'. *Last Christmas* won it by a nose, fracturing the night air with a love-lorn whine-fest about some irreplaceable bint or other. They were all interchangeable as far as I was concerned. Every single one.

I say night, but actually it was only late afternoon. It got dark in this godforsaken neck of the woods at 4pm in December and stayed that way until sometime after 9am, when it was replaced by a leprous twilight that leached colour from the world and joy from the soul.

And it wasn't as if the history of the place wasn't any cheerier. The Mound was an artificial hill constructed in the nineteenth century from tonnes of refuse excavated from a wealthier part of town and dumped where the poor no-accounts lived. And that was only the half of it. The artificial ice rink in Princes Street Gardens had been the site of the Nor' Loch, a sewage pit where they used to dunk old women to prove they were witches. I was betting the revellers had no idea they were partying on what had once been little better than a murderous cess-pit. As for me, I liked to see things as they really were - no rose-tinted, shit-denying glasses for me.

My current girlfriend, Louise, was just ahead of me with her best mate, Mia, and they were running, giggling, from one stall to the next, pointing at the more bizarre offerings for sale. I lost sight of them in the crowd, but not before I had exchanged a meaningful look with Mia. An innocent kiss and cuddle last November had mutated into a full-blown, raging affair and Mia was now putting pressure on me to leave poor, fat Louise.

Okay, so she wasn't fat exactly, but she had put on a few pounds this last year and I was concerned, for her own sake, that she had been letting herself go. Just as well I wasn't the superficial type.

Louise and Mia couldn't have been more different. Blond, curvy, sweet Louise just couldn't compete with brunette, willowy, hot-sex-on-legs Mia. Those honey-brown peepers of Mia's could melt a man to mush in under ten seconds. At least that was what I had told her in what proved to be a successful leg-over exercise. I was more interested in her surprisingly fulsome breasts than I was in her face, but that just meant I wasn't really cheating on Louise because it was only a physical thing. You couldn't exactly tell women that, though, could you?

Not if you wanted to get any. And blow me, because I did. I always had done, to the exclusion of everything else.

Something pushed past me with great force, small enough to be a child, but too fast to see. It wouldn't have registered with me in the touchy-feel fest of the heaving crowd, had it not left a rank stench like rotting meat spoiling in the sun.

Mia pursed those full, glossed lips, distracting me again. Though truth to tell, I was becoming a little bored with her, too, and had my eye on someone else who as yet hadn't responded to my boyish charms. This was still, however, a little inconvenient, given I was living with Louise and she was picking up all my bills.

"Derek," laughed Louise, popping up out of nowhere and tugging on my arm. "Go see Mia - she's got a surprise for you. I'll be over in a sec, I just want to check out a Rudolph glow toy for my godson."

Like the good-natured fool that I was, I walked over to Mia who was standing by a little stall, different from the rest. Lit only by four old-fashioned gas-lamps, it appeared gloomy and threadbare compared to all the others. Hanging from the roof were strings of drab, cloth dolls with buttons for eyes, interspersed with badly made wooden decorations each of which had a five pointed stick figure at the centre. There was a sign in the dingy interior that bore the legend:

Caveat Emptor

Buyer beware? Louise aside, who the hell fell for this demented, sub-standard goth shit? And while I hated the whole Christmas vibe, its absence in this stall irritated me even more. It also sold ugly-looking jewellery, as I found out when a prime example was thrust into my face by Mia, a small smile threatening to evict her usual sulky pout. Eyes bright, cheeks flushed with the cold, she gave my arm a furtive squeeze and there it was - that familiar little tingle that had gotten me into this in the first place. Maybe I wasn't through with her after all. Not yet, anyway.

Taking the item from her, I saw it was a necklace - a dull, grey pendant with a horned goat's head carved into its rough surface, hung on a discoloured chain.

"This is horrible," I laughed, handing it back, "just horrible."

"No," Mia hissed, pushing my hand back with some urgency. "It's for *you.* From Lou - I don't know why she wanted me to give it to you," Mia shrugged. "She got one for all three of us. Look, here's mine," she said, rolling her eyes and opening the palm of her other hand.

And so it was. An identical necklace, featuring a badly carved goat with tiny, indecipherable writing all the way around the edges, lay in centre of her palm.

"Lou's already wearing hers," said Mia as Louise returned laden with parcels and bags and beaming from ear to ear. "They're for good luck. Apparently."

"I see," I said, going over to Louise and taking her in my arms. "Well, what I meant was, I've always wanted to wear women's jewellery and now that my dream has come true, I might just go for a matching dress. And shoes. High heels, obviously. What do you think babes?"

I grinned down into Louise's upturned, trusting little face, taking in the neat, wheat-coloured hair held back with a red, silk bow. I always could literally charm the pants off birds and Louise was a particular sucker for what I had to give, even if I did say so myself. She looked at me with an indecipherable expression and, for a moment, I got the fear. She wasn't going to propose to me when we got home, was she? Her sister had died at this time of year and it always made her maudlin and needy.

"Put it on for me, sweets. We could really do with some good luck, couldn't we?" Louise said.

I hated it when she called me that.

"Couldn't hurt. Here, help me. will you?"

The seller, a sallow, sour-faced old bag I hadn't noticed until that instant offered to help, but was drowned out by Louise who, squealing with delight, beckoned me to bend down as she struggled with the clasp. I thought of my massive visa bill and did as I was bid.

"There."

"And, just so you know," said Louise, "It's an amulet, not a necklace."

The I-can't-believe-it's-not-a-necklace lay cold and heavy against my breast bone as though it had attached itself to my skin.

"Thanks babe. Wait till you see what I've got you."

The truth was I hadn't got her anything and wouldn't - not until she gave me some dosh.

Mia's mouth tightened, but she said nothing.

"Derek, why don't you help Mia put hers on," said Louise, smiling.

Mia turned around and moved the lush spill of her dark hair so I could fasten the damned thing. What had possessed Louise to buy this shit? My cold fingers brushed the warmth of Mia's neck and I inhaled that damned perfume of hers that always drove me wild. I had just started to concoct a plausible reason to get away from Louise so I could be with her tonight, when I pricked my finger on the stiff clasp.

'"Fuck," I muttered discovering a few drops of blood and sucking my finger.

"What is it, sweetheart?" asked Louise, face clouding.

"Nothing. Clasp's stiff, that's all. I think I need a drink."

She smiled. "I'm going to look for something for my nephews and then I'm done Christmas shopping. Why don't you go get some gluhwein and put your feet up 'til I'm finished, sweetheart. Do you fancy coming Mia?"

"Sounds like a plan," I said.

"I'm knackered Lou, I think I'll just stay here and have a drink with Derek," said Mia.

I gave her one of my looks. We had discussed this and I had been very clear about the affair protocol.

"That's fine. It'll give me time to get your real present, too," laughed Louise.

Mia gave her a playful shove. "It better be a car, that's all I'm saying. With a big bow."

"It'll be much better than a rotten old car," said Louise, turning to wink at us as she disappeared into the crowd.

We walked toward the mobbed gluhwein stall which, unbelievably, had a ringed off area of seats festooned in fairy lights. Sitting outside to enjoy a Scottish winter was for the suicidal and lunatics who wanted to say cheerio to their extremities, but as I took my first sips of the mulled wine concoction, bought and brought to me by the fair Mia, and the alcohol-fuelled warmth kicked in, I decided there were worse things.

"What the hell, Mia," I said, in between slurps. "I told you - I don't want Louise getting suspicious."

"You're never going to leave her, are you?" said Mia, sipping her drink and twirling a lock of hair between her fingers. "I don't know why I bother with you, I really don't."

“Yeah, you do,” I said, giving her the full-on Derek McVey experience, which consisted of gazing into her eyes as I moved my ungloved hand up her thigh to hotter climes under cover of the table.

She brushed it away.

“No, Derek. I don’t. And there hasn’t been a lot of *that* in the past few weeks.”

“I’ve been busy, babe.”

“Don’t. That’s what you call her. Maybe we should just end it. Right now. I mean it, Derek.”

She took out a powder compact, gazing at her reflection. “Look at the state of me. Jeez.”

I leaned in, risking a kiss full on the mouth just to shut her up. A woman leaving me was just not an option.

She tasted of spiced wine and the heat of her mouth on mine made me linger longer than was safe. Louise would be coming back any minute.

“Ouch! You bit me, you bastard! You actually bit me,” yelled Mia, thrusting her chair back and springing up.

“What? I did no such thing,” I protested, reaching out to her.

“I’m fucking bleeding!” she shouted, the smear of blood running down her chin, black against her pale face. “I’m going to tell Louise just what an animal you really are!” she screamed, whirling round and running into the crowd.

I absolutely had not bitten her, but there *was* a coppery taste in my mouth. Silly bitch probably had bleeding gums and wanted to blame me for her embarrassing lack of dental hygiene. I sighed, making a mental note that I was done with women.

I slid my chair back, noticing that the the lights had dimmed. Except that wasn’t quite right, it was as though all the brash colours that I’d enjoyed hating so much had been dimmed.

A brief but intense wave of nausea was chased by vomit as it scorched a trail from my stomach to the tarmacked ground. There were cries of disgust and outrage from the packed tables nearby, but I didn’t give a toss. Lurching from my chair, vision blurred, it looked as though I had been on the mother of all benders - but that wasn’t it. No, that wasn’t it at all.

The smell of vomit invited more of the same from both me and a woman at a table nearby who was shuddering with the dry heaves. For some reason this amused me and I laughed, a barking, guttural sound I didn’t recognise. I now had the crowd’s full attention and as I stared back, clots of darkness, blacker than the night itself, darted amongst those assembled making my vision flicker and spot. The clots formed and reformed into shapes that I couldn't make sense of, as though in perpetual, sickening motion. But that couldn't be, could it? Maybe I was coming down with some bug or other. Yes, that was it, all I needed was to head for home and a good night's sleep.

And then one of the amorphous shapes took on a structure, temporarily banishing all thought of flight.

It was a small, bent creature, no bigger than a child, and it whipped round to face me, huge head balancing on a spindle of a neck. Although it was solid enough, its outline was still moving as though the creature was infested with millions of burrowing things. As I stared, I realised that the thing was transforming again, from something almost human into something altogether more primal.

Large rabbit-like ears ripped themselves from the confines of the skull with a wet, thunk, even as the eyes elongated, revealing a dull-red sheen as though an invisible hand had slashed dead flesh, revealing the bled-out meat beneath. It snarled, revealing row upon row of pointed, gleaming incisors and then waved, an incongruous human gesture from something that could lay no such claim to that particular heritage. A warm trickle of urine down my left leg snapped me from my fugue and I ran.

I pushed past a family with two small toddlers and someone reached out to grab me as I went, but I was too fast. Spurred by the feel of hot breath on my neck, I raced with an awkward loping gait to the stairs that took me down into Santaland: consisting of a maze and Santa's Grotto, both of which were mercifully deserted. At least I could hide in the maze, courtesy of all the Christmas trees that formed it until either the creature went away, or I came to my senses, I didn't know which. There was a young man with a buzz cut dressed as the great man himself at the entrance, inspecting tickets, white beard askew, red suit drowning the thin body. By his side was a dirty sack tied at the neck.

Fuck. I didn't have a ticket and I had left my wallet at the gluhwein stall in my frenzy to leave. Where now? Glancing back the way I'd come, there was at least no sign of the creature.

"Got a ticket, mate?" asked Young Santa, poking the sack with a stick and eliciting a squeal from whatever was inside.

"Er, no. Can I get in anyway and owe you the money? I'm good for it, honest."

"Oh, I'm sure you are," he told me, grinning and rubbing his hands together so fast I half expected to see flames. "But that's the least of your problems, mate."

There was something about the cherubic roundness of his cheeks, so at odds with the cadaverous skinniness of his body that bothered me, but I couldn't quite pin it down. One of his eyes was opaque as though he had a cataract, but he didn't look more than nineteen or twenty. There was a scab on the end of his nose, freshly picked judging by the trail of blood down his cheek. It reminded me of Mia. Had she found Louise?

"You'd better run," he advised, sucking his teeth and snorting.

"What?"

"I said," he came closer, leaning in as though for a kiss, then, pausing for a heartbeat, he whispered, "run."

I froze, just as his massive clawed hand raked down my face and chest, the seeping warmth of my blood a momentary blessing before the pain set in.

In shock, I brought my hand up to touch my face, barely registering that the fingers had lengthened and acquired an extra joint. None of this could be real; it was obviously an nightmare and I'd wake up any second.

"Look," he said in an awed voice, drool running from his mouth to his chest in thick lines, "oh, *look.*"

He pointed behind me and I was so numbed that I obeyed.

Something was undulating towards us; gleaming, oily coils reflecting the reds, blues and greens from the Christmas lights. A wet, sucking sound accompanied the creature's progress, along with a low oddly familiar moaning.

It stopped. The head raised itself up in the air to eye-level, revealing a gaping, razor-toothed maw about four feet across which swayed in front of me like a snake being charmed. The fleshy frills around its thick, wrinkled lips vibrated as though responding to an electrical current. "*Aieeeeeee*," The thing screamed with a bowel-loosening intensity.

"As your official Santanic representative - did you see what I did there - I really recommend that you get out of here before the Yuletide Worm catches you. Lucky for you she's slow - and she's also a newbie at this - but if she catches you, well, you really are screwed. Eaten whole, as a python does, you'll be. Then all you'll have to look forward to is a slow, agonising death; eaten from the outside in by someone else's digestive juices. Bloody disgusting, if you ask me. Unless you're into that sort of thing of course. She's a bit of a screamer this one, I must say. Not used to her new role I expect. She'll soon settle. They all do."

Bloody disgusting. The very words I'd used earlier in connection with another female.

He stretched his now elongated lips in a grimace, revealing jagged, rotten teeth.

"Me, now, I've got manners. You won't catch me swallowing my food whole. I like to cut it up into small, easy pieces. Just like this," he turned, slicing a rust and blood encrusted scimitar through the air, taking most of my nose with it. He picked it up from the snowy ground, made a show of dusting it off and then popped it into his mouth like a bon bon, pinky raised as he suckled on it, groaning with pleasure.

"Please," I sobbed. "Why are you doing this?"

"Look at the state of me," the Yuletide Worm screamed. "*Look at the state of me*."

I recognised that voice - but that just wasn't possible.

Unperturbed, Young Santa made a show of feeling the tip of the scimitar as though checking it was still there.

"Oh, listen to her. But that's women for you eh? Never happy," he smirked, raising the bloodied weapon. "Let's really give you something to moan about, shall we?"

A surge of adrenalin and I barged past my assailant, blade whistling past my ear, just missing by centimetres. I bounded over the fence and into the Christmas tree maze, taking strings of lights with me and trailing blood.

"Don't look at me!" the worm-thing shrieked in that oh-so familiar voice.

It was only as I ran from that place of death that I realised that Mia, the newly crowned Yuletide Worm, and I were finally finished.

***

I burst into the start of the maze, stumbling and falling onto all fours before panic propelled me forward on hands and knees. The ground sped by, faster than if I had been upright, new-found claws cutting through snow and ice as I raced through the maze. A soft susurration of pine-needled branches, stirred by an arctic wind, heralded a heavier fall of snow, making the tree lights bob and weave, dappling the way ahead. A waxing, gibbous moon hidden behind massing snow clouds called to me in a language I hadn't realised I knew.

Reaching the maze's centre, my entire body itched with a raging intensity and I was burning up. Tearing my jacket and jumper off with clawed hands I discovered a dense furred pelt, long enough that it almost concealed Young Santa's slashes on my chest. Trousers and trainers were next and in seconds I stood naked but, as I looked down at myself, somehow not. If this wasn't a bug then I must be dreaming and here was the proof: I had become a beast.

But there was no time for fancy existential debates as a low growl sounded from a few feet away.

"Show yourself," I said. The truth was, dream or not, my new body was more powerful than the old and I knew I could take whatever fancied its chances. Colour had dimmed but my eyes were sharper, my sense of smell almost too acute and I felt renewed. Had I become I a werewolf or some other cool creature of the night? Maybe I had passed some sort of test and this new-found feeling of invincibility was my reward.

"Derek," said the growling voice as a furred nightmare stepped out of the trees.

Powerful jaws fought to contain large, gleaming teeth with an audible grating of tooth against bone. The corners of its lips lifted and its nose wrinkled - was it *smiling*? It towered over me, seven feet, easily, and I stepped back getting ready to run back the way I'd come, heroic invincibility evicted by the desire to survive.

It didn't look like anything I'd ever seen, but then that was proving to be the one consistent feature of this never-ending nightmare. The head resembled that of a dog, but the body was humanoid, covered in blond, glossy fur and, from the pendulous hanging breasts, clearly female.

Bloody disgusting.

"Derek," said the hateful, grating voice, struggling to shape words out of air with a mouth not built for such perversities. "Don't you recognise me?"

I snarled, a high pitched, fearful sound, about to turn tail and make a run for it, when I saw a red, silky ribbon stuck in the thing's long, flowing pelt.

Louise. It couldn't be. She had no survival instinct and should have succumbed to the horrors of this new world instantly. Mia and I, well, were a different story - but not sad, sappy Louise. And then a thought struck me.

"Did you do this?" I asked, struggling with my own new teeth gear.

"Do what?" The Louise-thing laughed, dugs quivering.

I shuddered and stepped back. It - she - came forward.

"Thiiss," I slurred with nervous bravado, waving a paw at the maze and the Christmas market beyond. In the distance, the sounds of people enjoying themselves on the artificial rink floated on the night air, oblivious and unconcerned. But that was another world now, one to which something told me I could never return.

A thought struck me.

"Is all this because of those fucking amulets you made us all wear?"

She stared at me, drool frothing in and out of her teeth in time with her breathing. Her eyes were a blazing, neon yellow, the pupils a narrow, vertical slit.

"I know about you and Mia, Derek," growled the monster. "I've always had my suspicions, you know. But we've had some interesting discussions since we…*changed,* Mia and I and she confirmed what I already knew. Of course, we have our differences," Louise laughed, an unpleasant, deep-throated gurgle, 'but we agree on one thing: something has to be done about you. Once and for all.'

'Who cares about that pish now?' My voice rose higher and faster until it reached a castrato scream. "Did you curse us? For Christ's sake woman, were the amulets cursed?"

"No," said a child's voice, giggling. "It was me. I chose you and then you chose…her." He pointed at the thing formerly known as Louise. "Your tasty little mistress, too. Greedy boy."

It was the small bent creature I'd seen at the gluhwein stall. The same absurdly big rabbit ears, flayed head and eyes like slashes in dead flesh, except now they had been stitched shut. From the stench of rotting meat I was guessing this was also the thing that had pushed past me unseen. It had touched me and then I had touched the girls - was that it meant by chosen? A game of contaminated tag which transformed all those caught into monsters…?

A roar from Louise as she leapt, knocking me to the floor. Straddling me, she snapped at and missed my jugular. I twisted and writhed, but she was too strong.

"No," screamed the Rabbit. "You'll kill him. We don't have time for a replacement."

But Louise wasn't listening. The dull staccato thud of her fists on my chest as she punched and clawed her way inside was accompanied by my screams. As I lay powerless, waves of excruciating pain took over as my lover scrabbled in the meat of my flesh.

"Fuck that," she snarled, "I always knew the way to Derek's heart was through his ribs."

She paused, tongue lolling out the side of her mouth, seconds before she slid off me, head parting company from her body and rolling to rest by the interloper's foot. The Rabbit stood over us both, axe in hand, blood dripping down the shaft to pool in a dark, congealed mass on the snow. The lights played over the flayed face, painting it red, green and blue. Relief swept over me in a scalding rush.

"You are mine," it whispered.

"Am I dead," I wheezed. Because I damn well should have been after that impromptu heart surgery. "What the fuck is going on? Am I a werewolf now? Am I?"

The Rabbit, despite its short stature, pulled me to my feet with ease and dragged me to a mirror at the centre of the maze that I could have sworn hadn't been there before. It held me up in front of the polished surface as though I weighed nothing.

"Behold the ravening werewolf, shit-for-brains."

A small, wizened creature with patchy white fur on leprous skin confronted me. Two, round, pink eyes stared out from a rodent-like face, rotten front teeth prominent against the snowy pelt. I wasn't a big, bad wolf after all - no, my inner beast had turned out to be a deformed rat. My legs were scaly like a chicken's, as was my long, curled tail, and I stood about three feet high on my hind legs. No wonder my dearly departed girlfriend had gotten the better of me. Women never fought fair though, did they? "I don't understand," I said, trailing off.

"I chose you. Don't you remember? The strength of your desire - its sheer insatiability - drew me to you. I brushed past you in the crowd and gave you the Gift of Becoming which you passed on to your little harem. But the true Gift is yours - and yours alone. You're the one the city needs on this, the shortest day of the year."

I struggled in his vice-like grip, biting and clawing, fuelled by a growing fear.

"Gibberish. Total gibberish. You can take your Becoming whotsit and stuff it up your arse," I squeaked, whiskers twitching.

The snow was now a blizzard and the chorus of REM's *It's The End Of The World* played through my head in a demented loop, blotting out all rational thought.

"Christmas is the time of year when the veil between worlds is thinnest and anything can cross over to this one. And I mean anything. Oh, I could tell you some tales, boy." The rabbit shook himself. "It's your job to make sure nothing does cross and you are the city's first line of defence. That is your honour, done you by the city of your birth. You should be grateful."

"Grateful? I'm not fucking doing it."

"Yes. You are." He let me go and I slumped onto the frozen, snow covered path.

"Wait. Why have I changed into - this? And why do I see monsters everywhere?"

The rabbit snorted.

"Changed? You haven't changed. This is your true self, Derek. It was your human form that was the lie."

"But the monsters…"

"Of which you are one, have always been among us. You are seeing the world as it really is. A world you have enthusiastically contributed to - and that's why you're here."

"What? What do you mean?"

"You've always been a monster Derek and deep down you've always known that. Now at least you can acknowledge it and put it to good use."

And with that he disappeared, leaving me to the howl of the wind and the strains of the fairground in the distance. I crumpled to the ground, put my head on my paws and wept for the man I'd been and the life I'd had.

And would have no more.

***

I must have passed out where I lay, because when I woke, there were no sounds of traffic or people nearby. The city was asleep, the cloud-covered, light-polluted sky the colour of old blood. I could hear the hum of electricity through pylons, smell the spoor of urban foxes as they hunted for the little, scurrying night creatures. Creatures like me. I even fancied I could feel the rotation of the earth as it hurtled through space and time like an ownerless, purposeless wind-up toy.

If I did have the Gift of Becoming, enhanced senses aside, what I had become did not please me at all. But what was I to do about it now?

My wallowing was interrupted by the swish of silk and a blast of warm green-scented air, as though someone had opened the door to a spring wood. The most beautiful woman I'd ever seen stepped out from the Christmas trees, smiling at me. Dressed in a tight-fitting, low cut scarlet evening dress, her pale, luminous skin was off-set by glittering obsidian eyes and a glossy, jetty tangle of hair that reached her tiny waist. The face was delicately boned with the barest flush of pink infusing her cheeks and her bee-stung mouth was a lush red. She laughed, the sound intimate and knowing as a lover's, and I was entranced in a way that I couldn't recall having ever experienced in my entire life.

"Come, my love," she said holding a small, white hand out to me, her mellifluous voice caressing its way down the length of my spine. "It's time."

"Time for what?" I mumbled, going to her and taking the proffered hand.

"Come see."

This was too much of an echo of Louise taking me to the benighted amulet stall and, alluring as she was, I tried to slip her grasp. Her shining black eyes blazed as she gripped me tighter, the corner of her lip curling.

"You are chosen."

"But what does that mean?" I pleaded, close to tears.

"You'll find out."

"No," I moaned. "Who are you and what do you want with me?"

Ignoring me, she dragged me out of the maze and we stepped out onto a dark, featureless landscape. The only light source was the faint glimmer of an almost total eclipse of a huge, rust-red moon that hung low in the sky.

"Where are we?" I asked through clenched teeth.

"Home," the woman said. "The heart of the city. Hush now. They come."

I almost didn't spot it at first. A blot on the empty, barren nowhere-scape that got bigger and was soon joined by lots of other blots, all heading in our direction.

"What's happening?" I asked my guide, having given up on an answer.

"I told you: you've been chosen," she replied.

"If I'm chosen, is that a good thing? Does that mean I'm going to live? To serve the city, or something? Because I'd like that, I really would," I gabbled.

Whatever was coming was getting closer by the second.

"Don't worry little rat, you will serve your city. It's an honour you were born for. The strength of your desire lights you up like a beacon to the ones who come."

"And who the fuck are they?"

"The Travellers, of course. Those who would cross between worlds - but they can only pass on the shortest day of the year."

The tumorous grey mass drew closer. I could see now that it was made up of individuals, running towards us.

"Yeah, but will I live?"

"Sacrifices by their nature do not live, Derek. Fear not though. Your death will cement the wards between worlds and keep the Travellers from crossing."

"What if I don't want that? What if I say, fuck your sacrifice, Derek McVey wants to live to fight another day?"

She turned to me, lights moving in the depths of her dark eyes, an expression of intense compassion on her face.

"Then you're screwed."

The first of the swarm reached us, red in eye and hooked in claw. I was going to be ripped apart by the mob and I wasn't going easy.

"God help me," I screamed as something hacked my leg off at the hip and I fell under the crush of heaving bodies.

“God is dead, Derek. It’s the Goddess you should be praying to,” was the last thing I heard before they took my head and stuck it on a pike while I was still alive.

***

I linger between worlds now. A puff of smoke, a tang of ozone on an autumn afternoon, a cold spot you pass through on your way to the warm pub to meet your friends and lovers.

Giving you the chills is the high point of this twilit eternal existence of mine.

That and the Christmas market of course - the only thing I’m allowed to haunt with impunity. Maybe you’ll feel me as I skim, light as a breeze, over your hair as you shop or swirl around your feet as you sip gluhwein, ready to trip you up.

Maybe though, on the shortest day of the year - if I’m in the mood - I’ll send the Rabbit your way.

To see if you’re worthy….

THE END

The Night Before Christmas

By

Suzanne Fox

Callum's eyes flashed open at the sound of creaking hinges and he raised his head to stare at the bedroom door as it slowly opened. His jaw fell open as he took in the image that was framed by the doorway. A pale figure clad in a red lace basque stood back-lit by the chandelier on the landing. Dark curls tumbled onto white shoulders and the curve of full breasts that were pushed even higher by the close-fitting underwear. His eyes lowered to take in long legs covered by the sheerest of stockings, and feet encased in four-inch high-heeled patent shoes. He pushed himself into a sitting position and the covers slipped from his chest, "Am I dreaming?"

The figure laughed. "No silly. I know it's still technically Christmas Eve, but I wanted to give you an early present for bringing me to this beautiful cottage." Jess stepped over to the window and drew back the curtain. "Look! It's snowing." Heavy, swollen flakes drifted lazily past the glass intensifying the cold moonlight's glow. "If it carries on like this we're going to be cut-off tonight." She shivered. "It's making me feel chilly. Any chance of warming things up?" She wiggled her way over to the four poster bed, kicked off her shoes and slid under the duvet beside Callum. She pressed herself close to him and he shuddered as the lace of her basque brushed the hairs on his chest.

"Can I unwrap my present now?" said Callum and a sly grin crossed his face. He reached around Jess's waist and grabbed her bottom, squeezing the flesh until she yelped.

"Hey! You need to learn how to treat a lady gently or you don't get to play with your pressie until tomorrow." She wriggled free of his grasp and rolled over, turning her back to him and then let out another high-pitched squeal as his arms wrapped around her. His fingers slipped inside the lacy cups of the basque to pinch her rapidly hardening nipples. Her squeal was immediately followed by a low moan of pleasure and she snuggled her bottom against his rapidly expanding cock.

He let his fingers explore Jess's warm, smooth skin, stroking, pinching and tickling. Every time she wriggled or jumped beneath his touch he felt himself grow a little harder until he could hold back no more. Callum grabbed her and flipped her onto her back. He twisted his fingers into the sides of her panties and the sound of tearing lace filled the room.

"Hey! They were expensive!" she laughed.

"I thought you said they were my Christmas present."

"They were the wrapping. Your present's what was inside."

"And now I'm going to have my present." He hooked his arms beneath Jess's knees and lifted her legs. "It looks like you've given me something I can wear." He let the tip of his cock brush her glistening cunt, pulling back slightly every time she tried to raise her hips to meet him. "Don't rush me. I'm going to enjoy this."

"So am I. Stop teasing and fuck me."

Callum reached down and guided the tip of his dick into her tight, wet pussy and then stopped, laughing as she tried to draw him deeper. "Patience, sweetheart."

Thud!

Both of them turned their heads towards the window, the source of the sound, and Callum jumped up. "What the fuck was that?" A white clump was slowly gliding down the glass.

A snowball.

He approached the window and cupped his hands above his eyes to look out into the dark night. "I can't see anyone out there and we're miles from the nearest house."

"Callum. Put some clothes on. There could be anyone out there." Jess's voice rose by an octave. She climbed off the bed and pulled on her robe, tying it tightly around her waist. She picked up Callum's robe and handed it to him.

"Don't you want to share the big feller with anyone," said Callum. He smiled and jiggled his hips so his cock swayed from side to side.

"Put your robe on. Who on earth could be out there?" She peered through the window. "The snow's getting pretty deep already. I think we're going to be stuck here."

"That's okay. We're not going anywhere for a few days and it'll probably have melted by tomorrow night."

"Yes. But we're here now and there's someone out there. It's the middle of the night on Christmas Eve and we're miles from anyone." She shivered and pulled her robe tighter. "There could be any kind of creep out there looking for a chance to get in. This is weird. Go and make sure the doors are locked."

"I locked them earlier. We're safe. What could possibly happen to you with a big strong guy like me around to take care of you?"

Jess's forehead creased into a frown. "I still don't like it." She pressed her nose against the cold pane, cupped her hands around her face and peered into the snowstorm. Her breath misted the glass and she wiped it with her hand. "Why would anyone be throwing snowballs in the middle of the night so far away from a village or town?"

"Don't worry about it Jess." Callum reached around her waist and pressed his recovering hardness against her bottom. "Come back to bed."

“In a minute. I just want to be sure.” She ignored the exaggerated sigh emanating from behind her and kept scouring the white landscape for any movement.

She jumped. “Cal! Look! Over there. By the line of trees.”

“What?”

She stepped back so that Callum could take her place. “Look over by the trees. Near the gate posts at the end of the drive.”

He duly did as he was told. “There’s no one there, Jess. It’s just the shadows and the snow. If there was anybody there, they’d have gone now. They’ve played their trick and they’ll be heading home out of this weather.” He stepped away from the window and walked over to the bed.

Jess looked again. “Oh my God!”

Callum was by her side in a heartbeat. “What is it?”

“It’s…it’s a child walking out from the trees. What’s a child doing out alone in the middle of the night? Maybe there’s been an accident on the road. Callum go and bring them in.”

“I can’t see-”

“Look!” she pointed towards the end of the quickly disappearing driveway. “There! Near the gate.”

“I don’t…no wait. I think I can see something.”

“See. I told you there was someone. Now get out there and bring them in before they freeze to death. The poor little thing must be terrified.”

Callum grabbed his jeans and sweater from the armchair where they lay in a crumpled heap and pulled them on as quickly as he could. He could feel the anxiety radiating from Jess and it was contagious. He wasn’t sure exactly what it was he had seen in the depths of the driving snow but there was definitely someone out there and, as far as he could tell, Jess was right, it was a child. But what the hell was a kid doing miles from anywhere in the middle of the night on Christmas Eve?

Jess followed him to the door of the cottage and watched as he pushed bare feet into unlaced boots and shrugged on a thick jacket. She kissed him on the cheek. “Be quick. The poor mite’s going to have frostbite.”

“I will.” Callum unlocked the door and opened it onto a wonderland of flurrying, white flakes. He put his head down and forged a path through the deepening snow towards the trees. Several inches had fallen already and there was no sign of it letting up. Come the morning they were going to be isolated from the rest of the world. The icy flakes stung his eyes as he plodded his way down the drive. Drawing closer to the tall firs he called out. "Who's there? Don't be scared. Come inside where it's warm." A heavy blanket of silence surrounded him, broken only by the crunch of snow beneath his steps. He shivered as a glacial gust of wind delved beneath his coat and nipped at his flesh.

He paused when he reached the trees and a different kind of shiver coursed through his body. The firs reached for the unseen stars, their crowns disappearing in the whirling maelstrom. The straight trunks shivered and seemed to huddle together creating a deep black void where the undergrowth should be. He called again. "Hello!" He strained his ears but there was no reply. Not even the sound of nocturnal creatures broke the silence. He could see nothing at all past the front line of trees. Just total blackness. He followed the tree line the short distance to the end of the drive. This was where he thought he had seen the small, childlike figure but the snow was unblemished. The only footprints to be seen were the ones he was making and they were disappearing as he watched. He turned slowly on the spot. The only other sign of life was Jess, silhouetted against the warm light spilling from the open doorway. Callum shook his head. *There's nobody out here*, he thought. No, he was just chasing shadows. The snow, the unfamiliar surroundings, not to mention the two bottles of wine they had shared earlier, had all conspired to play mind games on them both. A weight lifted from him at the realisation, and he began to turn around to make his way back into the warmth of the cottage.

A shrill scream pierced the night.

Jess!

He spun quickly, almost slipping in his haste, and looked towards the cottage doorway. Jess lay sprawled on the floor. Adrenaline gushed into his veins and Callum sprinted towards the cottage. The short distance felt like miles as the soft snow endeavoured to throw him off balance and denied traction to his steps.

Jess was staggering to her feet as he reached the cottage door. Her robe had slipped askew revealing pale breasts, pushed to seemingly impossible peaks by the cups of the basque, that were freckled with gooseflesh. He reached out and pulled her to him intending to warm and comfort her. Instead she jumped back as his snow-dusted jacket deposited a shower of white flakes on her bare skin.

"Jess. Are you okay" What happened?" Callum guided her inside and pushed the door closed behind him.

"I…I'm not sure." Jess sounded a little shaken.

Callum quickly checked her over to make she wasn't hurt. "Did you slip or trip over something?"

"No. No, it felt…" she thought for a moment. "It felt like someone pushed past me. I mean *really* pushed. Hard. But there was no one there so it couldn't have been that. I suppose it was just a big gust of wind. It must have caught me off balance.

Callum looked doubtful but said nothing. He took hold of her arm and led her into the cosy sitting room. Red embers glowed in the hollow belly of the wood-burner, casting a deep crimson hue across the room. He flicked a switch on a lamp and a small circle of light deepened the shadows in the corners. A woollen throw adorned the back of the sofa and Callum reached for it, draping it around Jess's shoulders. "Sit by the fire," he told her. "You're freezing. I'll make some drinks."

He stripped off his wet jacket and threw it over a chair as he walked into the kitchen. Grabbing a couple of glasses from a cupboard he splashed a generous amount of brandy in them from a bottle he had left on the counter. A creak resounded from the floor above and his head shot up. *Bloody old houses,* he thought. *Give me a new build every time.* By the time he returned to the warm comfort of the sitting room he had forgotten all about the creaks and groans of the old cottage.

Jess took a glass from him and sipped the warming liquid. She had stopped shivering. "There wasn't anyone out there," he said. "I think the snow and darkness were playing tricks on us. It must have been shadows from the trees against the snow."

She nodded, "I guess you're right. There wouldn't really be a child out alone this late on Christmas Eve." She glanced at the clock. "I mean Christmas Day."

Callum downed his drink in one swallow. The amber liquid burned a path down his throat but he relished the sensation after the biting cold of his search for the phantom child. He watched Jess sip hers more cautiously. "Shall we go back to bed and…finish what we started?" He smiled and waited for her reply. A lecherous grin in return gave him the answer he wanted. His fingers twisted in hers as he pulled her to her feet and towards the open staircase.

Bang!

A yelp escaped Jess's lips and her glass crashed to the floor in a thousand diamond shards. "What's up there?" she squealed.

Callum swallowed back his own cry that threatened to escape, "It's okay Jess." His voice sounded calmer than he felt. The noise had startled him and he guessed he was still a little strung out from imagining a kid wandering around in the midst of a snow storm. "It's just old house noises. Probably ancient plumbing or something." He picked her up and carried her to the stairs so she wouldn't step barefoot onto the broken glass. "You go to bed. I'll sweep this up and follow in a few minutes."

A frown flitted across her face before she smiled. "Thank you. I'm sorry I was so clumsy. It scared the crap out of me though."

Her eyes were still a little wide but Callum thought it was probably the effects of the brandy. He patted her bottom as she turned around and walked up the staircase. As soon as she disappeared from view he set about clearing up the glass and within a few minutes he entered the bedroom.

Jess lay on top of the duvet. She had discarded her robe and the basque covered very little of her body. Her knees were bent and slightly parted, welcoming him back to bed. A scrap of red silk, the remains of her torn panties, lay discarded on the rug. Any fears and uncertainties that had threatened to spoil their romantic Christmas retreat were being quickly banished by the anticipation of what would happen as soon as Callum climbed into bed.

The soft rug tickled his toes as he stepped closer and he pulled his sweater over his head as he went. He threw it to the floor and unzipped his jeans as he reached the side of the bed. Suddenly every hair on his body was erect. A primal fear held him in a grip of steel and dizziness threatened to engulf him as the blood drained from his face.

"Callum!" Jess's voice rose in a shaky crescendo. "What's wrong? You've gone white."

Adrenaline gushed through his veins. He wanted to run. He wanted to fight. But fight what? Confusion jostled at fear's shoulder. Why was he so anxious? Why was he so scared? Quickly regaining control of his limbs he jumped onto the bed and swung his legs up, abruptly anxious to have them above floor level in an echo of long-forgotten childhood neuroses.

"Callum?" Jess's voice pulled him back to earth.

"Huh." He looked at Jess and guilt superseded his unease. Concern had etched a clear course across her face. "I'm sorry sweetheart. I just freaked out for a minute. It's been a weird evening."

He slipped his hand between her thighs and squeezed her yielding flesh. He adored the throaty moan that escaped her whenever she was aroused and he felt his cock begin to revive at the sound. Jess parted her legs slightly and Callum traced his fingertips towards her dark, inviting core, brushing against the curls that framed his target. Jess's legs opened further and his hardness was now straining against the confines of his jeans. With his free hand he tugged at the zipper.

A scraping sound broke their focus and their heads jerked up simultaneously. A nefarious, ragged shape scuttled from beneath the shadows of the bed and raced across the floor towards the door. Jess screamed and pushed herself further up the bed trying to distance herself from the creature. A liquid heaviness settled in Callum's gut and he felt his cock shrivel like a crisp packet thrown into flames as the shape disappeared through the open door. Muffled chuckling rose up the staircase.

"What the fuck was that?" Callum was already on his feet zipping up his jeans. His fear had been surpassed by a primitive need to protect Jess. He grabbed a heavy decorative candlestick from the hearth and stalked towards the door.

"Wait!" Jess's demand cut through his impetus and he stopped. "It's…it's that child. The one we saw outside."

"Jess, it can't be. There was no-."

"Yes! There was." She had jumped off the bed and was pulling on her robe again. "He must have ran past you in the snow. I said it felt as though someone had pushed into me. I was watching you and didn't see him come through the door." She shrugged. "It makes sense."

There was an insane logic to her words. Callum's mind was desperately searching for a rational explanation for what had just happened and he couldn't think of one more believable than Jess's. Kids like to hide and where better than under a bed. It was always his favourite hiding place when he was little. His heart rate began to return to normal. Of course she was right. It couldn't possibly be anything else. It was far too big to be a squirrel or a rat, or any other wild animal that may have crept into the cottage to seek shelter. And yet…it didn't look like a child, he thought. He'd only caught a glimpse of the creature for a brief second but it looked, no not looked, it *felt* old. It resembled a very small man dressed in ragged, dirty clothes. He shook his head. *Pull yourself together. You've had a scare. Probably had too much to drink and it's been a long day stuck in Christmas traffic on the motorway for hours.* He replaced the candle stick. There was no way he could explain to the authorities that he had threatened a child with a blunt instrument.

Jess was already at the door. "Wait!" he called. "Let me go first." She pulled a face in protest but catching sight of his expression she kept quiet and waited for Callum to take the lead.

The staircase groaned as he took slow careful steps. He could feel Jess's eagerness almost like a physical force compelling him to go faster but he ignored her silent coercion. Their shadows followed them on the wall beside them until suddenly they were drowned in darkness.

Callum stumbled as Jess squealed and crashed into him. His fingers groped frantically until they latched onto the handrail and he managed to stop his uncontrolled descent into the abyss. The sound of malignant giggles drifted from the darkness, throatier and deeper than any child's voice he had ever heard. Splinters of ice stabbed at his spine and the hairs on his neck stood proud. "Go back to the bedroom and lock the door," he hissed.

"But it's just a child…" Jess's voice quivered. Her tone implied she was trying to convince herself as much as Callum of the creature's origin. Nevertheless she took a couple of steps back towards the bedroom.

"It…it didn't look like a child." Speaking his thoughts aloud gave life to Callum's fears. Whatever he had seen scramble across the floor of the bedroom was not a child, although there was a semblance of humanity to it.

"What! What do you mean?" Jess's voice trembled an octave higher. "What else could it be?"

"I don't know but I'm going to find out." It took all of his resolve to sound confident. He didn't want to alarm Jess any more than she already was. "Please do as I say." He sensed rather than saw her nod in the darkness but he heard the creak of the stair as she edged away. Knowing Jess was safer in the bedroom he felt a surge of confidence. Whoever the person was, he couldn't be a match for Callum. The intruder was small, very small, and Callum stood at six-foot two with a body that knew it's way around a gym. Callum had the upper hand now that the element of surprise was lost.

As soon as he heard the click of the bedroom door, Callum cautiously made his way downstairs, holding his breath so he could hear the slightest sound. A red glow emanated from the sitting room as the dying embers of the fire strived to bring cheer to his trepidation. The wall was rough beneath his fingertips as they explored their way towards the light switch. He flicked it and light filled the room, startling him, and he realised he hadn't been expecting it to work. His imagination had convinced him there was no power. That he would have to stumble around in the darkness searching for the creature.

A weight lifted from his shoulders and he almost felt himself grow in stature as his confidence returned. Quickly scanning the room he reassured himself there was no one there and he moved towards the kitchen. He flicked the light switch and another room flooded with harsh fluorescence. The stench of sour sweat and stale musk filled the room making his eyes water. He wiped his eyes with the back of his hand and looked around. Beneath the kitchen table, in a puddle of shadow, lurked a small hunched figure. Black eyes gleamed from deep sockets and dirty teeth were visible behind a malevolent grin. It was dressed in the strangest of clothes. Soiled red trousers tucked into worn-down, scuffed boots, a dirty, shabby jacket and what looked like an ancient Christmas hat. The point of the hat flopped to one side of his head and there dangled what looked like a rusted bell from its tip.

Callum took a step back before recovering his composure. He held the high ground. This less than a person that lurked beneath the table was no match for him. He crossed his arms and glared at the odorous creature. "I suggest you come out from there right now. I don't know what sick games you're playing but if you don't fuck off out of here this minute, you'll be leaving in an ambulance." He was answered with a gurgled chuckle.

"You think you're so fucking funny but you won't be laughing when I've finished with you." Callum's face burned with anger. He stomped towards the table and reached beneath, fingers outstretched in readiness to grab hold of his pathetic adversary. God help him, he was going to tear this piece of shit apart.

A scream ripped the night apart and it took Callum a moment to realise the shrieking came from himself. He staggered backwards into a dresser. China danced and chinked, and a teapot crashed to the floor. Agonising pain pulsed through his hand and he raised it before his face. Blood dripped from the stump of his thumb and flaps of ragged skin revealed the gleam of bone beneath. Dizziness swept over him in a wave weakening his legs. He grabbed hold of the dresser with his other hand to steady himself and more china skittered to the floor. Then he heard something that chilled his blood.

The bedroom door creaked open and soft footsteps padded across the landing. Jess had left her sanctuary and was on her way downstairs. "Callum," she called.

Her voice sounded distant yet Callum realised she was only moments away from encountering this vicious imp. He battled his shock and ran to stop her, gasping as shards of shattered porcelain buried themselves into the soles of his bare feet. He reached the bottom of the stairs at the same time as Jess. Her face was masked with fear and confusion.

"Get back upstairs!" he yelled. "Now!" He turned her around and pushed her back in the direction she had come from, smearing crimson stripes across her silk robe.

"Callum. What's happening?" Her head twisted around to look at him and her eyes widened in fear. "W...what's that?" Fear stiffened her body and the force of Callum's shoving unbalanced her. She landed on the stairs with a thud and Callum spun to see his attacker emerge from the kitchen.

The figure stretched himself to his full height. He was barely more than three-foot tall, but what he lacked in stature he remedied with muscle. Callum's view had been obstructed by the kitchen table but now he could clearly see his enemy as he moved like a hunter towards them. Its mouth was stretched into a wide grin displaying pointed teeth stained with Callum's blood and its tiny eyes shone with an evil lust. *He must be a dwarf,* he thought, but he knew he was miles from the truth. Something buried deep in his mind fought to get out. An echo of a memory swam just out of reach. There was something familiar about the stocky creature that stalked towards him. A scrabbling sound behind him alerted him to Jess's retreat upstairs and he followed her backwards, one slow step at a time, never taking his eyes off the figure that drew closer. He prayed that Jess would have the initiative to call the police. He had left his phone on the bedside table and it was fully charged.

"Oh Callum," snorted the creature and, at the sound of the phlegmy voice, Callum stumbled. His hand snaked towards the bannister banging the stump of his thumb against the oak rail.

He screamed with pain and the realisation that this thing knew his name. "Who are you?" Terror tinged his words and he heard Jess emerge once more from the bedroom, alerted by his cries. "Jess! Go back," he yelled. "Call the police! Now!"

"I tried. There's no signal."

"Oh my. You've got a pretty one there. Do you deserve her though?"

The lasciviousness in his voice sent a shudder through Callum's body and he retreated a couple of more steps. "Leave her alone," he hissed.

"Oh. Leave her alone, he says. Don't touch her, he says. Leave her pretty little pussy alone, he says." His hand rubbed against his rapidly swelling crotch.

"I never said-."

"But you were thinking it Callum. Yes you were." He was creeping closer to the stairs, his eyes shining gleefully as mischief danced across his face.

Callum's arse hit one of the steps as he fell backwards. His legs kicked out and he pushed himself further towards the landing. Fear squeezed its grip tight around his chest. Why should he be so afraid of this little man? He'd bested far bigger men than this one, but something crawled beneath his skin at the sight of this malignant imp.

The little man reached the bottom step and started to crawl up towards Callum. He licked his bloodied lips as his smile widened and his greedy little eyes narrowed.

Callum found himself hauled to his feet as Jess's hands were thrust under his arms and she pulled. Her robe gaped open and her nipples had escaped the tight confines of her basque. Callum noticed but arousal was a million miles away. *Don't let him see them. Don't let him see them,* played on a loop inside his head. Thrusting Jess before him they tumbled into the bedroom. There was only a flimsy lock on the heavy door but he slid the bolt anyway. A chunky chest of drawers stood to the side of the door. Wedging his shoulder against the chest, Callum pushed as hard as he could. The furniture was weightier than he imagined and he thought it wasn't going to budge but inch by slow inch he manoeuvred it across the doorway. Nothing was getting through.

Jess had pulled her robe closed again. "Who…Who is that. Why does he know you?" There was accusation in her tone.

"I don't know," snapped Callum. He looked at his hand. The stump of his thumb was throbbing in time with his heartbeat but at least it seemed to have stopped bleeding. The blood had congealed in a thick, viscous clot. His stomach clenched as he wondered what had become of his thumb. Had it been swallowed? "Did you call the police?"

"I said there's no-."

"Pass me the phone." Jess scrambled across the bed and picked up the phone. Callum snatched it from her trembling fingers.

"Oh my God! Your thumb." Her face whitened to match the thick blanket of snow outside.

Callum jabbed at the screen and held the phone to his ear. "Fuck!" He tried again.

Jess jumped as the phone smashed into pieces against the wall beside her.

"There's. No. Fucking. Signal!" Callum paced the floor, his hands gripping the sides of his head. "Why the fuck did we come here, to the middle of nowhere. Fuck! Fuck! Fuck!"

Jess ran over and hugged him. "It's okay. Nothing's going to get through that door. We can wait it out. We're safe in here."

He took a few deep breaths letting Jess's words soothe his fractured nerves. Maybe she was right and they were safe. He had struggled to move the large cupboard so the little guy wouldn't stand a chance. He flopped down on the edge of the bed taking Jess with him. She took hold of his hand and inspected his thumb. "How did he…?"

Callum shook his head, "I don't know. I…I guess he bit it."

Jess shuddered and nestled in closer to his chest.

Bang!

The door shook and the chest jumped a couple of inches. *It's not possible,* he thought. *There's no way he can get through that.*

As if to prove him wrong the door was pounded again, the lock snapped and the chest creaked further forward. Long, dirty fingers reached around the door and Jess screamed. Callum startled by Jess's scream jumped up looking around for something to defend them with. The candlestick. He grabbed it again and waited.

The next assault splintered the door and the chest skidded several feet across the floor gouging furrows in the wooden boards. *It's not possible.* The phrase had almost become a prayer to Callum. If he kept thinking it, the words would eventually ring true. They didn't. The nightmare man stood framed by the doorway and in his hand was the bottle of brandy from the kitchen. Before Callum had time to react the bottle flew through the air and shattered against his temple. The room blurred as blood ran into his eyes and nerves exploded in his skull. The muscles in his legs failed him and he slid to the floor. The candlestick rolled from his grip as he watched the stranger saunter into the room. Somewhere in the distance he could hear Jess screaming.

The grubby figure swaggered towards Jess who had backed herself into a corner, her arms outstretched to ward him off. It was a futile attempt. His hands grabbed her wrists and her shrieks grew as he crushed the bones in his grip. He dragged her towards where Callum slumped bleeding and weakened on the floor. "Let her go," Callum slurred.

"Let her go," mimicked the man. "I don't think so." He wound the long fingers of one hand around both of Jess's wrists and she whimpered in pain as her bones crunched. He extended a finger of his free hand and drew a pointed, black fingernail down the front of her basque. The lace fell apart revealing her pale trembling flesh. A crimson line bloomed from between her breasts to her navel following the path where his nail had travelled. Without releasing his grip on the girl, he kicked out sharply, landing a booted foot in Callum's groin.

Callum shrieked and tears of pain and fear tracked down his cheeks. "W…why are you doing this. Let Jess go. Please." His hands cupped his aching balls and his knees were drawn up in a belated attempt at self-protection.

"Oh dear, Callum. Do I really have to explain why I'm here? I thought you were smarter than this."

"I…I don't understand," he sobbed. "Who are you and why are you doing this?" Callum's bloodshot eyes begged for mercy but none was forthcoming.

"My name is Malgath," came the reply. "But the name won't mean anything to you, though we have met before."

"No. You're wrong. I'd know if I'd met you before."

"You've just forgotten Callum. It's been a long time. Twenty years in fact."

"But I would have only been nine then."

The imp laughed and a dislodged lump of grey phlegm splattered the floor next to Callum. "And what a nasty little nine-year old you were." To add emphasis to his statement he kicked Jess's ankle, the crack of splintered bone was briefly audible before being drowned by her scream of agony. She collapsed to the floor and a gash opened on her cheek as he once more dragged a blackened fingernail across her skin.

"I don't understand-."

"No. Of course you don't. You've always been too selfish, too mean and too cruel to understand how your actions damage other people. You're the reason I have to mutilate this pretty little plaything you brought with you." He plunged a fat thumb deep into Jess's right eye. It slithered from her socket with a wet plop.

Jess screamed and convulsed in her torture and Callum tried to crawl towards her. A crunch of shattered teeth halted him in his tracks and pain exploded through his shattered jaw. Through a crimson haze he saw their tormentor absently rub the blood from his boot down the back of his stained trouser leg.

"Still can't remember can you? That was the year you found your sister's Christmas presents and smashed every single one. You told her Santa had sent his elves to break them because she had been such a naughty girl. She was only four years old."

Callum recalled something from his past. He'd never told anyone what he'd done. How could this freak possibly know?

"It was the same year you told all the kiddies in the queue waiting to see Santa Claus, that he was dead and no one would be getting any presents that year."

Callum shook his head from side to side, instantly regretting the movement. He remembered that day. The tears and cries of the other children. The angry parents. It had been a wonderful day. Well worth being grounded for a week. He'd done something else that day too. But what?

"And there was the elf you kicked. The one who had to stand there in silence when he really wanted to slap the mean little smirk from your face. Yes, I can see you remember now. That was me."

Disbelief possessed Callum. This thing couldn't be the man who was dressed as an elf all those years ago, and why would he do this because a little boy was a bit naughty twenty years ago?

“I can see you still don’t believe in me Callum but you will.” He fish-hooked a finger into the corner of Jess’s mouth and pulled, ripping her lips into an extended bloody grin. “Poor, poor little girl,” he sang. “But you don’t care about ruining Christmas for anyone. Do you Callum?”

Callum tried to phrase some words but his flapping jaw refused to comply with what his brain commanded. Blubbering noises slipped from his ruined mouth along with bloodied saliva.

The elf giggled, an obscene resonance in the room. “You never grew out of your spiteful streak either. You stabbed your best friend in the back to steal his promotion and screwed his wife at the same time.”

Tears streamed from Callum’s eyes. He had no idea how this vile creature knew his darkest secrets.

“What kind of man let’s his grandmother think she’s lost her wedding ring when he’s sold it to pay his cocaine dealer? Oh dearie me, Callum. You have been a naughty boy. But do you know what? Santa knows every bad thing that you’ve ever done and once you’re on his naughty list there’s only one way to get your name taken off it.” The elf turned his attention towards Jess. “You look a little uncomfortable sweetie. Let me put you out of your misery.” He released her wrists and using both hands snapped her neck. Her head fell to one side like a marionette with snipped strings. She collapsed to the floor. “Such a shame. Her only crime was being with you, but such is life.”

The elf knelt next to Callum and put his face close. His breath caused the broken man to recoil. “Santa was very disappointed when you told all the kiddies that he was dead. Don’t you know you shouldn’t make Santa angry? He has a very bad temper when he gets upset and it’s my job to help him deal with his naughty list.”

Bile burned its way up Callum’s throat and he coughed and spluttered, igniting fresh flames of pain in his jaw. His mouth flapped wildly but no words came forth to beg for salvation.

“Save your breath Callum. It’s going to be a long night and I’ve got a few friends waiting to meet you.” Malgath walked over to the window and yanked it open. Icy air flooded the room carrying with it the sound of singing.

Jingle bells. Jingle bells. Jingle all the way...

“Up here boys,” called the elf. “It’s time for a little festive fun and games…”

The End

In The Bag

By

Tim Curran

So it's Christmas Eve and the dirty snow falls on the dirty city, making a bad situation worse for the street people who huddle under ratty blankets on street corners and shiver in piss-stained cardboard boxes in narrow, trash-blown alleys. Through the bitter wind and swirling snowflakes comes Johnny Puckett, pushing his old grocery cart. Squeak-squeak-squeak! You can hear it coming a block away, on account of the bad wheel which will never be fixed.

Johnny pauses, resting, because it's no easy bit on a night like this. His breath puffs out in rolling white clouds as he warms his hands and surveys the streets. He winces inside as he sees the homeless pressed together for warmth.

Some live on the streets by choice, others are mentally ill or elderly, stewpots or junkies, war vets whose brains are scrambled from combat, the unemployable, the disenfranchised, and the forgotten.

Funny. Seems like there are more every year.

Johnny sees a Lexus sedan drive by followed by a high-end SUV that splatters gray road slush at his feet. Some have so much and others not a damn thing.

Go figure.

He looks from the bums on the corner sharing bottles of Formula 44D and cans of Sterno to the bag inside his cart, the gray sack.

It's the most wonderful time of the year, he thinks.

From beneath the canopy of a department store, he hears strains of John Lennon singing "Merry Xmas (War is Over)" as he is pushing out into the storm.

"Yeah, so this is Christmas," he says under his breath. "And what the fuck have you done?"

He stands there, a rail-thin black dude with squinty eyes set in a face marred by street life: old knife scars, razor cuts, a sandpaper complexion, and a twisted nose that was broken in a fight and never set properly. He wears a dingy, soiled Santa suit he pulled out of a dumpster whose white fur trim has gone the color of slate. Fishing out an old Sucrets tin, he selects one of the choice cigarette butts he has collected. Lighting up, he thinks, *hey, a good one. A Camel only half-smoked.*

When he's done, he pushes on down the sidewalk, ignoring the dirty looks he gets from shopkeepers. That's okay, that's okay. He comes around the corner and smells hot food, seasoned and succulent. The juice runs in his mouth and a tiger roars in his belly.

"Hey, Johnny!" a voice calls.

It's Mr. Santorini over in his sheltered cul-de-sac, still at it with his food cart beneath the red-striped umbrella despite the weather. And Johnny knows why. His wife died seven long years ago and his kids never call. It's only the cart that keeps him fluid, keeps him from begging with the others and gives him a sense of purpose.

Johnny wheels over there. "Merry Christmas, Mr. S. How's business tonight?"

"Not bad," says the little old man. He's compressed by the years, worn thin as sticks, shivering and stomping his numb feet but never giving in. "Two things you can count on come Christmas Eve, Johnny. People gonna want to eat and they gonna want to get drunk."

He talks on and on about the weather, blizzards he's seen other years, friends he's buried and will never see again. But Johnny can't pay attention. It's those Italian sausages. Nobody makes 'em like Mr. Santorini. Slow-smoked, seasoned with a family recipe straight out of Naples, then pressed hot and juicy into a butter-soft deep-fried bun, slathered with onions and peppers, melted provolone and some kind of sauce that's sweet and hot and sour all at the same time.

Mr. Santorini prepares one and hands it to Johnny, foil-wrapped.

"No, no," Johnny protests. "Ain't got no scratch, Mr. S."

The old man laughs. "And on Christmas Eve, you don't need any. Enjoy."

Johnny does and it's complete mouth-orgasm. His taste buds tap-dance on his tongue. His stomach grows teeth. Then it's gone, and he's licking his fingers; a beautiful torrid zone of warmth at his core.

"You handing out goodies again this year, Santa?" Mr. Santorini asks.

"Was, Mr. S., was. Ran fresh out."

"Well, bless you, Johnny! You're one of the good ones."

Johnny's not so sure about that, but he does render a service; he does at that. And it goes far beyond the cheap combs, scarves, and slippers he hands out to the destitute every year.

Twenty minutes later, still warm inside from the kindness of Mr. Santorini, Johnny cuts off West 23rd into an alley, knowing what waits there. He goes anyway because he needs to.

He brushes snow from his face and shakes himself like a wet dog. Christmas…damn the chill of it! He spies a snow-covered refrigerator box pushed real snug-like between a dumpster and a row of green plastic recycling bins that are overflowing.

"Kathleen," he says. "Kathleen, it's time."

There's a scrambling sound in the box like rats fighting, a raw-lunged tubercular coughing that becomes a gagging and then a wheezing.

Kathleen claws her way out like an ogre from a cave. She snarls at Johnny, and spits at him. She stands uneasily on feet wrapped in rags and stuffed in bread bags, secured with sealing tape. She's a bestial, hunched-over, delirious troll in a threadbare, olive-drab overcoat encrusted with feces and other nameless stains. Her face is caked with filth. It clings to her cheeks, fills the crevices and deep-set wrinkles like mud. Her eyes are feral, her hair ratty steel wool. Her cracked lips part, revealing splintered yellow-brown teeth broken into stubs. There is black grit seamed between them.

She growls.

She hisses.

Johnny knows she's crazy so he keeps his distance. Whatever she once was, she's an animal now. Rabid, lips slavered with white foam, fingers like black split claws, mind sucked into a whirlpool-pit of decay, dementia, and delusion, she's ready to fight for her lair.

But Johnny's voice, like a cooling balm to her fevered mind, was calming. "It's all right now, Kathleen. Everything's gonna be all right now. Look in the bag and know peace."

Kathleen is unsure of his words.

She is a deranged territorial beast used to fighting for those few scant pathetic possessions she can call her own. Slowly, though, she mellows. She can sense something in Johnny's form, his intent. Something in the placid, sad pools of his eyes. There is mercy there and though she is unfamiliar with it, it moves her.

"That's it, Kathleen," he says softly. "In the bag. There's something for you in the bag."

She advances to the cart, pointing at it, jibbering, jabbering. Drool runs down her chin and tears well in her eyes. She remains uncertain. Now she reaches into the cart, placing her hands on the bag, the gray canvas sack. She strokes it lovingly. There is confusion in her rheumy eyes. It does not feel like canvas...it is warm, pliable. It feels like—

Whatever the bag is and whatever it isn't, it opens now like lips sliding back to expose gums and huge teeth. Kathleen shrieks and the mouth darts forward with incredible speed, faster than the strike of a rattlesnake. Before she can hope to escape, she is pulled in up to her shoulder blades. The jaws close like a man-trap, serrated teeth piercing her, cracking through vertebrae and severing her spine. She flops limply like a crushed rat in the jaws of a mastiff...then she is drawn into the sack.

There are crunching sounds from within, chewing sounds. Then a gurgling noise like the agitator of a washing machine. Before the lips of the sack close, a jet of blood sprays into the air.

Johnny can feel wet, warm droplets break against his face. He staggers back, sickened as always.

The sack is stained a vibrant, Technicolor red. Then slowly, slowly, the stain is completely absorbed. The sack is just a sack again.

Breathing hard, Johnny pushes the cart out of the alley. The sack looks deflated now, flaccid. The cycle continues.

On 27th Street, down by Cement Park where the junkies share needles, he runs into Georgia Stan holding court with a couple winos whose eyes are like cigarette burns in vellum, reflections of the ash-pit desolation of their minds. They move on, but Georgia Stan squats on his rug, chattering away as if his friends are still there. He seems oblivious to the fact that he's nearly covered in snow.

"Stanny, how you doing?"

Georgia Stan cocks his head, eyeballing Johnny, but there is no real recognition in his glassy eyes. In fact, there's not much of anything. They are as shallow as rain puddles.

"Got me this," he says, holding up an empty bottle of cheap cooking sherry. "Lady...lady she gimme it. She put it in my hands, gimme it. Say...she say...you have this for Christmas. This all yours. You drink it and you don't have to give none to others save them you want to. You can't have what she gimme."

"That's cool, Stanny. You hang onto it."

"I do, I do." He looks around, narrows his eyes, seeing someone that Johnny cannot. "You ain't gettin' none. No sir. This mine. Lady gimme it. She gimme it for me. Not for you."

Stanny rocks back and forth on his rug, clutching his empty bottle as he probably will be clutching it a week from then. And he'll be here, too, because he doesn't have any feet, just stumps. He lost them to frostbite two winters back.

"Well, later, Stanny," Johnny says, pushing his cart off down the sidewalk, leaving Georgia Stan alone to speak with his friends about the lady that gave him the bottle.

In the cart, the sack rustles.

"No, not that one," Johnny tells it. "Not just yet."

The sack trembles. It shudders. A muscular spasm sweeps through it. It is clearly agitated but Johnny is holding firm. If he doesn't hold firm, the sack will get out of control and if too many people go missing, questions will be asked and those questions might lead back to Johnny and if they lead to Johnny they might lead to—

But he isn't going to think about that.

He's in the park now, fighting down the path, pushing through drifts and feeling that cold locked down in his bones. He makes his way over to the band shell. This is the place. This is where the desperate, the dying, and the damaged come to roost and rot. Usually, there's dozens of junkies hanging around, begging and caging and stealing, comparing tracks and collapsed veins. But the storm has pushed them under cover—sewers and culverts, rat-infested warehouses and sterile methadone clinics and homeless shelters.

There's only one left just as Johnny figured.

He doesn't have a name and maybe he doesn't even have a soul any longer. Whoever he was and whatever he might have been is long buried. All that's left is this ghost. It haunts the park, the band shell, but mostly, it haunts itself.

When Johnny steps under the light, the junkie—folded up in the corner and layered in old newspapers stained with dog piss—begins to moan.

"Oh, Santy, Santy Claus. I'm dying inside. I'm just *dying*. It hurts soooo bad," he whimpers. "God help me, but it hurts so bad."

He's a living skeleton in a dirty track suit, loafers, and a split-seamed parka. His hair is black-brown frosted white, his beard like a dark smear of burnt cork, his face wrinkled like branching lightning. He's maybe twenty or fifty.

"You want the pain to go away, my brother?" Johnny asks him.

"Yeah...yes, oh please."

"Then come to me. There's deliverance through me."

The very idea of such a thing is enough to get the junkie moving. Crick-crack-crack go his ancient icy joints and ligaments. He clings to Johnny's legs like a starving cat, the way the crippled and infirm, diseased and maimed must have clung to Jesus at Galilee.

Johnny helped the poor nameless junkie to his feet. "In that bag. What you want is in that bag. Go ahead, my brother, reach in there. Lay your hands on what is inside and it'll be done with. No more suffering."

Words. They mean very little to the junkie. Just roads that lead back into one another.

He stands on his own.

Grinning at Johnny, he reaches into the bag.

Whatever's in there, takes hold of him. It seizes his arms with blinding speed and devastating killing power, the way an owl takes a mouse. The junkie cries out, flashes a look of utter contempt at Johnny. That look says, *betrayer, goddamn betrayer! I might be nothing but a used-up addict, but even I know better than to betray a fellow human being to this...thing.*

He manages to almost pull himself free, but Johnny knows there's no getting away. The junkie's arms are peeled down to red meat, muscle and tendon. He screams and shouts, pure pain and pure terror, then the sack pulls him in, gulping him down and there is the crunching of bones and a perfectly horrible slurping, sucking sound like a kid with a melting Popsicle.

Then the junkie is gone, just gone.

The sounds that follow are repulsive: a chewing, licking, crackling noise followed by a gurgling. The sack deflates. It's larger after consuming two adults in one evening, but not by much. What it does with what it eats, Johnny does not know.

Ten minutes later, back into the storm. The snow keeps coming down and Johnny is chilled to the bone. He grumbles and groans under his breath and then he sees Georgia Stan up the block, still ranting and raving and carrying on heated conversations with people that exist only in his mind. The sack convulses with a sound like wet leather. It is growing excited.

In the back of Johnny's head, a forlorn voice begins to speak: *who are you to complain when others are suffering so terribly? Look at that poor, poor man. Society's trash dumped in the streets. Have you no sympathy on this most holy of nights for the destitute, the needy, the indigent?*

Johnny knows it's all about mercy and who is he to deny those in need? It makes him think of that night he found the sack in the attic of the ruined church. How it was just hanging there, empty and limp. And he thought, *that's a good bag for my stuff.* Then he touched it. And freezing cold teeth like icepicks sank into his palm. They didn't just pump him full of venom that turned his willpower to mush, they filled him with the knowledge of how it had to be, how they, together, would show mercy unto the needy for that was their calling.

Remembering, he pushes his cart over near Georgia Stan, very near.

"Hey, Stanny."

Georgia Stan holds up his empty bottle. "Lady gimme it. She gimme it so it's mine."

"Sure it is. She left something in this bag for you. She wants you to have it."

"For me? She leave it for me?"

"Yes. Something that's gonna make you feel all better. No more hurt."

Georgia Stan looks confused, uncertain. What little is left of his mind does not know what to think. In fact, he's not sure if Johnny is even there just as he's not sure about a lot of things.

"For me?"

"All for you."

"You gimme it. It's mine. You gimme it. You can't have it. It's mine."

Johnny, feeling the spirit of the season moving him, boosts Georgia Stan up and tells him to reach inside that bag and he does. It's over fast. A scream echoes off into the blizzard and there's a mist of blood in the air, terrible sounds coming from inside the sack. But it's over, it's finally over.

Johnny hears the clock at St. Anthony's ring twelve times. It's Christmas and it fills him, overflows him, makes tears run from his eyes. In his brain, which isn't so right anymore, he feels good about those who will no longer have to suffer.

God bless us one and all, he thinks.

Later, he's up in the attic of the ruined church at 33rd and Piedmont, in his little crib there, warming his hands before the woodstove. The sack has crawled away now. He watched it creep up the wall into the corner where it hung itself from the rafters, looking much like the cocoon it actually was. It would not move again until next year and by then it would be very hungry. Then, together, they would venture out to help the homeless and poverty-stricken.

Staring into the flames that burn as bright and hot as the hellfire in his soul, he whispers, "Merry Christmas, Merry Christmas."

The End

Afterword

Well it looks like you have made it to the end of our little book. I hope you enjoyed it.

I had planned to put together a little Christmas collection this year and add a few bonus stories from other authors in the back. I started contacting some authors that I have spoken to in the past to see what the interest would be and the response was overwhelming. It meant the book was going to be bigger than I expected and a lot more work to put together. With the help of a wonderful editor I had been working with, some great stories from a group of my favourite authors and an excellent cover designer we managed to put this book together in 6 weeks. It was a lot of work and stress but I think the end result is worth it.

I only became a part of the writing world just over a year ago so this was a big step for me to take and I only hope everyone involved and everyone who reads it enjoys it as much as I have. I'd highly recommend checking out some work from any of the authors in the book that you hadn't read before.

If you have a few minutes to spare, please consider leaving a review on Amazon or Goodreads as it truly helps authors more than you might realize.

From everyone involved at 'Collected Christmas Horror Shorts', we wish you a very Merry Christmas and hope the New Year ahead brings you an abundance of scary reads!

Thanks again for your support,
Kevin J. Kennedy

About the Authors

Willow Rose

Willow Rose also goes by the name The Queen of Scream. She is the author of 45 novels most of them horror and mystery. She lives on Florida's Space Coast where many of her books take place. She has sold more than a million books.

http://willow-rose.net/

https://www.amazon.com/WillowRose/e/B004X2WHBQ/ref=sr_tc_2_0?qid=1478535218&sr=1-2-ent

John R. Little

John R. Little is an award-winning author of suspense, dark fantasy, and horror.

He currently lives in Ayr, a small town near Kitchener, Canada, and is always at work on his next book. John has published 14 books to date, and most of them are available on Amazon. He hopes you enjoy his work.

https://www.facebook.com/profile.php?id=670108452&fref=ts

http://www.johnrlittle.com/

Veronica Smith

Veronica Smith lives in Katy, Texas, a suburb west of Houston. She has been married to her husband, Kelly, for over 25 year and has a son, Zach, who just graduated from college and is also a writer. She's always loved writing and although her overall school grades were only average, she always got A's in English.

Her current project is her first full-length novel, Salvation, for Helheim Games Studios. It is based on the Survive: Zombie Apocalypse CCG and should be published soon. She also has several short stories published in anthologies.

https://www.facebook.com/Veronica.Smith.Author/?fref=ts

Michael A. Arnzen

Michael A. Arnzen (gorelets.com) teaches fulltime in the MFA in Writing Popular Fiction program at Seton Hill University, and has been publishing sick and funny horror for about twenty-five years. He is author of the novels, Grave Markings and Play Dead, and you can catch "the best of Arnzen" in the recent re-release of his Bram Stoker Award-winning collection, Proverbs for Monsters from Dark Regions Press. Also look for his series, "55 Ways I'd Prefer Not To Die," in The Year's Best Hardcore Horror in 2017.

http://gorelets.com/

Weston Kincade

Weston Kincade has helped invest in future writers for years while teaching. He also writes fantasy and horror novels which have hit Amazon's best seller lists. His non-fiction works have been published in the Ohio Journal of English Language Arts and Cleveland.com, his fiction published by Books of the Dead Press and in anthologies by Alucard Press and TPP Presents. When not writing, Weston makes time for his wife and Maine Coon cat Hermes, who talks so much he must be a speaker for the gods.

Author Site - http://kincadefiction.blogspot.com

Twitter - https://twitter.com/WestonKincade

Facebook - https://www.facebook.com/WAKincade

J.L. Lane

J. L. Lane is an English author, poet and artist, currently residing in the county of Cheshire. She is best known for her short stories in many horror anthologies, including two in the anthology entitled 'Fifty Shades of Slay' by Alucard Press, and has many more short stories due to be released. She has previous published work in the mythical fantasy genre and has a completed horror novel.

She is active on social media and shares news of her work there.

She is also the Founder of Anthology House Publishing, an up and coming publishing service which serves as a completely free platform for authors and readers alike.

She has enjoyed writing for as long as she can remember. It was a passion she inherited from her father and one she hopes her sons will inherit from her one day. Writing has always been her dream.

https://www.twitter.com/J_L_Lane

https://www.facebook.com/J.L.LaneAuthor/

Lisa Morton

Lisa Morton is a screenwriter, author of non-fiction books, Bram Stoker Award-winning prose writer, and Halloween expert whose work was described by the American Library Association's Readers' Advisory Guide to Horror as "consistently dark, unsettling, and frightening." Her most recent releases include Ghosts: A Haunted History and Cemetery Dance Select: Lisa Morton. She lives in the San Fernando Valley, and can be found online at www.lisamorton.com .

Website: http://www.lisamorton.com

Facebook: https://www.facebook.com/lisa.morton.165

J.C. Michael

J.C. Michael is an English writer of Horror and Dark Fiction. He is the author of the novel "Discoredia", which was released by Books of the Dead Press in 2013, and has had a number of short stories published since then. These have included "Reasons To Kill" in the Amazon bestselling anthology "Suspended in Dusk" and "When Death Walks The Field Of Battle" in "Savage Beasts" from Grey Matter Press.

Taking his inspiration from Stephen King and James Herbert his writing frequently explores the dark side of human nature where moral boundaries are questioned, and the difference between good and evil is far from clear.

For more information on his writing please find him on Facebook, or take a look at his author profile on Amazon.

https://www.facebook.com/james.c.michael1

https://www.amazon.com/J-C-Michael/e/B00AX8BFIK

Rick Gualtieri

Rick Gualtieri lives alone in central New Jersey with only his wife, three kids, and countless pets to both keep him company and constantly plot against him. When he's not busy monkey-clicking words, he can typically be found jealously guarding his collection of vintage Transformers from all who would seek to defile them.

Defilers beware!

To contact Rick (with either undying praise or rude comments) please visit:

Rick's Website: www.rickgualtieri.com

Facebook: www.facebook.com/RickGualtieriAuthor

Twitter: www.twitter.com/RickGualtieri

Amy Cross

Amy Cross is the author of more than fifty horror, paranormal and fantasy novels. Her books include Asylum, The Farm, A House in London and the collection Perfect Little Monsters and Other Stories.

Website: https://amycrossbooks.wordpress.com/

https://www.facebook.com/Amy-Cross-308979449122729/?fref=ts

Xtina Marie

The Accidental Poet:

Xtina Marie is an avid horror and fiction genre reader, who became a blogger; who became a published poet; who became an editor; who now is a podcaster and an aspiring novelist—and why not?

People love her words. Her first book of poetry: Dark Musings has received outstanding reviews. It is likely she was born to this calling. Writing elaborate twisted tales, to entertain her classmates in middle school, would later lead Xtina to use her poetry writing as a private emotional outlet in adult life—words she was hesitant to share publicly—but the more she shared; the more accolades her writing received.

Light Musings is close to being ready for publication and her first novel: Desiree is well under way.

https://www.facebook.com/darkpoetprincess?fref=ts

@Xtina0321

Kevin J. Kennedy

Kevin J. Kennedy's short stories have appeared in several top selling horror anthologies and he is also the publisher of the book you are holding in your hands right now.

He fell in love with the horror world at an early age watching shows like the Munster's and Eerie Indiana before moving on to movies like the Lost Boys. (The eighties was a good time to grow up and his mum and dad kept him stocked up on horror movies.) In his teens he became an avid reader when he found the work of Richard Laymon. After reading everything Laymon had written Kevin found other authors like Keene, Garton, Lee, Smith, Strand, Little, Mellick and the list goes on. At the age of thirty four Kevin wrote his first story and it was accepted by Chuck Anderson of Alucard Press for the Fifty Shades of Slay anthology. He has never looked back.

Kevin lives in a small town in Scotland with his beautiful wife Pamela, his step daughter Rachel and two strange little cats, Carlito and Ariel.

Facebook: https://www.facebook.com/authorkevinjkennedy/

Blog: http://kevinjkennedywriter.blogspot.co.uk/

Amazon: https://www.amazon.com/Kevin-J-Kennedy/e/B016V0NA7M/ref=dp_byline_cont_ebooks_1

Peter Oliver Wonder

Hidden in a remote location in California lives a man that responds to the name Peter Oliver Wonder. Though little is known about him, several written works that may or may not be fictional have been found featuring a character of the same name.

Devilishly handsome, quick witted, and as charming as an asshole can be, Peter has come a long way since his time in the United States Marine Corps. Making friends wherever he goes, there is never a shortage of adventure when he is around.

The works that have been penned under this name are full of horror, romance, adventure, and comedy just as every life should be. It is assumed that these works are an attempt at a drug fueled autobiography of sorts. Through these texts, we can learn much about this incredible man.

http://peterowonder.wix.com/peteroliverwonder

https://www.facebook.com/PeterOliverWonderAuthor/

@PeteOWonder

Ty Schwamberger

Ty Schwamberger is an award-winning author & editor in the horror genre. He is the author of a novel, multiple novellas, collections and editor on several anthologies. In addition, he's had many short stories published online and in print. Three stories, "Cake Batter" (released in 2010), "House Call" (released in June 2013) and DININ' (optioned in July 2013), have been optioned for film adaptation. He is an Active Member of the International Thriller Writers.

Learn more at http://tyschwamberger

follow at @SchwambergerTy

Andrew Lennon

Andrew Lennon is the author of A Life to Waste, Keith and Twisted Shorts. He has featured in numerous anthologies and is successfully becoming a recognised name in horror and thriller writing. Andrew is a happily married man living in the North West of England with his wife Hazel & their children.

Andrew grew up in Ormskirk, which is a small market town. During his school years he enjoyed writing stories. These were kept locked away at home because he did not have the confidence to show the outside world.

Having always being a big horror fan, Andrew spent a lot of his time watching scary movies or playing scary games, but it wasn't until his mid twenties that he developed a taste for reading. His wife, also being a big horror fan, had a very large Stephen King collection which Andrew began to consume. Once hooked into reading horror, he started to discover new authors like Thomas Ligotti & Ryan C Thomas. It was while reading work from these authors that he decided to try writing something himself and there came the idea for "A Life to Waste"

He enjoys spending his time with his family and watching or reading new horror.

For more information go to: www.andrewlennon.co.uk

C.S. Anderson

C.S Anderson dwells in the soggy Pacific Northwest and has been writing since he could form written letters. Hee is married to the most patient woman on Earth is one of the founders of Alucard Pess. He is the author of The Black Irish Chronicles, The Dark Molly Trilogy, The Zombie Extinction Event Novels and Sin City Succubus. He loves to hear from fans and can be reached at alucardpress@yahoo.com

https://www.facebook.com/soontobeworldfamousauthorcsanderson/?fref=ts

Israel Finn

Israel Finn is a horror, dark fantasy, and speculative fiction writer, and a winner of the 80th Annual Writer's Digest Short Story Competition. He's had a life-long love affair with books, and was weaned on authors like Kurt Vonnegut, Ray Bradbury, Richard Matheson, Arthur C.

Clarke and H.G. Wells. Books were always strewn everywhere about the big white house in the Midwest where he grew up.

He loves literary works (Dickens and Twain, for instance), but his main fascination lies in the fantastic and the macabre, probably because he was so heavily exposed to it early on.

Later he discovered Stephen King, Robert McCammon, Dean Koontz, Dan Simmons, Ramsey Campbell, and F. Paul Wilson, as well as several others, and the die was indelibly cast.

He's been a factory worker, a delivery driver, a singer/songwriter in several rock bands, and a sailor, among other things. But throughout he's always maintained his love of storytelling.

Right now you can find Israel in sunny southern California.

https://israelfinn.com/

Lisa Vasquez

This story introduces Heresy, The Anti-God (the Beast), and Lucifer's game of cat and mouse from my other book, 'The Unsaintly Chronicles' due for release next year. Heresy is the dark Void that existed before Creation. When God brought light to the universe, Heresy vowed to destroy all of His creations. Because she is the "original entity", her powers are a threat to the kingdom of God. The Father sends out Lucifer to hunt her but he can only detect her when she manifests, physically. Want to know more? Visit my website at www.unsaintly.com or follow me on facebook at www.facebook.com/unsaintlyhalo. Excerpts of my work, including

The Unsaintly Chronicles are available to read on my WattPad:
www.wattpad.com/user/unsaintly-author.

Steven Casey Murray

Steven Casey Murray has been writing since Junior School. His love for horror began when he watched 'A Nightmare On Elm Street ' at age 13 and decided Nancy was his heroine. He has written for numerous horror magazines such as 'Gorezone' & 'Scream'; & has written for websites on horror and graphic novels. He collects Catwoman memorabilia (mainly, Michelle Pfeiffer''s iconic take) and loves cat's.
Steven graduated First Class Honors from Bath University in 'English Literature & Creative English.' His favourite book is 'Cujo' by Stephen King, and he is currently working on his first major novel. Steven lives in Llandaff with his Bengal cat, Isis.

www.screamhorrormag.com

www.bellaonline.com/articles/art37257.asp

www.thesidekickcast.com

Christina Bergling

Colorado- bred writer, Christina Bergling, sold her soul early into the writing game. By fourth grade, she knew she wanted to be an author. In college, she studied English with a Professional Writing emphasis.

Her creative nonfiction class yielded two pieces that were later published—Tell Me About Your First Time in the college literary magazine riverrun and How to Kill Yourself Slowly on denversyntax.com.

However, with the realities of eating and paying bills, the survivalist in her hocked her passion for dystopian horror for a profession as a technical writer and document manager. Bergling published the short story Death and Other Disappointments while working as a technical writer for a Department of

Defense contractor. That job took her to Iraq for one rotation, which cracked her mind open to a whole new perspective and started infecting her writing. She blogged from Iraq and during pregnancy and now continues another blog centered on running.

Her debut novella, Savages, was released in December 2014 and followed by her second, The Waning, in July 2015.

Bergling is a mother of two young children and lives with her family in Colorado Springs.

christinabergling.com

facebook.com/chrstnabergling

@ChrstnaBergling

chrstnaberglingfierypen.wordpress.com

pinterest.com/chrstnabergling

Rose Garnett

Rose Garnett is the author of Carnalis, (Winlock Press 2017) first novel of three in the Dead Central series. Other assorted monstrosities liberated from the oubliette of Scottish Urban Horror can be found on her author page at https://www.amazon.co.uk/-/e/B01N52B87N

Story fragments opening the oubliette on Rose's world are available on her blog at http://www.rosegarnett.com. Visit her on Facebook at https://www.facebook.com/profile.php?id=100004133444829. or follow her on Twitter @dead_central for updates. The horror....

Suzanne Fox

Suzanne lives and works in the wild and wonderful county of Cornwall. She has a taste for all things erotic and this is a fundamental element of her writing. She usually writes erotic fiction but has recently been seduced to the dark side by some very bad people who have tempted her to try her hand at horror. The story in this anthology is a direct result of her seduction. She hopes you enjoy it and she invites you join her on her facebook page.

https://www.facebook.com/suzannefoxerotica/?ref=aymt_homepage_panel

Tim Curran

Tim Curran lives in Michigan and is the author of the novels Skin Medicine, Hive, Dead Sea, and Skull Moon. Upcoming projects include the novels Resurrection, The Devil Next Door, and Hive 2, as well as The Corpse King, a novella from Cemetery Dance, and Four Rode Out, a collection of four weird-western novellas by Curran, Tim Lebbon, Brian Keene, and Steve Vernon. His short stories have appeared in such magazines as City Slab, Flesh&Blood, Book of Dark Wisdom, and Inhuman, as well as anthologies such as Flesh Feast, Shivers IV, High Seas Cthulhu, and, Vile Things. Find him on the web at: www.corpseking.com

66513074R00143

Made in the USA
Columbia, SC
17 July 2019